The Menu

Also by the Author

The Alcrest Mysteries

The Cistern

The Menu

The Sgt. Reid Series

Red Island

Red Serge

The Menu

An Alcrest Mystery

Lorne Oliver

THE MENU
Copyright © 2015 by Lorne Oliver

ISBN 978-0-9738132-7-2

Cover Photo: Kassandra Arsenault
Cover Model: Hanni Vale
Cover Design: C.D. Breadner

Jordann and Wylie

Always…always seek out adventure

ACKNOWLEDGMENTS

I can't even start this without first thanking Brandi, Jordann and Wylie for their support. Without their encouragement and understanding when I'm off talking to the voices in my head I'd be nothing.

Thank you, thank you, thank you to all those who have helped me out through this entire process. Elizabeth you inspire me. Trinky, Louise, Eryn, Allison - without guinea pigs reading your work before it goes out to the public I'm sure there'd be a lot more mistakes. They are not to be blamed for any of it. It's all me. Donna, thanks for your hard work. Sorry I tortured you.

Hanni, Kassandra and Cara thank you for your creative hard work. It's hard to believe, but even the cover was 4 months work. It came out better than I thought.

Lastly to you dear reader. Thank you so much for joining the journey.

Menu
"Men-you"

A list of foods that may be ordered at a restaurant

Foods that are to be served at a meal

A list of things you can choose from

Chapter 1

If it wasn't for her mother disappearing twenty-two years ago, Chrys Alcrest would not have been where she was now – The Alcrest Gastropub Barbeque for Foster Families.

"Chrys."

She smiled and looked around, her ponytail flicking back and forth. Untethered, her dark hair fell to mid-back. Most times it was almost black, but in the sunlight the chestnut shone through. She had a gorgeous movie-star smile with her Angelina Jolie lips (in Tomb Raider when they seemed fullest) and exotic Aboriginal features. She wore denim cut-off shorts (showing off her muscular dancer's legs) and an Alcrest T-shirt. An artist would have described her skin as mocha-caramel with a touch of sunshine. She was what most would call a natural beauty. She was just as happy on a runway as she was tackling the boys on a football field.

When she was only four Chrys went to live with the Alcrests as a foster child. For as long as she could remember they'd hold a barbeque for foster families, foster children and their actual parents as a way to bring them all together. After Mr. Alcrest passed away and Chrys' brother Spencer bought the restaurant from their mom, the two of them continued the tradition.

"Chrysanthemum, over here."

She saw a woman break through the crowd. There was nothing too outstanding about Mrs. Staples except that she was a spectacular woman. On the outside she was a little plump; her blouse bunched up around a couple of rolls on her belly. She wore a long pleated skirt that was not long enough to hide somewhat hairy calves or the grey wool socks she wore with sandals. Her hair was a wild nest of shades of grey held up with pencils. She had a bit of a waddle to her walk. Since she'd dedicated the past twenty years to fostering dozens and dozens of kids who needed her help, she earned the right to waddle.

Chrys stopped and shifted the tray of drinks she was carrying from one hand to the other. "Mrs. S, you really should call me Chrys." Only a handful of people used her full first name, Chrysanthemum.

Mrs. Staples was a little out of breath. Chrys was surprised she wasn't sweating in the May heat with all the layers she was wearing. She smelled stale like her clothes had been in the closet for a long time.

"Sorry, sorry." She put a hand on Chrys' arm. Her fingers were rough. "Your name is so lovely though."

"How can I help you? Do you like the menu today? Do you need drinks?"

"No, no. I'm fine. The menu is fantastic like always. I have some friends who need your help - yours and Spencer's."

~ * ~

Spencer didn't mind holding the barbeque because all he had to do was flip burgers and turn hotdogs. The serving staff volunteered their time to look after everything else. It was the cost of the food that was on his mind. Every year the need for foster families was greater, so every year there were more and more people at the party. Burgers by the case, buns, condiments, paper plates, cups, balloons – it all added up. As if on cue a balloon string slipped from a little kid's hand and the yellow ball floated up to the heavens dragging the red ribbon behind it. Fifty cents wasted. It wasn't bad last year when the restaurant was doing well, but sales had dropped over the past six months. Having a headless body found in your oven could taint your reputation. Even with brand new ovens the customers still weren't coming back.

He jumped as though a furry spider had just crossed his skin as he felt fingertips graze his back. "What the hell?"

"What?" said the voice behind him.

All Spencer had for safety were a couple of folding tables and a large rented barbeque. Back at The Alcrest Gastropub the kitchen was a part of the dining room and practically blocked off on all sides, so nobody could get to him. The servers were certainly not allowed down "the line." That was the cook's sacred ground. Here in the park he wasn't safe.

Hanni, (pronounced Honey which always made Spencer feel awkward) one of his best servers, leaned back against a table. She wore extremely short shorts that exposed her smooth legs and an Alcrest T-shirt she had tied in the back so that the front pulled against her chest and exposed a flat stomach. The girls had been told to be comfortable but not too scantily dressed. She hadn't paid attention. At work Hanni flirted with all of her male customers for bigger tips. Spencer's girlfriend (Hanni's direct supervisor) hated the way she acted around him. Spencer said it was just harmless teasing, but he knew he liked it too much, so much so that he tried not to be alone with her.

"Did you need something?" He asked as he adjusted his backward cap over his short sandy-blond hair. Sweat had made the short spikes collapse long ago.

"Not right now." She tossed her straight golden hair over her shoulder. She didn't like tying it up like she was supposed to. As she made a sniffed her nose scrunched. "Where's Jessie today? How did she get out of this charity stuff?"

"Doctor's appointment." He turned back the grill. His eyes searched around to find someone to save him. He was certain he felt Hanni's eyes move over his body. He worked out when he could and took pride in keeping things firm.

"On a Sunday? Is she sick?"

Spencer suddenly smelled flowers. He felt her close to him, close enough to touch him. He felt something get excited inside his pants. He loved his girlfriend, but that didn't stop the thoughts and he knew Hanni would test how far he would let her go. "No, she just wanted to see her doctor." Jessie's doctor did shifts in a walk-in clinic, so his patients could see him even on weekends.

"I guess." Hanni stepped close enough that Spencer was certain he could feel her breath on his cheek. Her fingers reached out and ran the length of his forearm over his tattoo - the one that reminded him to suck the marrow out of each day and get everything you could out of it. A manicured nail scratched his skin as she continued, "She's just not as much of a giver as I can be."

If he were a teenager he would have bolted to his bunk for some alone time.

"What's going on?"

The two looked at Chrys standing on the other side of a table. From the moment she arrived at the Alcrest home, Spencer considered her his sister. When he moved into the apartment above the restaurant four years ago he didn't have to think twice about asking her to be his roommate. She was six years younger than him, and felt she had to be his moral compass. Of course that never stopped her from going over the line with her own agenda. Spencer had regretted the decision to have her as his roommate a few times since, but there had been no question at the time he first asked her.

Chrys stared at the woman. She didn't hate her, but something about the flirty-slut rubbed her the wrong way. Her dark eyes spoke volumes as she glowered at Hanni.

Hanni stared back at her for a long moment. Her own blue eyes were thin slits as she tried to get the upper-hand. She said, "I should go see if anyone needs anything," and left.

Spencer watched her walk away. The tattoo on her back peaked out from under her shirt. He stopped looking the moment his sister hit him.

"What the monkey-fuck are you doing?" Chrys asked the moment the two of them were alone. "What if Jessie were here? You know how damned insecure she is about you two, about you and any woman. She'd blow her top and you'd have a bitch on your hands for the next week." She was more concerned about having *her* boss being a bitch. Jessie was front-of-house manager and (though Chrys barely listened to what she said) her boss.

"She's not ..."

"Where is she anyway?"

"She's…" He started to tell her, but changed his mind. "Did you want something?" Spencer knew if he said Jessie was at the doctor's he would have been hit with a load of questions that he wouldn't be able to avoid. And that he *wanted* to avoid.

Chrys' oval cocoa eyes glared at him. She knew something was wrong. Her pouty lips pouted some more. She'd get it out of him eventually. "Yeah, Mrs. Staples wants to talk to us."

"What about?"

"I don't fucking know." Her voice rose to a high squeal. Nobody knew where it came from, but Chrys could curse like a sailor. Hell, even a sailor would get offended to some of the profanity chains she could create. No matter how much Spencer's dad tried to get her to stop she couldn't. "Does it really matter? She wants to see us. Let's go, numb-nuts."

"I have burgers on the grill. I can't leave them."

Without a word Chrys stormed off. Spencer mumbled to himself about not leaving the grill and just stood there flipping the burgers. His sister was back in less than a minute pulling a young woman, who was also wearing an Alcrest shirt and shorts. Her shorts were more respectable than Hanni's. "Izzy can watch the burgers."

The redhead looked from one to the other. She said, "Yeah, sure," between quick breaths. She wore oval black-framed glasses and had freckles like constellations across her cheeks. "What?" She looked at each of them again as she tried to catch her breath. "I was playing with the kids."

Spencer had asked his staff to serve the food and drinks then make sure everyone had fun. For Izzy that meant playing games with the kids. For Hanni it meant barely wearing anything and flashing her ass to all the men. To each his own. He nodded and handed over his tongs. His sister pulled on his arm.

As soon as they were away from the barbeque she said, "I can't believe you let that skank get her claws on you."

"Who?"

15

"Hanni. She'll go after anything. I've never liked the way she flirts with you. Jessie sure as shit doesn't."

They headed off across the park. "She didn't have her claws on me," Spencer said.

"Oh come on. She was stroking your arm like it was your ..." Her hand flittered around.

"Chrys."

"And I'm pretty sure the size is nowhere the same." This comment made her smile at her brother's expense.

The City of Middleton was lucky to be on the coast where spring arrived at least a month or more before it reached the rest of the country. The grass was a vibrant green and all of the trees were full of leaves and life. Tables were scattered all around the park, mostly under trees for shade.

Spencer and Chrys walked through crowds of people all smiling and having fun. Kids chased each other while parents sat at the picnic tables talking and visiting. Somebody had brought a soccer ball and a small game had started off to the side. Sitting at a picnic table next to a crooked pine tree Spencer saw the woman who had been close friends with his parents. They'd helped each other care for their foster children when they needed help. When his father died, Mrs. Staples organized a collection to assist with the expenses. Six months ago the two siblings found the body of one of her former foster children as well as identity of the killer. Spencer recognized some of her current foster kids in the grass bouncing their balloons around. He hoped the end of the ribbons were tied to their arms.

"What's this about?" Spencer whispered in Chrys' ear.

She shrugged her shoulders. "She said she wanted us to meet some people who need our help."

With a groan Mrs. Staples pushed herself to her feet and stepped to meet them. "Spencer," grabbed the thirty-one year old's shoulders and, with a firm grip, pulled him in to kiss his cheek. "I'm glad Chrysanthemum could pull you away."

"Mrs. S, remember what I said." Chrys smiled.

"Sorry, Chrys. It was just that Rene always loved your name. He always told me it was nice having two flowers in the family."

"Yeah, I remember that." Whenever Spencer really smiled his dimples were evident.

"How is Rose?"

The chef nodded. For this cooking adventure he'd worn tan cargo pants which clung to his buttock and a black Alcrest T-shirt – sweat had pasted it to his skin. He said, "Mom's good, enjoying retirement."

Mrs. Staples took a deep breath as though to signal that part of the conversation was over. Her voice suddenly became serious. "I have some friends who need your help."

Right away Spencer had a bad feeling. He hoped it wasn't someone needing a job. He hated giving jobs to friends or friends of friends. It never worked out right. Not to mention hiring new people was not really an option. He had just hired a new cook and wasn't sure how that was going to work out.

Chrys wondered if there was money involved. Yes, she worked at The Alcrest and taught dance, but her lifestyle and extra-curriculars meant she had to stay

17

flexible and compensate with small side jobs. Of course that was how she and her brother came face to face with a serial killer that one time. *Shit happens,* she thought.

"Meet Anne and James Carol." Mrs. Staples signaled three people to join them. "They have been foster parents for five years. Five years right? And this is Emma Weston."

The Carols looked like your average middle-class couple that were pushing the high ages. Neither seemed to move quickly. Jim's hair was receding from his forehead, his cheeks were round, and he was growing small breasts above a belly. Anne slouched; her hair looked like it was coloured and fashioned in an eighties style. It was Emma who was interesting. She didn't seem that old, no older than Spencer, but she already had wrinkles. There were old scars down both sides of her face. She wasn't beautiful, but could have been considered pretty if not for the marks on her face.

"Let's sit down," Mrs. Staples suggested.

They all sat around the weathered picnic table. Joints creaked with the added weight.

Mrs. Staples sat on the same side as the Alcrests. She took a moment to adjust herself to a side sitting position before continuing. "Four years ago…was it four years ago?" The others all nodded. "Four years ago Emma's son, Luke, was put in the foster system and came to the Carols. How old was he then?"

"Fourteen." Emma Weston took a moment. "It wasn't me. My boyfriend at the time did…we were involved in drugs and he was a bad man." She dropped her eyes as a sheet of shame fell over her.

Anne Carol wrapped her arms around the woman's shoulders. Both Spencer and Chrys remembered other foster kids coming into their home. Their parents tried creating a comfortable relationship with the biological parents, but it honestly did not always work that way. It was nice to see that the Carols genuinely cared for this woman.

Mrs. Staples waited a few minutes before going on. "This year Luke turned eighteen and aged out of the foster system."

"He's not one of those troubled kids," James Carol took over. "He had some bad things happen to him, but he was still respectful. He did chores, his homework. He rarely got upset with anything. He kept to himself and was quiet, but was a good kid."

Chrys saw Emma Weston flinch every time the man referred to Luke in the past tense. Chrys was getting excited. This was starting to sound like a mystery. Though six months ago her life had been on the line more than once and she lost part of her earlobe, it had been one of the most exciting times in her life. She glanced at her brother. He was checking the time on his phone. She flicked her foot at where his calf should have been under the table.

"Luke moved out on his own. He had a job." Mr. Carol became quiet. Foster parenting was usually supposed to be a part-time thing. When a kid needed to get out of his real home due to abuse or neglect or just because the parents needed help, it was never the plan for them to go to a foster home for a long time period. Still, the kids and the part-time parents often cared for each other. Looking at the Carols it was obvious they had loved this boy.

"Luke has gone missing," Mrs. Staples stated.

Spencer's first thought was, *what the heck do you want us to do?* He said, "What do you mean he's missing?"

James cleared his throat. "Every Sunday Luke, Emma and some of the other foster children and families come to our house for dinner. For the past three months," he looked to his wife to see if he had the number right, "Luke has had one excuse or another for not joining us. A week ago was the last time we heard from him."

"He calls me every couple of days." Emma Weston began. Her voice caught in her throat, almost like she was a long-time smoker. "The last time I heard from him was a week ago today. He called to say he couldn't make dinner. We were told you helped the police and might be able to help us." She squeezed Anne Carol's arm. They all gazed across the table with hopeful eyes.

Spencer faced to his sister. She looked back at him. The two of them turned to the woman they knew with confused expressions plastered on their faces.

Mrs. Staples bit down on a knuckle. "You're the only people I know who've caught a serial killer, so I thought maybe you could help find Luke. I know it's not your thing, but we don't know what to do. We filed a police report but they can only do so much."

James mumbled, "Nothing is what they're doing."

"And since reports of the bodies found outside of the city have been in the news we're all getting worried."

Spencer gazed around the park – everywhere but at the people in front of him. He had heard the news

20

about the men's bodies that had been found, brutally beaten and left for dead, on country roads east of Middleton. They were older men though. This kid was eighteen. And the police spokesperson said there was no reason to believe they were anything but isolated incidents. Still, this kid was gone. *No.* He was a chef – that was it. The last time was dumb luck. Both of them were nearly killed and a friend *was* murdered. "Mrs. Staples, I really wouldn't know where to start."

"Where does he live? Have you been there?" Chrys chirped. She was practically dancing in her seat. Her brother hoped she'd get a sliver.

"We did." Mr. Carol scratched his face which was bristled with whiskers. "He's staying at a hostel downtown. I went there. I knocked on his door, but he wasn't there. The people at the front desk wouldn't let me in his room and said he was paid up until the end of the month."

"Is he into anything like drugs or gangs or anything?"

"No. He hates drugs because of my past. He's a good kid. He can be depressed and withdrawn, but with what he's been through you can't blame him." Emma Weston looked ready to cry. "I've tried to find him. I call and I drive around where he should be. I'm just so afraid of what I might find. The police aren't really doing anything. They say he might have run away or something. I'm worried. My son wouldn't do that. He wouldn't leave without telling me." Her hand brushed tears from one cheek, then the other.

Spencer found he couldn't focus his eyes on the group of people in front of him. He started, "Like I said we, ah, wouldn't know where to ..." He had to get them out of this.

"But we'll do what we can," Chrys blurted. While her brother couldn't look at the mother and foster parents of the missing boy, they were all she could look at. She had been in that boy's place. The only difference was that her mother had disappeared before she ever went into the foster care system and in the end the Alcrests adopted her. This was a mother who admitted she had problems and foster parents who obviously cared for the kids they looked after. There was no reason for Luke to flake out and run. She looked at her brother. His aquamarine eyes glared at her. She didn't care. She had to help. She still had one earlobe left.

Chapter 2

"Seriously, Spencer, are you not going to help?"

As Spencer lifted the folding table into the back of his truck he thought for a moment of throwing it at his sister. "Are you?" he strained to find the right words.

Who was she to stand there, arms crossed over her chest, yelling about how he wasn't helping while watching him pack everything back into the truck? The equipment rental had already picked up their barbeque. The other staff members were going around making sure any loose garbage was picked up. She was the only one not doing anything.

"I'm serious, Spence."

"We're not cops, Chrys."

"We caught a serial killer."

He grunted as he pushed the table into place. "I think you're remembering things wrong. The police caught the bad guys. *We* almost got killed. Look at your ear."

Chrys untied her ponytail and adjusted her hair over the front of her shoulder to keep her deformed ear hidden. It wasn't that bad. Her earring had been torn off taking part of the lobe with it. She pierced the top of the ear instead.

Spencer continued, "I'm not sticking my neck out there anymore. It was too big a price. Do you know how many customers we lost because of ..." He bit his lip and wouldn't say the words. He grabbed the bin holding the cooking utensils. "We're still not back to what we were. I have to worry about that, not some runaway."

"This has nothing to do with that. This is a missing kid. He didn't run away, he's missing. Don't be such a feneuter."

"A what? I'm not ... he's not a kid. He's an adult and adults don't have to talk to their parents. Maybe they had a fight. Either way, nothing good is going to come of this."

Chrys side-stepped so her brother could lift the bin into the truck. "After you left I asked his mom and foster parents more questions. They all said their last conversation was good. Luke told them about making some positive changes in his life and that he had something very important to tell them. Then they heard nothing else."

Spencer closed the tailgate and leaned back against it. Sweat covered his face. His foster sister's excitement could often get intoxicating. He hated that. "Maybe he's into bad stuff."

"Both his mom and foster mom said no way. He's going to college in the fall and doesn't do drugs or anything. He had good grades in school and was never in trouble. They said he doesn't even drink."

"Yeah, and kids tell their parents everything. Mom know you're a lesbian yet?"

"I'm not a lesbian," Chrys shrieked. Her hands flew to her hips and her face scrunched up like a little kid ready to hold her breath until she got her way.

"What was Dawn then?"

She punched her brother's shoulder. Pain shot back into her wrist. "Just because I date and screw women doesn't make me a lesbian. I'm a person. That's it, that's all. I date men too remember."

"Bisexual then."

"No, Spence. I don't like labels. Labels hold you back." It was an argument the two of them had before and one they would have again. Chrys knew the real point of it was to distract her anyway. She took a breath and said, "Are you going to help me or not?"

"I'm going with not."

"They texted me his picture. Look at it." She held it up for him, but he wouldn't look.

Chrys stared at her brother for a long moment. She looked up to the guy, but the older he got the more he could be a prick. "You're an ass." She turned her back to him and marched off, stomping her black ankle boots in the grass. She decided right there that, with or without help, she was going to find out what happened to this boy.

Her choices for a ride, however, were slim. Most of the people from the barbeque were gone and of those remaining Chrys didn't know anyone. It was a strange feeling, usually she knew everyone. As she surveyed the park she realized she had three choices: forget about it and go with Spencer, call a taxi, or ask Hanni for a ride. It was mid-pay period, so her financial situation was grim. Well, even the word grim hinted that she had some money, which she didn't. Taxi was out. Her brother was being a dick, so he was out. Hanni it was then. Or she could do a GoogleMaps check and see how far it was to walk.

Chrys walked toward her nemesis with fake determination. She went over what to say in her head. Starting off by yelling, "hey bitch," would not be a good choice. Just calling out her name like they were friends felt icky, but she shouted, "Hanni."

Hanni stopped her conversation with Izzy and slowly turned. The statuesque blond conjured up thoughts of every bad witch in every Disney movie. A beauty with wickedness inside. She had to have a cauldron and jars of eye of newt or wolfsbane somewhere.

Chrys fought the impulse to turn away.

"What?" Hanni's hands rested on her hips. She always appeared as though she were posing.

"Can I," Chrys dug her fingernails into her own palm, "get a ride? Spencer's being a dick."

"Where to?"

"Cumberland."

"That's across town." Hanni's expression was the same as when there was a foul smell in the air.

Chrys ran her fingers through her hair. This was proving to be a much longer day than originally anticipated. "Look, I was asked to check on this missing kid. Spencer can't take me and I can't afford a cab. Can you give me a ride there and back or not?" She thought she should throw out the, *and back,* part or risk being stranded on the other side of the city.

Middleton was the eighth largest city in Canada with over half a million people in a relatively small area and that brought its own problems. As it was the largest port city on the West coast there were a large number of immigrants and individuals who arrived on their way to someplace else, something else, somewhere better, but Middleton was where they stayed. It had a vast array of cultures that seemed to gather in certain neighborhoods, as did families, people with similar interests and sexual orientation. It did have great cultural events and venues, an amazing assortment of restaurant choices, and top-draw sporting events, but for a lot of people it was still a stepping stone to the other side of the fence.

Cumberland was along the southern shore. It was a multi-ethnic area with much low-income housing. Many families and local businesses had been there for years. It was known as the place to go for hookers when the sun went down - that and drugs. The locals were trying to take it back, but a couple of streets were never going to get away from it and fighting fire with spit never turned out right.

"What's in it for me?" Hanni sniffed and twitched her nose. She always seemed to do that.

"The gratitude of helping out a dear friend." Ew.

"Right."

"I don't know. I'll owe you a favor, holy hell!" Chrys was ready to give up. Walking had to be easier.

Hanni pursed her lips. "Fine, but when I ask you, you better not go back on it." She turned and strutted off toward the closest parking lot.

Chrys glanced at her brother getting in his truck. She was hoping he would change his mind and call her over. No such luck. He wouldn't even look in her direction. What a dick.

"Can I come?" Izzy asked. All three women walked beside each other. The blond and brunette both shrugged their shoulders. The girl's red hair swayed back and forth. A rolling giggle escaped the younger woman. She had joined the staff at a time when others were leaving and had become a bubbly mascot.

As soon as Chrys was in the passenger seat she slipped her shoes off, sat on one foot and put one bare foot up on the dashboard (ignoring the dirty look from Hanni) and Googled the Greenleaf Hostel. She stayed in a few hostels when she went on a trip with friends to Australia after high school. She remembered debauchery and bed bugs. According to the Greenleaf website they offered beds ranging from $25 a night to $35 a night depending on whether you wanted privacy or were willing to bunk in a dormitory-style room. Each floor had a communal sitting room, kitchen, and washrooms. This hostel offered a more than the ones she'd experienced. Laundry facilities, video rentals, free wireless internet, no curfew, and long term rooms were available. Chrys guessed that Luke Weston had one of those since his mother said he had stayed at the same place for a few months. The hostel also boasted close proximity to shopping, clubs, tourist attractions, and a beach.

Cumberland was far from the behemoth skyscrapers of downtown, but still had tall apartment buildings and business offices along some of the streets. Tall groomed trees lined every street making the metropolis disappear. It was known for having a lot of different shops. The South Shore Beach and hotels with ocean views brought in tourists who wanted to be in the city, but not too close to the bustle. As long as they didn't venture out at night past the streets they were located on it was all good. Get into the heart of Cumberland, where the Greenleaf was located and all bets were off. Nothing too bad would happen. You wouldn't get killed or anything, but you would be asked if you wanted a date by a few women. Some men.

"What the hell?" Hanni exclaimed as she rubbed her nose. A sign reading Closed for Street Fair blocked the road. A man in a florescent yellow vest waved in the direction of a parking garage.

"At least parking is free," Izzy stated in her giddy tone from the back seat.

"You guys can wait in the car if you want."

Hanni didn't hesitate. "Sounds good to me."

"I'll go with you Chrys." Izzy saw the driver staring at her through the rearview mirror.

"And leave me all alone?" Hanni made a sound of derision as she pulled into the first empty parking spot which was three levels up. "I'm coming too, I guess."

As the three of them walked through the parking garage exit it was as though they stepped into a different world. The wind they'd felt at Marina Park couldn't get through the tall trees here, so all that touched them was the sun's heat. The street was alive with colour and sound. Street-lamp poles had been decorated like old-fashioned May poles with colourful ribbons twisting their way upward. Colourful plastic patio lanterns were strung between the trees like in that Kim Mitchel song. More streamers and banners were spread across the street above everyone's heads. One announced that this was an Artisans' Fair. The aromas of cotton candy and popcorn were thick. Booths set up on the wide sidewalks displayed various foods and items for sale. Chrys recognized a couple of local artists selling their paintings; they'd previously displayed their work at The Alcrest. She waved at a blond woman who was singing to a small crowd. The singer looked much better than she did when they met six months prior. There were a number of busy buskers up and down the street. The three ladies stopped now and then to watch or listen. The crowd was a mixture of families (little children had their faces painted like animals, butterflies, and super heroes) and those who longed for the hippie days of yore. Everyone looked to be having fun except for Hanni who grimaced every time a child came near.

"This is wild," Izzy exclaimed. Her entire body bopped along to whatever music was loudest. What she lacked in rhythm she made up for in enthusiasm.

Chrys found the hostel sign further down the street. "This way." She had to yell to be heard. She plowed through the crowd. A little boy with his face painted like Spiderman made her stop for a second.

Izzy grabbed her arm. "Look, a clown."

"Oh God!" Hanni squealed.

Izzy continued, "He's doing magic. I'm going to stay out here."

"Yeah, you both stay." Chrys started up the hostel's stairs.

Hanni stayed at her side, her oval browns looking at Chrys as she said, "I'm not staying out here with a clown. What? They're creepy."

The Greenleaf Hostel was not what the women expected. The lobby was clean and tidy. Behind a registration desk off to the side, a woman looked up when they entered, but quickly went back to her computer. A collection of couches and chairs filled the room. A flat-screen television on a wall above an aquarium of tropical fish seemed to be the focal point. At the moment the TV was silently displaying *Sports Center*. An open doorway on the side led to a dining area. A chalkboard beside it announced that breakfast was from 7 am to 10 am. The woman behind the counter was the only person in the lobby; everyone else was probably out at the street fair.

"His mom said he's on the fourth floor. The stairs are over here." Chrys flashed a quick smile in the direction of the woman behind the counter as they walked past. She barely moved her eyes.

Hanni signal her discontent with a huff. Today she wore Jesus sandals with straps around her ankles and a flat base instead of her spiked heeled boots. Any time she was out of her "hooker boots" for long she complained about pain in her Achilles tendons on the backs of her ankles. That was all she did up the stairs. "I should have waited outside. My ankles hurt. This is stupid."

31

"We'll see if he's here or not then we can fuck off." Chrys looked up and down the fourth floor hallway. Again there was not a soul. "Don't get your panties in a bunch."

"First of all," Hanni waved a defiant finger in the air, "I wear thongs, so my panties are never in a bunch."

Just stuck up your ass, Chrys thought.

"Secondly, are you serious? We came all this way and you don't even know if he's here? My ankles really hurt." She sniffed.

"He wouldn't be missing if he was that easy to find." Chrys wished she knew the Chinese phrase for "dumb blond."

The fourth floor hallway was not kept as presentable as the lobby. Carpeting ran its length. There was obvious wear and tear in the middle, however, close to the walls it seemed to be in good shape. The walls were a faded yellow (or maybe it was dust) with patch marks here and there and black marks where furniture or bags hit. The artwork was reminiscent of old peoples' yard sales - a lot of cabins in the woods painted on canvas. The only thing that looked new and alive was an over-filled corkboard. As Chrys walked past she saw a notice for the street fair, a couple of job ads and something called Club 22. She wondered how far back in time the notices over notices over notices went. From what she found out online about the Greenleaf, this floor was for men's long term stays. Each room on the fourth floor had its own washroom. On the lower floors only a few did. The others had to share a public washroom. This floor did have a living and kitchen area shared by all. It was right next to the corkboard. As they passed they saw it

32

was empty and furnished with a table and chairs, couch and television.

"Number six. This is it." Some of the doors had been decorated. Number six was plain except for the plastic copper number screwed into it. There was no peephole. They both stood in front of it just staring.

"Are you going to knock or not?" Hanni finally asked.

As if in answer there was a noise behind the door. Chrys thought it sounded like something being kicked over.

She rapped three times. "Luke?" There was no other noise. Maybe it was the air conditioning kicking in. "My name is Chrys. Your mom asked me to drop by."

"Don't say that." Hanni scrunched her face up. She smacked her hand against the door. "There's two hot chicks out here. Open up if you want a good time."

Chrys gave her a sideways glare.

Hanni's arms crossed in front of her and rested most of her weight on one leg. "I'm not serious. We want him to open the door, don't we?"

"I'm just surprised you'd refer to me as a hot chick."

"Don't get any ideas, lesbo."

"Excuse me?" Chrys mirrored the blonde's stance. "I am not a lesbian." That was twice in one day that she was called a lesbian. Did she give off a scent or something?

"Really? Your last serious relationship was with a woman, wasn't it? A cop?" Hanni said the last sentence loudly and toward the door.

"What's your point?" Chrys felt the rage rising inside her and she didn't know why. It wasn't the word.

She had been called a lesbian before and would again. There was nothing wrong with it. She dated women and men and didn't see anything wrong with it. There were complications that came with her lifestyle, she knew that. Most of it involved an asshole on the other end of a stupid comment. It was Hanni's tone of voice she didn't like. She said "lesbian" like it was a bad word.

"My point is," Hanni leaned in so close to Chrys they both felt each other's breath, "I want to go home." She stood in front of the door and began banging her fist against it. "Open up!" *Bang, bang* "Open up or we're calling the cops."

"Hanni, don't."

"What?"

The door flew open. For a few seconds time stood still. Chrys stared at the man in the doorway. Hanni took a step back. The man looked from one to the other. He wore a grey hoodie sweatshirt, the hood over his head, and a baseball cap underneath. Sweat trickled down his dark skin. His eyes were wild, black dots inside enormous whites. He looked more surprised than mean. He didn't expect them as much as they didn't expect him.

Chrys held her breath. She didn't think anyone would be there. Her heart was beating in her chest. Who was this guy?

He moved. His arm hit Hanni across the chest. The blond flew backwards. Her shoulder collided with the wall behind her. Chrys quickly stepped back as the man sprinted down the hallway toward the stairs. On the back of his hoodie were tire tracks and the words, "I should have run faster." The papers on the corkboard danced as he flew past. Hanni slumped to the floor, sobbing uncontrollably.

Chrys looked down at her, then she looked at the back of the man heading for the stairs. That wasn't Luke Weston. "Stop!" She jumped over the blond woman and exploded down the hallway. Her heels pounded on the worn carpet.

Once inside the stairwell she heard the man running down. She took two stairs then jumped the rest to the next landing. Her ankle wrenched on the second jump. She grabbed the railing and pulled herself around the corners. Her shoes slipped on the tiles. *Who was this guy? What did he have to do with Luke? What was she going to do when she caught up to him?* On the last set of stairs she saw his back. Chrys plowed through the door into the lobby just seconds behind him. The woman behind the counter protested.

He dashed through the front door.

Chrys hit the door and pushed it open. Izzy was there at the bottom of the front stairs. She was bopping to music again. "Izzy, stop him!"

Izzy turned. She saw the man. She saw Chrys. Her hands grasped at his shirt. A fist connected with her cheek. She screamed. Her glasses soared from her face as he continued twisting and turning into the crowd. The young woman flew backward away from the stairs. Her body bounced off another man then dropped to the ground. Her hands went to her face.

Chrys stopped at the bottom of the stairs. Hopelessly, she watched the grey hoodie disappear into the crowd. Other people were coming to them closing in the circle and any sign of the direction he had gone. She looked down at her co-worker and all thoughts about the chase left her. "Izzy, are you okay?" Chrys knelt down beside her. "Holy fuck, are you okay?"

The side of her face was already turning an unhealthy shade of purple. There was a bleeding cut on her temple just a centimeter from her left eye. "Where are my glasses?" Izzy's eyes looked stunned.

Chrys crawled across the paved ground Velma-style to where the redhead's glasses had come to rest. The lenses were still intact but one arm was broken. After a couple minutes of pushing people's feet out of her way she grabbed them. To Izzy she said, "I have them." She placed the pieces into Izzy's hands. "Can you get up?" Chrys wrapped her arm around the woman and freely took most of her weight. The younger woman was suddenly having trouble catching her breath. "Take it easy, Izzy. Deep breaths."

"Who ... was ..." Izzy tried taking a breath. As she exhaled in tiny puffs, she began to sob. "Who was that?"

"I don't know," Chrys said as she took the lead pulling Izzy up the stairs to the hostel. She thanked those who offered help, but replied with, "We'll be fine." At the top of the stairs she looked again in the direction the grey hoodie had vanished. The crowd was too thick to see anything as the fair continued.

Who was he? She wondered.

Then she had another thought which trumped everything. It was enough to give her chills. *Spencer had been right.*

Chapter 3

Spencer parked his truck behind The Alcrest Gastropub next to the wooden stairs that provided access to his apartment. There were three other vehicles in the parking lot, none were the one he was hoping to see. He glanced upward with the thought that he should take the dogs for a walk. They could wait a few more minutes; his staff always took them anyway. He went through the door under the stairs and stepped from the hot air outside to the air-conditioned dishpit of the restaurant. A teenager stood at the table with his back to the door. As Spencer walked in the kid finished peeling a carrot and dropped it into a bucket on the floor. Spencer moved rapidly through the restaurant, past the bathrooms in the hallway to the main dining room. He crossed in front of the high ledge separating the open kitchen and bar from the diners to the frame room around the corner and even looked in the private dining room with barely acknowledging anyone who said, "Hello." He returned to the front counter which was located between the front door in the corner and hallway. It had a glass front and held muffins and goodies made fresh most mornings. A coffee maker and cappuccino machine were behind it. Jessie's bag and spare shoes weren't behind the hostess stand.

"Everything alright, Chef?"

Spencer looked up at Wylie, one of his servers. Three words to describe him were blond, attractive and tall. He was the only staff member who had to duck when he walked through a doorway. "Everything's fine." Spencer said. "Has Jessie been here?"

Wylie nodded as his sandy hair flowed with every move and fell back into place. "Better part of an hour ago, she came and left."

"She was looking for you." Gordie was never shy about his eavesdropping. The large sous chef stepped from the kitchen line. He had a pencil sticking out from under a crooked cap and the crumbs of something he had eaten were still entwined in his bushy beard. Spencer didn't say a word about it. He was hoping it would fix itself.

"We thought she might have caught you at the park."

"No, I left there a while ago. I had to return the barbeque." He checked his cellphone but saw there were no messages. His aquamarine eyes looked up and actually saw what was happening in the restaurant.

Not much. A few tables were occupied by customers drinking coffee or beer and having loud conversations. There had been three people reading in the frame room (called such because it was separated from the rest of the restaurant by a wall made up of mostly empty window frames hanging from the ceiling and attached to each other by chains) and two playing cards. In short, nobody was spending much money. For the second time today Spencer ran the numbers through his head: one dishwasher/prep guy, Gordie and Ranger in the kitchen, Wylie as acting manager and two servers with not much to serve. It was just past 5:00 pm. There were no reservations for the night, so he would have to start sending people home if it didn't get busy. It was Sunday night, basically a crap shoot when it came to predicting how many customers they might have.

Once Spencer passed on instructions to Ranger and the dishwasher kid to empty the truck, he ascended the inside stairs to the second floor.

As he opened the door and stepped into the apartment, a very distinct odor met him. He knew this smell from all the times he had visited farms or taken the dogs for walks and picked up their deposits with tiny plastic bags with paw prints painted on them.

"It smells like dog shit," Spencer growled aloud.

His sister's chocolate Chihuahua, Breeze, bound from wherever she had been hiding and yapped franticly at his feet.

Spencer's dog was a faun and white British bulldog named Bullet. The overweight beast eased off the couch like melting wax falling down the side of a candle. He took two steps then settled on his haunches.

All the wrinkles in his face made the animal look both guilty and clinically depressed at the same time. One eyebrow went up. The owner and dog stared at each other. Bullet's other eyebrow went up again as the first one went down.

Twenty minutes later Spencer stepped through the door to the top landing of the outside stairs. The clouds had rolled in. Bullet swaggered and stopped at the first step. Breeze wiggled around in Spencer's arms. She was too small to get down all of the stairs by herself. Bullet dropped down from one stair to the next. A couple of times Spencer had to pull back on the leash to stop the bulldog from tumbling.

As Spencer reached the bottom he placed Breeze on the ground and Bullet sat with his front paws on the ground, his back half sitting on the last step panting. Spencer watched a canary yellow Volkswagen Beetle pull up beside his truck then noticed with annoyance that the boys had left his tailgate open. Jessie exited and stepped up to them. Spencer's eyes flashed to the restaurants back door then he leaned in and planted a kiss on her cheek.

"How are you?" He asked.

"Good." Jessie took Breeze's leash from his hand. She wore sweats, a hooded sweatshirt zipped up to her neck and a dark grey twill golfer's hat. She wasn't Hanni, who knew she was beautiful and used it, or Chrys, who knew she was beautiful and just went along with it. Jessie didn't think she was beautiful or sexy. Spencer thought she was gorgeous, but rarely said it. "How was the barbeque?"

"It was great. Lots of people this year." He gave a tug on the leash he was still holding. Bullet stayed where he was and looked up with the same expression Spencer's sister got when she went on a cursing tirade. If he could speak, the profanity would be flying.

"Where's your sister?"

Spencer tugged Bullet's leash again. "She's on another adventure." He tugged and Bullet leaned forward dropping off the step. Instead of going out to the street in front of the restaurant Spencer lead the way down one of the side residential streets. The Fairmont area had a fair amount of greenery, but it was closer to the downtown. It was touristy with little shops and a variety of eateries, museums and market areas. Behind The Alcrest were a few streets of affluent homes; people with money. Why the hell weren't they spending it at his restaurant?

Bullet trotted along in front of them while Breeze ran as far ahead as her leash would allow.

Spencer and Jessie walked close enough to hold hands, but neither bothered to reach out. They had dated off and on for years and Spencer was always uncomfortable showing affection in front of people. He left Middleton for culinary school after graduating high school, then took five years to work at different restaurants before his mother asked him to return home. His father was getting sick and Mom hoped the prodigal son would assume some of the burden of the restaurant. That was when he met Jessie. She had been a server at the restaurant then and the two of them hated each other. Things changed over time, feelings grew, she became front-of-house manager, and he took over operations. In the past seven years, however, this current eighteen-month stint they were on had been the longest.

41

"Are we going to talk about it?" Spencer gave Bullet a tug.

Jessie shrugged her shoulders. She knew what he meant. She stared down at the sidewalk. "I don't know." Her voice had a husky scratch to it.

Spencer didn't know what to say. He was involved, but what she told him was at her discretion. He glanced at her face. The area around her eyes had taken on a dark smoky look. As he breathed, he noted the subtle notes of her vanilla perfume. He had been battling the same thing over and over in his own mind. He loved everything about her that was there to love and missed her imperfections when she wasn't around. Yet he still had trouble showing his feelings and giving himself to her completely. He was struggling to get over his hang-ups.

"What adventure is Chrys on this time?" Jessie had some tension in her tone. She and Chrys did not always harmonize.

They stopped so the dogs could sniff a pile of sticks some kid had stacked on the sidewalk.

"Some eighteen year-old hasn't called his mommy in a while."

"How much is this one going to cost?"

Spencer was certain she didn't mean money.

Satisfied that the pile of sticks was only a pile of sticks the dogs continued. Bullet waddled his butt while Breeze zigzagged back and forth across the sidewalk.

Spencer responded, "It's nothing. Some kid got too busy with life to check in. He probably found a girl or doesn't want to hang out with his parents." *But she probably should have been back by now.*

"Spence, I'm pregnant." Jessie threw it out there. Spencer forgot to breathe for a moment. Both continued walking.

This was what Spencer was expecting. Of course no matter how much he was waiting for it he still didn't know what to say. "Are you okay? Is he, she ... it okay?"

"It's all fine." Jessie's shoulders shook. "Can we not talk about it right now? I just don't want to talk about it."

Chapter 4

Hanni was still where Chrys left her, sitting on the floor. Her back was against the wall, mascara smeared down her cheeks. She rubbed her shoulder where she had hit the wall. Izzy was walking by herself as she and Chrys reached the second floor. She was a lot worse off than the blond, but from looking at the two of them you couldn't tell, unless you looked at the redhead's face.

"Holy hell!" Hanni pushed herself to a more upright sitting position. She swiped black tears away. "What happened?"

"I got punched."

"She got fucking punched," Chrys repeated. "The douche-bag punched her and took off into the crowd."

"Nobody stopped him?"

"Nobody knew what was going on."

Izzy backed up against the wall and slid down to the well-used carpet. Her orangey-red hair scrunched up behind her head like a deflated ball. "Was that the guy we were looking for?"

Chrys shook her head. The door of Luke Weston's room was still open. There was enough space between the door and the jamb for someone to squeeze through. All she could see were a pair of used running shoes that had simply been discarded beside the door as if someone had flipped them off when they last entered and forgot about them. Only one was on the plastic matt. Chrys placed a flat hand against the door. Her thumb ring clicked against the wood.

"Chrys, what are you doing?" Hanni had panic in her voice. As she tried moving a moan slipped from her lips.

"Someone might be in there." Chrys said with a little too much excitement in her voice.

"That's why you shouldn't go in there."

Chrys craned her neck to get a better angle around the door. She said, "I mean Luke could be in there hurt or something. We have to check." She slowly pushed the door. Her neck began to grow as she stretched to see more. She suddenly spun around. Her eyes moved to her arm where Hanni's handmade white marks on her skin.

"We're not going in there. That guy was just some punk thief looking for whatever this Luke guy left in his room. Obviously he's not here. I don't care what you say about it, we're not going in there." Hanni glared at Chrys shooting spears with her eyes. She flexed her fingers. "We're not going in."

Thirty seconds of staring, six colourful curses, one tongue sticking out and Chrys finally pushed the door in. There was no reason for Hanni to be worried about anyone hiding in the room because there was nowhere to hide. It was barely bigger than the walk-in cooler back at The Alcrest. There was a single bed (*not much room for recreational activities*), a small dresser, an apartment size refrigerator that doubled as a bedside table and a desk and chair by a tiny window. Other furnishings included a lamp with a western motif shade and a digital alarm clock/radio atop the fridge, a 13" television on one corner of the desk and that was about it. It didn't smell like she thought it would. It smelled "girlish." There was the faint aroma of perfume in the air. The blankets from the bed had been tossed across the floor where they lay in front of a closet door. Papers and magazines (they must have originally been on the fridge next to the clock) were half-hazardly thrown on the floor beside the bed. Either Luke was a horrible housekeeper or *Hoodie* was looking for something.

"This is smaller than my bedroom." Izzy walked in and sat on the bed. Her face looked terrible. Her left cheek had swollen so much the eye was half closed. At least the cut had stopped bleeding. Blood had dried down her face and neck and soaked into the dark Alcrest shirt. She still had the pieces of her glasses in her hand.

Chrys looked at her a moment then remembered what Hanni had said about how someone else could be in the room. There was space under the bed. It had

47

been a long time since she'd hidden under a bed. Did people still think that was a good place to hide? She got down on her hands and knees and looked between Izzy's white-skinned legs to see underneath. Two maroon suitcases. No boogieman.

"Seriously, Chrys? Can't you keep your mind on the task at hand?"

Chrys looked up from the floor at Hanni who leaned on the door frame rubbing where Hoodie had pushed her, or fondling her own boobs. It was hard to tell. Different place and time Chrys would have thought she was trying to seduce her. "Just admiring her pretty anklet. Real gold?"

Izzy nodded. "Birthday present from my dad."

While Chrys was down there she thought she might as well look through the papers. She sat Indian style, an expression she always found funny since she was Aboriginal, (different kind of Indian – dots, not feathers) and began going through them. Some were bills, some receipts for clothes or food, but most looked like poems. All were written in the same handwriting. The first three she read were about being alone and sad. Next came the magazines. It was not the typical selection one expected to find in a man's room. There was a Men's Health and People and then there were two Cosmopolitans, (both with dog-eared pages), Glamour and Life & Style. It wasn't against all odds that he would have them. She caught Spencer reading a Cosmo the few times she had one. It just seemed odd. In Chrys' mind an eighteen year old man without any nudie magazines was just strange.

As she pulled two magazines apart, a small rectangle piece of white paper fluttered to the floor like a feather. It was just big enough for the typed phone number printed on it. One of the edges had a ragged edge like it had been torn from something. She put it in her pocket.

She got up and went to the dresser. All of the drawers were ajar and the clothes messed up. She quickly went through them moving things aside to see if there was anything underneath or behind. It was all standard fair. The only things out of the ordinary were a collection of women's lacey underwear in the back of one drawer. Some of them were kind of nice looking. A collection donated from dates maybe? She found a bra back there too.

"Are you done yet?" Hanni kept looking up and down the hallway when she was not watching what was going on inside the room. She sniffed and ran a finger under her nose.

Izzy had found a small compact mirror on the bed next to the pillow. She studied her reflection and pushed her finger into the swollen side.

"I'm almost done." Chrys got down on her knees gain and pulled the suitcases from under the bed. Both were empty. Her body folded to the side until she landed on her bum. The only place left to look was the closet. If Hanni was right, there could be someone waiting inside there. If Hanni was right, Chrys would hit her face against the wall until the world went right.

She rose to her feet with a slight grunt. The blond snickered as she peered down the hallway. Chrys kicked the blankets away from the closet door. If someone was in there he would have had to go in before Hoodie destroyed the place. Or perhaps that was where Luke had been all along. She put her hand on the handle and took a breath. She knew what a dead body smelled like and she didn't get the scent at all. *Did a freshly killed body smell?* She wondered. She tore open the door.

Five hangers dangled from the rod. There was a white dress shirt on one, a black shirt on another. Both looked a little rough around the cuff. A pair of faded blue jeans were folded over a hanger next to the black shirt. She fingered the jeans and saw there was a design on the back pockets. She didn't think a man would wear those. On the third hanger was a navy blue dress with matching shawl. It was pretty. She checked the tag. It said size 14. The other two hangers were empty. Chrys got down on her knees to examine a pair of black wedge heels, size 13. They were not well worn. It didn't seem right. Luke's parents said nothing about a girlfriend. However, having a girlfriend would make his disappearance seem more possible. Women made men do all sorts of things.

"Those are pretty. Izzy had crossed to stand behind Chrys, not that it took too many steps.

"Why they are here, is my question."

"Maybe the guy got lucky. Can we go? I'm tired of wasting time." Hanni stomped her foot and stared at the other two. "This is bullshit. I'm going back to my car and I'm leaving."

"We can't leave all of his stuff here. What if that Hoodie guy comes back?" Chrys said.

Hanni crossed her arms. "What the hell do you want to do then?"

Chrys looked around at everything. Her eyes fell on the suitcases. "Let's pack everything and take it with us."

"Are you serious?" Hanni squealed.

Izzy just opened the smaller case and started loading the papers.

"You're going to steal his shit so that someone else can't steal his shit. I'm not doing this." She turned and stomped away down the hallway.

Izzy didn't say anything. As soon as she had the small suitcase full she vanished into the hallway pulling the case behind her.

Chrys took another look around the room. She had searched through everything she could. There was no sign that Luke had been in his room recently. There was dust on the fridge top. The earliest date on a magazine was a month prior. She picked up a pen from the floor and wrote a quick note on the back of one of the Alcrest business cards she carried with her. Usually they were for random guys she met. She had all of the clothes packed into the large suitcase. The last thing she added were the heels.

Her name reverberated down the hallway.

"I'm coming," Chrys called out. She locked the door as she closed it. The other two had already descended the stairs. She quickly headed toward that end of the hallway rolling the larger of the maroon set of cases behind her. She wasn't looking forward to the stairs where she'd have to lift it down. It wasn't heavy, but it was bulky. Her eyes caught the bulletin board again. The job ads were there with small rectangles of paper hanging from the bottom waiting to be torn off. A few were missing. She took the slip from her pocket and scanned all of the ads. One, hidden half under the Club 22 poster, had the same number as the small piece she found in the room. All but one of the number strips were missing. The name on the solid part read, McClean Contracting.

Outside the street fair continued. Izzy stood on the stairs waiting for her. She said Hanni promised to wait at the car. As they walked through the crowd, people took a look at the bruised woman. At the first stand selling drinks, they bought a soda in a can so she could put it against her face. It didn't really make her look any better. Chrys scanned the crowd and continued to look behind them every few steps. Part of her was looking to see if Hoodie was anywhere around, but most of her was looking for something else. She had the feeling like they were being watched. Perhaps they were being followed.

Izzy stopped and grabbed Chrys by the arm.

Chrys looked at her friend who stared ahead with wide eyes. Hoodie stood in front of them, his hood still pulled up. Most of his dark face hid inside the shadows, but the whites of his eyes seemed to glow. This weren't the startled eyes Chrys saw in Luke's doorway. These were confident eyes, probably because of the two men standing with him, one behind each shoulder. One wore dark sunglasses with a ball cap holding down long black hair. The other had pale skin with tattoos crawling up his neck from under his shirt. Both of them appeared to have more muscles than the first one.

"Where are you going, Sweet Thing?" Hoodie asked. He was staring directly into Chrys' brown eyes. His hands were hidden in the pouch of his sweatshirt.

"That's original," she smirked. Chrys didn't like the way they were looking at her body. It wasn't lust, she knew what that was like; it was more like they were sizing up her worth. The way their eyes looked up and down made her feel like she had bugs crawling over her skin. Perhaps it was her fault for wearing so little. Her cut-off shorts suddenly felt shorter. Her T-shirt hid her well though, but judging by the way they leered, she could have been wearing nothing at all. She had to shake the feeling. They were in the wrong, not her. Chrys began backing away. She pushed Izzy behind her. "What the fuck do you want?"

All three of the men laughed. *Was this just a game to them?* Maybe harassing women was how they got their kicks. They weren't giants, but neither looked like they were going to back down from a couple of women in tight shorts dragging suitcases. Tattoo's right hand was in his pocket. Weapon?

Without taking her eyes from the men Chrys did a rapid assessment of where they were. They were closer to the parking garage than the hostel and on the edge of the fair. People walked by pretending not to see the awkward meeting. They had to get past the men to get to the garage where Hanni had gone, alone. She hoped Hanni was all right. She would have nobody to blame but herself if anything happened. There was that icky feeling again. No, she couldn't put Izzy and Hanni at risk. Giving them the suitcases was probably the only choice. What did they want with them?

"Well?" Chrys hadn't realized the hand not holding the suitcase had balled into a fist.

"I bet this one could do good if we put her to work." Tattoo licked his lips. "She'd bring in a good price on the menu."

"Go fuck yourself you gorram…" even she lost track of how man expletives she used. "What the fuck do you want?" Chrys raised her voice hoping to gain attention from the people pretending to ignore them.

"Maybe to smack you around like I did her." An empty hand came out of Hoodie's pocket and pointed two fingers at Izzy. The left hand. Chrys was pretty sure he was right handed, so what was so important that he kept that hand in the pouch?

Izzy squeezed Chrys' arm and yelled, "Just you try it you, you monkey-ass-kisser."

Chrys focused on Hoodie's eyes (she had taken a few kickboxing classes and knew to watch the eyes, not the hands) and tried to stop herself from bursting out laughing. She had never heard Izzy raise her voice, let alone call someone a monkey-ass-kisser. Her foot hit something. She looked down.

Hoodie took his chance. He leapt forward and grabbed for the arm holding the suitcase. Thick fingers locked around her thin forearm.

Chrys didn't think. Her hips pivoted. Her free fist jabbed. She felt the soft tissue as her knuckles connected with his throat. A choking noise escaped his open mouth. He let go of her arm and grasped his throat. Chrys saw his friends register that something was happening.

Tattoo's hand came free of his pocket. A flick of his wrist revealed a blade with a *thack!*

A sudden loud scream echoed into the air. Chrys looked to her side. Izzy's mouth was wide open in a bellowing screech that gained instant attention from anyone near. Her good eye spat fire. She grasped the pull-out handle of the smaller case with both hands. Her body cranked back. With another scream she unwound and the suitcase arched into the air. Tattoo and Glasses stepped back out of its path. Hoodie never saw it coming. The case pommeled him square in the back sending him sprawling past Chrys onto the paved ground.

Izzy's teeth glistened. Chrys couldn't believe what was happening. This timid young girl seemed to have fangs and her eyes were wide. She let out another howl as the bag swung back the other way. This time the corner of the suitcase stabbed Tattoo's hand sending the knife into the air. The last time they saw it, it skidded across the ground.

Chrys grabbed Izzy's arm. For a moment she wondered if the redhead was going to swing the case at her.

"Run." She pushed Izzy to the side. The two of them took off into the crowd that had gathered. The suitcases bounced behind them. Chrys wanted to look back, but wouldn't dare. Her eyes searched. They charged around people. As they reached the door to the parking garage there was a car horn honking.

Hanni leaned out the driver's window. "Get your skinny butts in the car." She rubbed her nose.

Chrys opened the passenger door and let Izzy scramble into the back seat followed by both suitcases. Chrys slammed the door. "Go, go, go."

"What's your..."

"Just go!"

Hanni stepped on the gas sending pedestrians out of way. Chrys and Izzy spun in their seats. They couldn't see the three men at all. All of this was getting way too real.

Chapter 5

"Dude, come here."

Spencer looked up. He sat at a corner table with Jessie. Neither of them were actually supposed to work today, but after depositing the dogs upstairs they ended up down at the corner table going over restaurant bills and staff schedules. Anything to keep their minds off their other problems. Neither wanted to talk about it, but they didn't want to leave the other alone either. Of course, they barely spoke to each other about anything else either. "Did you just call me Dude?"

Gordie threw his head back in frustration. "Chef Dude. That better?" He said. Though almost all of the staff called Spencer "Chef" the two of them had worked together so long that simple things slipped. "We're having a very important discussion that you *need* to be part of."

Gordie and Ranger had been over in the bar with Wylie for a good fifteen minutes discussing something. Wylie was as tall as Gordie was round, so how the three of them squeezed into the small bar area was tricky. As other staff members came by, they asked a question, gave their response, and moved on.

Sunday nights just sucked. A group of four played a board game in the frame room (tonight it was Settlers of Catan) and a few new people were out in the dining room. Spencer really had to send some people home.

"I'm working over here. I'm not even supposed to be here." He really didn't want to get involved in whatever they were talking about. Past "Important discussions" included: the greatest cinematic achievements off Arnold Schwarzenegger, which fast-food restaurant had the tastiest fries, the best Ninja Turtle, and craziest place anyone had sex. The most popular answers by the way were: Terminator, McDonalds, and Michelangelo and with your mom.

"Just come on. This is so important."

Spencer looked at Jessie. She hadn't really met his eyes since she gave him the news. She didn't look up and moved some papers around. He shrugged his shoulders, got to his feet and carried his empty glass to the bar. Wylie took it and filled it with The Alcrest house-made iced tea. Today's iced tea was supposed to have a handful of wild berries, but Spencer opted out. He slipped onto one of the stools and took a long swig. Gordie, Wylie and Ranger were all squished into the small bar looking at him and waiting.

58

"Okay," he placed his glass on a coaster, "what is this important question? Ranger, can I get some fries?"

"Yes Chef." Ranger adjusted his hat and started walking backward. The bar and kitchen were all along the same line - bar, cold side and hot kitchen, with on open space between the cold and hot side.

Gordie took a breath for dramatic effect. "Zombies are attacking the restaurant. Which two women and two men of the staff would you want on your survival team?

Now that was an important question!

"Ranger wants Chrys, Sue, you and me on his team, but I don't trust any of his answers." Gordie ignored the fry cook's protest from behind him. "Mr. Wylie here has picked you, Chrys, Jessie and Ranger. I'm a little reluctant to pick you. You have too many attachments. Ranger would be perfect because he was nobody."

"Screw you guys." Ranger turned toward the fryer. He took two steps and his toe snagged on the hectogram floor mat. One hand shot out, and touched the basket in the fryer then grabbed onto the edge of the machine. His feet caught up beneath him and as he stood he turned to the others.

"Watch your step, Ranger," Spencer called down the line. He had held his breath as he watched the other stumble. "You don't want to know what happens when your hand falls in 375 degree oil."

Gordie's eyes opened wide and rolled back in his head. He reached out like Frankenstein's monster and started taking stiff-legged steps. "Unimaginable pain and horror." He let out a howl. As soon as he was

59

back to normal he said, "I once saw a girl reach into a fryer. Her hand came out and the skin literally peeled off like a glove."

Just the thought of it made Spencer's stomach churn and there was a twitch in his groin. "What the hell did she put her hand in there for?"

The big man scratched his beard. "She was walking by on her way for a smoke break and her lighter fell in."

"Was she blond?" Wylie asked.

Ranger stood back from the fryer a moment as if it had just appeared.

The front door opened. Hanni came through first. She took her sunglasses off with a little flair in her movements and marched toward the bar. Izzy came in next followed by Chrys. She whispered something to the redhead before disappearing down the hallway to the back.

"Izzy, what happened?" Dee, one of the servers, asked.

Jessie quickly crossed the room. "What the hell?" Her arms went out to her sides. Hanni sidestepped around her and continued to the bar. Izzy shrugged and shook her head. As Chrys came from the back Jessie marched right to her. "Did you do this?"

"What?" Chrys' face scrunched up. "No."

Hanni sat kitty-corner to the chef. To Wylie she said, "Can I get a Dirty Hooker?"

"What happened?" Spencer asked in Hanni's direction.

"Nothing happened." Chrys blasted and actually nudged Jessie as she walked past.

"Bullshit, Chrys. Look at her face." As Jessie realized how loud she was she took a quick look around. There were a few customers in the main restaurant, but most were in the Frame Room.

"We went looking for, for that kid." Chrys motioned toward her brother. "And some fucking gangbanger punched Izzy in the face."

"Oh my God," was one remark.

"What the hell?" asked Jessie as she put her arm around Izzy.

"She came back and beat the shit out of three of them though." It was a little embellishment. Chrys lowered her eyes and hoped the others would be quiet.

"Ah, guys." Ranger's timid voice could barely be heard.

Jessie folded her arms over her chest. "I can't believe you're doing this again, Chrys. But this time you're putting people directly in the line of fire."

"Ah, guys."

"Jess your mouth is talking. You might want to look into that," Chrys said keeping her back to the other woman.

Everyone who heard gasped. They all seemed to take a step away and held their breath. Spencer felt both women watching him, waiting to see whom he would support.

Jessie made a noise to try and get him to say something. She moved toward Chrys. "Who the hell do you think you are? This is the second time you've done this."

Chrys shook her head. She stepped toward her manager. "Who the fuck do you think you are? This has nothing to do with work, so it has nothing to do with you."

"You really don't want to get on my bad side right now, Chrys."

Chrys did one of her award-winning eye rolls. "And what the fuck are you going to do?" She leaned in.

"Chrys!" Spencer jumped off the stool, the legs scratching on the floor. Both women stopped talking but didn't move. He stared at his sister for a long moment trying to will her to look in his direction.

The stare down was only broken when a couple walked through the front door reminding everyone that they were still in a restaurant. Other customers were staring waiting for something to happen.

Spencer swiftly rounded the bar. He grabbed Chrys' arm where Hoodie had grabbed her and pulled her the other way. Her eyes looked from the other woman and locked on his. "Can I see you in my office?" It wasn't really a question. He tugged again. She stumbled at first then followed him like a pouting child.

"Are you seriously taking her side?" Chrys ripped her arm from his grip before they got to the hostess stand. They both looked at the couple who had come in as Dee walked them past. "I can't believe you're taking her side," she continued. She looked behind her. Jessie was still standing where she had been, glaring in their direction. The others were trying to act as though they weren't paying attention. "Seriously? I can't fucking believe this."

Spencer looked back at Jessie. His eyes dropped to her belly. He turned back to his sister. "This isn't the place to be having this discussion. I'm not choosing anyone's side."

"Of course you are." She took two steps toward the hall leading to the back then stopped and turned around again. "You think I'm stupid for looking for this guy, don't you?"

"I didn't..."

Chrys' hand went up. "You just said enough. I'm so sorry I'm a foster kid who would hope someone would look for me if anything ever went wrong."

"And you know I would..."

"But Luke has no one. You made your choice, Spencer. I get it." She glanced over at Jessie. "I'm on my own." Chrys whipped around and walked swiftly out the front door.

Spencer wondered where she was going. He honestly expected to find her upstairs in their apartment when he went up there later. She wasn't there, however. He didn't know where she was.

Chapter 6

Walking back into his bedroom after taking the dogs for a short walk early Monday morning, Spencer tried to be as quiet as he could. He checked his sister's room as he passed. Her bed was all a mess (it was always a mess) and she wasn't there. In his room Jessie was asleep. She stirred a little when Breeze jumped on the bed and Bullet started snorting that he wanted out. She had kicked off all of the blankets and lay there on her side completely naked except for a gold watch on the wrist draped over her hip. Tattooed on that arm was the phrase "Candle within the Chaos." Spencer was surprised at how seamless her body was. She had a couple of moles on her skin, but otherwise she was perfect. He could sit and watch her sleep for hours. Her short sun-kissed brown hair was in a crazy mess around her head. He sat down on his side of the bed. She rolled onto her back. She didn't have the flat toned stomach like his sister (Chrys was a dance instructor, so nobody had a flat stomach like her) but she was still in shape. In that belly could be his son or daughter. He was suddenly afraid to touch her. If he did she would be real. The whole situation would be real. Or maybe she would vanish in the wisp of a breath. He wasn't sure which made him more fearful.

"Spence?"

She speaks.

Jessie rubbed her eye with the back of her hand. Nothing could make a naked woman seem less sexy than watching her mine the crud from the corner of her eye. "What time is it?"

"Early. Just past seven."

"Sandra's downstairs?"

"Yes." Sandra was the morning cook. Spencer could smell some of the baked goods she had made. He watched as Jessie checked the time on the digital alarm clock, as though he had lied to her. He pushed his back against the wall. The cold forced a breath to escape his lungs.

Jessie rolled toward him. "What's wrong?"

"Nothing's wrong. I was just watching you."

"Right. Still no word from Chrys?" Jessie started rubbing his hairy leg. He wore surfing shorts with bright hibiscus pictures on them.

Spencer grabbed his phone. He said, "No, not yet. I texted her but she hasn't responded. I'm sure she's fine."

"She probably found a warm bed to sleep in."

"Jess." He knew what she meant.

"What? You know it's true." She rolled away from him and sat up.

Spencer took a few breaths. He didn't want to fight with her. He really hated some of the things she said about his sister – of course some of the things his sister said about her were not good either. It was one of the things he wasn't sure he could get past. In one move he grabbed a shirt from the floor, smelled it, and put it on. He found a clean pair of black chef pants, slipped the shorts off and replaced them with those. "I have some running around to do this morning. I should be back before lunch time."

"You have the new guy working with Gordie, remember. Gordie doesn't like him that much."

"I'm sure I'll be back before lunch."

"How many times have I heard that before?"

Spencer had the urge to tell her she was gorgeous, but held back. She would have said something like – she was naked in his bed, so of course he thought she was gorgeous. He stared at her bare back, her skin fair and smooth. "And if I'm not, I'm sure they can get along without me." He didn't even have to see her face to know her expression. "You don't trust Gordo's ability to bite his tongue?"

"No." She couldn't find her panties. Last night wasn't that wild and Spencer kept his room freakishly tidy, so there was a good chance Bullet took them for a walk. "The last time you weren't there to train a new dishwasher Gordie handed him a knife and sent him up the back stairs to, *get the chickens for supper*."

Spencer tried his best not to laugh. At the time he wasn't sure who was more freaked out - Chrys or the dishwasher, probably his sister considering she was in the living room barely wearing any clothes as she exercised. Gordie was sure the kid fell down the stairs. He still worked on weekends and couldn't look Chrys in the eyes. "I'll be here," he said. "Look, I'll put a reminder in my phone."

"That'll help. I'm going to take a shower. Care to join me?"

For a second Spencer stayed focused on his phone. As he looked up Jessie was backing away toward the hall. Her naked body seemed to glow in the morning light. The curves of motherhood were far from taking over her form. Would he love her body more or less then, he wondered. It didn't really matter in the moment. He put his phone down.

Chapter 7

Chrys opened one eye. For a few moments she didn't have a clue where she was and was cautious. She could smell coffee (which could have been coming from the restaurant) but she was on a couch that creaked like leather. They didn't own a leather couch. On the far side of a red oak coffee table (with no glass rings stained on the surface) was a giant flat-screen television mounted above a brick fireplace. She and her brother didn't own either of those and there wasn't a dog licking her face while another one stared at her with a sad expression.

Her first thought, *she sure as fuck wasn't home*.

She did recognize it, however, as everything from the night before flooded back. After leaving The

Alcrest she ran up the back stairs to the apartment; changed her clothes, gave Breeze and Bullet a good rub and headed off toward the dance studio. She wasn't sure she wanted to go there, but she could at least burn off some steam and someone there could give her a ride. She walked with her head down texting everyone she could think of who might have a spare place for her to sleep for the night. A couple of former mistakes reminded her why they *were* mistakes. "Yeah, I have some spare room, but you'll have to sleep with me on top of you. Lol" *Really?* She was just about to hit the last resort button and message Hanni when Roy answered her text.

She opened both eyes and focused on the framed photo of Roy and his husband that sat on the fireplace mantle. The three met when the couple came to the Elizabeth Frances Dance Studio for ballroom dance lessons before their wedding. Since then they had become Chrys' BGF's - *Best-Gay-Friends.*

"Oh look who stirs. How do you want your coffee, Honey?" Roy's voice was always so soothing.

Chrys pushed herself to a sitting position and slowly turned her head. Something inside her skull wasn't quite right. Roy was behind a kitchen island dressed in a tailored business suit. He was immaculate - hair perfect, shaved smooth, manicured nails, professionally dry-cleaned suit with matching tie and pocket square. The kitchen around him was immaculate. Everything was in its place without a crumb or speck of dust anywhere. Yeah, Chrys could never live here. Spencer too was a clean-freak, but could never achieve the perfect magazine setting of this apartment. She stretched her arms and felt the muscles in her back pop into place. "Do you have any hot chocolate mix?"

"I don't think so. Wes might have some in his secret stash. He likes to move it to a new place in the condo every few days to try and keep it hidden. He thinks he's being sneaky." He shook his head.

Chrys tried getting to her feet. For a moment she thought she wasn't going to stand. "A shit load of cream and four, five sugars."

"What's the point in the coffee?" He queried, but prepared the cup as she'd asked.

"Do you have any Aspirin?"

He already had the bottle on the island by the time she made it there. "Too much Kiki?"

"Is that what we were drinking last night?"

Kiki liquor and Orange Crush together made a creamy-orange creamsicle-flavoured drink. The trouble was you couldn't taste the alcohol. For Chrys that was both a problem and a benefit.

"That was what we started with, then Wes made extra-strong margaritas. I hope we didn't keep you up last night. Get too much booze in him and he gets a little frisky."

Chrys shook her head as she sipped the hot liquid. A phone on the island beside a bowl of fruit pinged and she realized it was hers.

"Honey that thing has been going off all morning."

"Just my stupid brother. See - *Where are you?*" She texted him back saying, "Go fuck yourself."

"You really need to get over yourself."

Chrys screwed her face up like a little kid not getting what she wanted. "Whose side are you on?"

71

Roy exhaled, "The side that gets you off my sofa." He reached out placing his hand over hers. "I love you, Chrys, and you can stay here as long as you want, but I just can't drink like that on a work night. Luckily today is an office day. Tomorrow I'm going to be in court all day."

"You look fine." Chrys tried running her fingers through her hair, but they got caught in the tangles. "Probably better than me."

"I don't feel fine," Roy said.

"Sorry. Next time I have a crisis I'll plan it for a weekend." Chrys asked if she could have a shower before she left. When she got in there she wasn't surprised to discover the boys had more hair and body products than she did.

As she let the water fall over her, tiny beads of heat pricking her skin, she wondered what was next. The problem with Spencer would fix itself, always had; it was Luke Weston she thought about. He was out there somewhere. The questions she wanted to answer were where was he and was he okay. She had to figure out where to start. The suitcases had been left at the restaurant (Izzy texted her to let her know), so she couldn't go there. She couldn't think of anything that had been in them which would help anyway. She could always return to the hostel in the hopes there would be guests she could talk to; however, she didn't want to go alone. She wasn't going to push her luck with last night's roommates. There was no way she would ask Hanni and no way the blond would go with her if she did. Luke had the number for that construction contractor in his room. She could start there. It was as good a place as any.

She stepped from the shower, dried off and dressed in her black jeans, white tank-top and pale blue hooded sweater with the zippered front. It was her outfit from last night and she had slept in the tank-top and panties. She didn't think about taking extra clothes when she left her place yesterday. She liked playing and getting dirty, but Chrys really hated wearing dirty clothes. She usually changed a couple of times throughout the day. She didn't want to go home though. She pulled on her ankle boots and headed out the door with a fresh peach in her pocket.

Chapter 8

Spencer was lucky enough to find a parking spot right in front of the Greenleaf Hostel. The street fair was gone. In fact the only way to tell it had even been there were piles of road barriers (disassembled and left on the sidewalk at cross streets) and some signs that still remained taped to lamp posts. Cumberland was back to normal. People sauntered through the street, dropping into some of the artistic boutiques which lined the street. Spencer wondered if he should cross over to the psychic's for a good old-fashioned palm read to figure out his life. He saw a woman step from the small, Bohemian-decorated shop, sobbing into the shoulder of another woman and decided against it.

The inside of the hostel was not what he expected. It was clean and modern. It was much more like a hotel lobby than what he thought a hostel would be. In a sitting area, two women and a guy huddled around a map of the city. Spencer was pretty sure they were speaking German.

The man behind the front desk was tall and skinny with an eagle-like nose and long greasy hair. He did look like he belonged in a hostel, just maybe not behind the front counter.

"Hi." Spencer flashed a smile.

"Hey, mornin'. How's it going'?"

"Good. Look, I'm wondering if you can help me out. I'm looking for my friend. I know he's supposed to be staying here, but nobody's heard from him in a while. Luke Weston."

The tall skinny guy shrugged his shoulders. "I can check the computer for his name, but I can't, like, tell you much."

"That's okay. My sister came here yesterday, so I know he's still registered." He didn't know that, but the greasy guy didn't need to know. "I'm more interested if anyone's seen him lately." After the morning shower with Jessie, Spencer called Mrs. Staples and was able to get the same photo of Luke that Chrys had sent to his cellphone. He showed it to the front desk guy.

"That guy? Yeah, I've seen him around. Not for a while though."

"When was the last time?"

"Shoot man, I don't know. It's been a while though, like, a long while."

"Can I ask around?" As soon as Spencer got the nod he turned around and crossed to the trio still huddled around a map. "Hi guys." He pushed the sleeves of his shirt up to his elbows and settled his behind on the arm of the sofa the girls sat on. "Can I ask you some questions?"

"Yes, I guess so." The woman closest to him answered in broken English.

All three of them were young and relatively good-looking. Spencer knew that the majority of people staying at a hostel didn't have much money, but that wasn't always the case. He wondered if he should put brochures in some of the city's hostels. It might be a good way to get the out-of-town crowd to come in.

"How long have you guys been staying here?"

The closest woman said, "We only two days."

"I been three weeks," said the man in the same accent.

"Have any of you seen my friend?" In turn, Spencer showed the photo on his phone to all three of them. The ladies shook their heads. The man leaned in for a closer look. "Have you seen him?"

"I think when I first come here."

"And that was three weeks ago? Did you talk to him at all?"

He shook his head in the negative.

A possible sighting had to be better than no sighting at all. The next two people to pass through the lobby had never seen Luke. Spencer wasn't sure what else to do. He thought about calling his sister, but the only message he had received from her since yesterday told him to go fuck himself. Anyway, she wouldn't be interested in helping him prove this Weston kid just didn't' want to talk to anyone. This was the only lead that he had, but a lot of the people who stayed here were in and out just as fast. Luke had been missing for a week, so Spencer had to talk to people who had been there longer than a few days.

The fourth floor was quiet; in fact, he saw only one person on the floor. A woman stood at a bulletin board flipping through the pages. Waves of dark-blond hair cascaded over her shoulders. Her skin looked bronzed. She wore a dress what looked like a white tank-top over a long black skirt, so long that her feet were not visible. She turned in his direction for a second, didn't pay him any attention and went back to what she was doing. All of her attention was directed toward the bulletin board and the papers covering it.

"Excuse me." Spencer's breath caught at the woman's green eyes as she faced him. He also noticed the even dark space between her healthy breasts.

A paper fell from her hands.

"Did I startle you? I didn't mean…"

"You didn't." Her words bit.

Before she could bend down Spencer had the paper in his hands. On the front was the silhouette of a beautiful woman dancing on a blue background. The biggest lettering said, "Club 22." She snatched it out of his hand.

"Do you work here?" he asked.

"No." The paper got unceremoniously stuffed into her designer purse. She focused her attention on the bulletin board basically ignoring the man. She no longer shuffled through the papers, but her eyes searched all around not seeming to lock on anything in particular.

"Do you work there? Club 22? I've heard of it, but I've never been there."

The woman turned toward him. A smirk crossed thin red lips. Her hands clutched onto the bag. Her eyes quickly looked up and down his body as though she were sizing him up to decide what to do with him. A perfectly formed eyebrow arched up.

Something inside Spencer didn't like the way it made him feel. He thought he knew what lobsters in a tank must feel like.

"You should come check it out." she said quickly. Her voice was sharp and demanding. She moved to step around him.

"Have you seen this guy?" Spencer held up his phone. "He lives right there."

She looked to where he pointed. For a long moment she was still. "What's your name?" the woman asked as she turned back toward him. Her head tilted to the side. She smelled like wildflowers.

For a moment he either couldn't remember his name or couldn't understand the question. "Spencer Alcrest. Have you heard of The Alcrest Gastropub?" There was no acknowledgment from the woman. He wanted to know her name, but for some reason couldn't bring himself to ask. Maybe thinking of her as *The Woman* was just better. "Can you look at this picture? My sister was here yesterday looking for him and…"

She shook her head making the blond hair roll over both shoulders like actual waves. The scent of wildflowers was suddenly stronger, almost intoxicating. She said, "Sorry I couldn't help you," and stepped around him.

He was stunned for a moment at the harshness in her voice. His eyes stayed on her as she walked around him and down the hallway. His gaze lingered on the way her dress hugged the curves of her hips like a second skin. Everything about her walk said she knew what she was doing. Hanni had a good walk, but this woman's he wouldn't mind watching again. He blinked and realized she never did answer his question. She pushed open the door to the stairs and slipped through. The door clicked. Spencer took a step and the door opened again. Two men stepped onto the fourth floor. Their necks stretched back to see the woman they had just passed.

Chrys said her attackers were black. One of them at least. Or did Izzy say it? It didn't matter, these two were Caucasian. They both wore jeans and T-shirts. Spencer's body tensed. His hand grazed his pants pocket. At work he always had a knife hooked on the edge for cutting open boxes and plastic bags. It wasn't there. He wasn't at work, so why did he need the knife? Spencer took a step back leaving plenty of room to pass. They weren't speaking to each other. One looked at the chef. This was it. His head nodded as they walked by.

Spencer let out a breath he didn't know he was holding. "Excuse me."

The men turned and side-stepped a little before stopping.

It was then Spencer realized they were still boys, barely men. "Can you guys take a look at something?"

"You sure you haven't seen him?" Spencer asked after explaining everything and showing the picture. "How long have you lived here?"

"Yeah, like, almost two months, man. I don't remember him. What room was he in?"

"This one," Spencer looked around. He had moved a few feet to catch their attention, "406 -right there."

"That's Luca's room," the second one said.

"His name is Luke. I thought you didn't see him."

"Who's Luke?"

"The guy who lived in 406." Spencer felt like he was stuck in a loop.

"Her name is Luca. A chick lives there, or lived. Haven't seen her in over a week or so, man." He pulled his cellphone from his pocket. The other one was nodding along.

"A woman?" Spencer was getting a headache. If this was all just going to turn out to that Luke got lucky and took off, he was going to be pissed.

"That the one with the nice ass?" The first one said to his friend. "Hey," his attention was back on Spencer, "did you see that blond that was just here?"

Spencer just nodded. "I thought the woman's long-stay rooms were on the third floor."

"They are." The second one scrolled through something on his phone. "Luca said she was staying in her cousin's room since he'd already paid and didn't need it. Here, this is her." He handed his phone to Spencer. The picture on the screen was the back view of a woman in tight fitting pants and a brown bomber jacket. Chestnut hair fell over her shoulders hiding her face. "That is Luca. I had to take a picture from behind because of that ass. She wasn't too bad from the front either."

"And when was the last time you saw her?"

81

"When this pic was taken. Just over two weeks ago."

"Can you send it to me?" Spencer took the man's phone and typed his information into it. Seconds later the picture of Luca was on his phone. As the men went into their rooms, Spencer headed for the stairs. Now he had two mysteries - where was Luke and who was this Luca? Damn his sister.

Chapter 9

Chrys looked up from her cellphone. At least she could finally see the sign for McClean Contracting. It took her two buses to get close to their offices and then she still had to walk a few blocks. Her hair was tied back since she didn't dry it all the way, though the sun was doing a good job. It was still early in the day, but perspiration (hell it was good-old-fashioned sweat) soaked her entire body. Her damp hair cooled the back of her neck for a while. If she had slept at home she would have dressed in shorts and maybe borrowed Spencer's truck, but no - he had to be an ass. She didn't even know if Luke had actually worked for this contracting company. All she knew was that he had the number. If this was going to be the loss of a day Spencer would have every opportunity to laugh at her.

As she opened the door a rush of cold air chilled the sweat covering her body. It felt so refreshing she just wanted to stand there and enjoy it.

"Can I help you?" A woman sat behind a desk facing two computer monitors. One set of fingers hovered over an adding machine. Papers covered an L-shaped desk in some sort of organized confusion.

"Hi," Chrys suddenly realized she had no idea what to say. "I'm looking for someone."

"Who is that dear?"

There was another office across a small corridor. The man in there looked briefly at the woman at the door before his attention returned to whatever he was frantically doing. One table in his office held blueprints, which were rolled up, secured with rubber-bands and stood on end like a forest of birch trees.

Chrys turned her back to him and leaned over the counter that separated her from the woman. An air conditioning grate in the floor blew cold air right up her front to her armpits. "I'm looking for Luke Weston. His mother is worried about him." Not the butchest thing to say at a construction company, but the woman looked like a mother. She would care. "I think he worked here."

"You think he worked here?" The hand reluctantly left the adding machine. With a mouse she clicked a few things on the computer before her fingers settled on the keyboard. "Weston, you said?"

Chrys nodded. "Luke Weston."

"He was on Andrachuk's crew." the man said as he crossed through the corridor. He had a bushy moustache and dark bags under his eyes. His clothing sagged on his body. He stacked papers on top of the others on the desk. "File these and pay these." To Chrys he said, "He didn't work long, I don't think."

"I know I haven't issued him a pay cheque in a while." the woman said, suddenly sounding like she knew exactly who Luke was.

"What's a while?" Chrys received a grunt from the man as he headed back to the other office.

"A couple of months or more. I can't really comment on staff." The woman got up from her desk and quickly filed the papers the boss had given her.

Chrys said she understood. She did, but it wasn't going to help. She needed information on this guy before her brother got her to stop the whole thing. He had to be somewhere. Someone had to know something. "Why did he stop working for you?"

"I can't say."

"He wasn't fired was he? His mom would be so pissed." Chrys giggled hoping to break the tension. She bet she could get the woman to tell her everything if the man wasn't there. Using a little charm she could usually talk anyone into telling her what she wanted to know. Emphasize that a mother was looking for her child and another mother would usually do all she could to help.

The woman shook her head. She looked like all she wanted to do was get back to her work. "I don't really know."

"He wasn't fired," the man said in the same voice he would use to ask you to pass the salt. Chrys watched him move from one desk to another. He stacked papers and binders as though he were getting ready to take them somewhere. "Pretty sure he quit."

"Any idea why?" Chrys leaned on the door to his office. She heard the sound of numbers on an adding machine rapidly being punched behind her. If she couldn't use motherly sensibilities then maybe she could use her sexuality to get what she needed. Covered in cold sweat she didn't feel that sexy, but she could act like it.

He didn't look up. "No idea."

Luke stopped talking to his mom a week ago and stopped working months before that, stopped working for McClean anyway. She had no idea what any of it meant. Luke could have quit this job and taken one that put him on the road, so he was out of touch for long periods. Maybe he took a new job that had him so busy he couldn't even call. Maybe he answered an ad for people to do science experiments for cash and one went terribly wrong? Alien abduction? Hired to find proof of the ever elusive bamashous creature? He had to be out there somewhere.

"Could I talk to other members of his crew and see if they know anything?" Chrys asked.

For the first time the boss man slowly looked her up and down, though he may have checked out her backside earlier. Chrys was very aware of her shirt clinging to her body and the pinup calendar on the wall behind him. He said, "Andrachuk's crew is doing a house in the Blue Meadows housing area. I can't call them in or anything."

"Can I go to them? Maybe when they go for lunch I could ask them if they knew him or something. Do any buses go up there?"

He stared at her for a long moment. Thirty seconds ago he was leering and now he looked like he was ready to throw her out on the street. "I can give you a lift there. You might have to find your own way back, however. The white truck outside." He grabbed his pile of papers and binders and nodded toward the door.

~ * ~

Blue Meadows was a new housing development just east of the city. Middleton was surrounded by water on three sides (it sat on the Thunder Bay Peninsula), so the only direction there was to expand was the farmland to the east. Chrys was lucky she had a ride as city buses came nowhere near the area. Over a dozen houses were complete with families living in them already, another dozen houses were at different stages of construction. There had been times when she thought about one day having a two-story house with attached two-car garage and fenced-in yard, maybe a couple of kids chasing Breeze around a swing set. Chrys imagined many things for her future. She was almost twenty-six, so she kept telling herself she had plenty of time to decide what she wanted. Her brother was set. He had the career he wanted and would keep for the rest of his life. Sooner or later Jessie was going to trap him and start popping out kids and the two of them would get married. Then Chrys would be forced to find her own life plan. Roller derby was fun, but she knew it wasn't going to last, same with the dance instructing. These brought in a little money each week, but where would she really go with that? Any thoughts of being a professional dancer were long gone. She modeled occasionally and was doing a little acting, but that was only locally. She sure as hell didn't want to be a waitress the rest of her life! Chrys suddenly had an image in her head of herself years from now with leathery skin, pink lipstick, a pudgy body, wearing stained clothes, chewing bubble gum and asking, "What'll it be?" at some crappy diner.

"Here you are." The truck stopped next to another white truck with McClean Contracting stenciled on the door. There were several other vehicles parked along the curb in front of a house. It looked nearly finished from where Chrys sat except for tape on the windows and a yard that was still covered with dirt and rock. "I can't let you go on the property, but the boys should be going for lunch in about a half-hour. I have to go see another site, so you'll have to wait here. You sure you want to stay here?"

No, she wasn't sure, but she didn't know what else to do. Chrys gave the man a meek smile. "I'm sure there are a lot of people out here who will give a pretty girl a ride." She blew him a kiss after stepping to the ground.

"Good luck then." He picked up his cellphone signalling any conversation was over. The truck sped away the second the passenger door slammed shut.

Broken by the sound of power tools faint music came from open windows of the house. Further down the street construction machinery was busy. Between a couple of houses she saw a yellow backhoe attack the ground like a hungry beast. Besides the company truck parked at the curb, there were two cars and a motorbike. The bike was something special. Though she could see no brand name, the paint job was obviously custom. Every part of the painting appeared three-dimensional as though you were looking into a child's marble. Depending on what part you looked at there were skulls and grim reapers on horseback going into battle. They weren't depictions of evil. They were paintings of beauty.

One of her boyfriends in high school had a motorbike. She didn't love him, but she did love riding on that bike. If she closed her eyes now she was pretty sure she could still feel the vibration in her thighs. She missed that feeling. The way she remembered it, it was as close to sexual release as one could get without having another body or something with batteries between your legs. She was certain her dad hated the bike more than the boy. Of course Dad was gone, and Chrys did need a vehicle. When she had the time she was going to have to check out bikes.

By the time Chrys saw men walking out of the house toward her, her backside hurt from sitting on the curb. She had been "relaxing" with her legs stretched out, crossed at the ankles, fielding texts from friends.

Yes, she would teach the little kids class tomorrow night.

No, she wasn't at the restaurant.

Yes, I'm still working tonight. Spencer's still a dick.

There was nothing special about the men on Andrachuck's crew. She wasn't sure what she expected - muscles maybe. They were a group of skinny guys covered in dust and clomping around with oversized work boots. Two wore long surfing shorts. The others all wore pants that seemed to sag low on their hips. One carried a full-face motorbike helmet.

They all carried white hard hats that seemed to have slipped from head to hand the second they stepped from the house.

"Can I ask you guys something?" Chrys had let her hair loose again. She flipped it in her best "flirty-girl" way. The men didn't stop, though they did slow down to look at her. She continued, "I'm trying to find Luke Weston. Does anyone remember him?"

"Did he knock you up?" the tallest one asked to a spattering of laughter. He walked toward the company truck.

Chrys tried to show his comment was funny. "No, his mother hasn't heard from him in a while. She's worried about him. Are you Andrachuk?"

He let out a sigh as if this interruption was ruining his day. "He quit like two months ago; said he had family issues or some bullshit. That's all I know." He climbed in the truck. The door shut and the engine started. Others got into the cars without a word.

Chrys remembered she was about to be stuck there.

The owner of the motorbike was taking off his boots and replacing them with a pair of Nike running shoes he pulled from saddlebags on the back. He tied the laces of his boots together and hung them over the seat. His arms were not as thick as Chrys thought they would be, but she was learning today not to bother with pre-conceived thoughts about people. He was one of the guys wearing shorts. His thin face was clean-shaven. His toast-brown hair was short and brushed back. His features were distinguished for what she thought a construction worker would have. She really had to stop listening to what she thought.

"Hi." Chrys didn't really know what to do with herself. She didn't know where to put her hands. It had been a while since she had been that nervous. Was it him or the bike? "That's a nice bike."

"It's for sale," he said as if he was offering it to her. His eyes were hidden behind reflective sunglasses. He looked healthy and strong. His legs were well muscled and smooth. In fact Chrys felt a warmth in her chest.

"What kind of bike is it?"

"It's a mutt. I built it myself from a bunch of different bikes and had someone paint it."

"You built it?"

"I did. That's what I do in my spare time. But now it's time to sell it and build something new." He smiled showing perfect upper teeth.

Chrys liked his smile. She felt a warmth inside her. *Damn.* "I'm Chrys, by the way."

"Colby." He attached the work hardhat to the back of the bike. "Are you a friend of Luke's?" The bike helmet slipped from the seat and hit the ground. He bent at the waist to snatch it up.

Double Damn! "Ah, no. His mom asked me to see if I could find him." Chrys made sure she was looking at his eyes when he stood.

"You a cop or something?"

"Fuck no. I'm just a friend of a friend of the family, I guess. Did you work with him?"

"Yeah." his head bounced up and down. He seemed to suddenly get lost in his thoughts.

"Were you friends?"

"Not really." He looked around the two of them. There was nobody else left. "We were similar in a few ways, so I helped him out with something. I think it

91

might have been one of the reasons he quit." He put the helmet on and fastened it under his chin.

"Helped him with what?" Chrys asked.

Colby reached for the far saddlebag. He unclipped the latch, flipped the top and pulled a small helmet from inside. He held it out to her. "I'll show you if you want. I know nobody's around, but I really don't want to talk about it here."

Chrys didn't know what she was supposed to do. She didn't know this guy and she was there for something other than herself. What was the big secret? She looked up and down the street. There was no one else around. All the other construction crews had broken for lunch. She didn't have any bad feelings about the situation, but she knew from experience what could happen. "I don't know. Can't you just tell me how you helped him?" She realized that they were completely alone, so anything he was going to do to her on the back of a bike he could do better right there.

He threw one leg over the bike and relaxed on the seat. He turned back to here with a sexy Tom Cruise Top Gun smile. "I saw Bryan drop you off, so I know you don't have a car. It would just be easier to show you than tell you about it, but I don't have much time for lunch so I have to get going." Colby offered the helmet again and Chrys took it.

She strapped it beneath her chin and climbed onto the back of the bike. There wasn't really a back seat, so she had to press her body up against Colby's. Her hands fell to her thighs. The engine beneath her revved to life and her arms reflexively wrapped around his midsection and squeezed. There were the powerful

92

vibrations through her thighs that she remembered. As the bike took off, Chrys' bum slipped back. She spread her fingers across the man's stomach and pulled herself closer. *Jesus his stomach is flat*, she thought as she buried her face behind his shoulders blocking out the wind. She suddenly realized how close her "yum-yum" was to him and wished she hadn't pulled in so close. She had to get her mind somewhere else. She tried paying attention to where they were going instead of what she felt.

Within minutes they were back in the city. Colby weaved the bike along the streets without going too crazy with the turns. Chrys knew they were not going toward The Alcrest or go anywhere near the downtown. She ran through the city map inside her head as best she could. It wasn't a reliable map. Spencer actually had a city map in the glove compartment of his truck because neither of them ventured too far out of their comfort zones, she more than he. The water was on their left, so she knew they had to be near the south end of the city. Some shops and buildings started to look familiar. She had been in this neighborhood before. As the bike slowed and eased toward the curb it came to her – Luke Weston lived just three blocks east. They were in the Cumberland neighborhood, almost in the area referred to as the Clothes Line.

As Chrys climbed off the bike she straightened out her clothes. Her thighs were warm and vibrated in a good way enough that her knees felt weak. She took the helmet off and tried adjusting her hair. She knew there were strands going in all directions. She watched as Colby slipped from his bike and took his helmet off.

One swipe with his hand through his hair and it was perfect.

"What are we doing here? Luke lives like…"

"I know. I don't know if I can say Luke and I were friends, but I recognized something in him. He was uncomfortable with everyone and especially himself. We had some good talks about it."

"I don't get what you mean."

He pulled a pack of cigarettes from one of the saddle bags. "He wasn't happy with himself. Even when he laughed he didn't really, you know, laugh. It was for show. I brought him here." He pointed across the street.

A sign above a dark door read, Ms. Kara's Pride. Chrys could tell that at night the words would all be lit. Next to the door was a tall sign. On it was a notice for a drag show from Wednesday to Saturday.

"This is a gay bar." Chrys stated.

Colby nodded and flashed his lovely smile. "Yes it is."

Things started turning in her head. "Is Luke gay?"

"No. He is confused about himself, but not gay."

"Oh." The thoughts churned. Thoughts developed inside her brain. Her eyes suddenly got large. "Are you gay?"

Colby smiled and dropped his gaze. "Yes."

Noooooooo!!! Chrys' knees buckled. "Come on, seriously? Fuck!"

Colby looked like he was enjoying the moment way too much. "Sorry. I can't say anything about it at work. It's my big secret. Nobody knows who I really am. I don't think they would understand, you know. When Luke started working with us I saw something in him that I recognized. I didn't know exactly what it was, but I felt like he was different, so I brought him here."

"But you said he's not gay."

"He's not."

"But," Chrys' train of thought was getting all twisted and lost. Part of the puzzle was missing.

"Look, I brought you here because of that." He pointed across the street.

"But you said he isn't gay."

"You don't have to be gay to go to a gay bar. I promised Luke I wouldn't say anything about what we talked about and I hold promises to be very important, especially since I have my own secrets. Look, go to Pride on Wednesday night and talk to Ms. Kara. I haven't seen Luke in a while, but she was pretty close to him. Maybe she'll be able to tell you where he is. She goes on at 10:00 pm. Stay for the show; it's really great. You'll be impressed." Colby donned his helmet. "Can I drop you off somewhere?"

Chrys stared at the club. She imagined at night that it was going to be all lit up and full of excitement. She loved a good gay bar. She hated waiting.

Chapter 10

"Can I get a server here?" Spencer slapped his hand on the tiles beneath the hanging heat lamps.

Dee suddenly appeared slipping a handwritten blue order ticket across. "Order in, Chef." She flipped her jet black ponytail from her shoulder.

"Thanks Dee. Can you take these to table twelve? I don't know where Chrys is." Spencer slid two dinner plates across the pass before turning to his kitchen crew. "Order in. Four covers on table six. Two oysters, one Alcrest salad, one soup. Second course. Two strips medium, shrimp taco, and a pickerel."

"One soup, one taco," Ranger replied.

Gordie grunted with, "Two medium." The new guy at the cold table didn't respond with anything. This was his third day on the job. Gordie slapped his tongs against the charbroil grill. "Jonas, are you gonna to answer the chef?"

The new guy looked up from his table. He wore an Alcrest Gastropub hat with the front bill turned up. He stood there for a moment then raised his hands, slapped them twice with straight arms and barked like a seal.

"What the hell is that?" Gordie squared off toward Jonas. The only thing between the two of them was Chef Spencer. "Answer the damn chef."

Spencer raised his hand to the sous chef. He was making sauce for the steaks and had the pan ready to cook the fish. "Jonas, did you hear the order?"

"Aye, captain." He saluted.

Spencer took the few steps to be right in front of the cold table. The new garde-manger cook was already shucking oysters for the ordered plates. The chef lowered his voice and leaned in. His aqua eyes stared at Jonas until he looked up. "I need you to answer me when an order is called. I need to know you heard the order."

The new guy responded, "You bet." with a giant smile.

"Plate them just like you were shown." Gordie said from his position.

There was a tapping noise behind Spencer. As he turned his sister was at the pass tapping her thumb ring against the tile.

"Where the hell's my table twelve?" she blurted out.

"I had Dee take it.

"What the…"

98

"The food was ready and you weren't around. You're all spacey tonight," Spencer said.

"I've got things on my mind, Spence. Shit you don't care about. You gave away my table." She stared across at her brother. Actually she stared at his chest because the hanging lamp was in the way of seeing his eyes and she was glad for it. No words had passed between them about last night and they probably never would. That was the way their relationship worked for them. Spencer and Chrys were as close as people who were not blood-related could be. They argued and then, with a nod, all was forgotten.

"I didn't give away your table. She just delivered their plates."

Out of the corner of his eyes Spencer saw Gordie charge along the line behind him. "What the hell are you doing?" came from the bull as he pushed his Chef out of the way.

Spencer leaned down to see his sister's chestnut oval eyes. "Food doesn't sit …"

"What's your problem?" Jonas yelled.

"…on the pass, Chrys. That's always been the rule."

"Whatever Spence." Chrys flashed him the finger, spun and walked across the dining room. The clip clop of her boots was lost in the noise of the crowd. The restaurant wasn't full, but it was busy enough that the two of them arguing was not a good thing.

Spencer still hadn't told her about his trip down to the Greenleaf. He didn't know if he wanted to. It would just give her the upper-hand. And he really didn't find much out.

"Does that look like a round damn plate?" Gordie seemed to be in his own world as he raised his voice at the new cook.

As spencer turned to his sous chef he realized the bigger man's body was shaking like he had an uncontrollable shiver. One hand formed a tight meaty fist, the other held onto the rag folded over the back of his apron strings. Spencer had seen him angry before, but this was beyond that. Tonight Gordie wore a white bandana, with black skulls printed on it, on his head. It was already soaked through. Curls of copper hair snaked under the bottom. His jaw was clenched tight enough to show bone through his beard and round face.

Spencer wished he could get between the two. "What the hell is going on?" he asked through his own grinding teeth trying to sound like he was yelling without raising his voice.

Gordie's fist uncurled and flashed over the made-up plates. Two white rectangle plates were on the table with crushed ice, eight shucked oysters, lemon wedges and two ramekins of different sauces on each. "He's got the wrong frigging plates."

"Oh blimey, me boy's cracking up," Jonas announced in a horrible English accent. He wasn't English.

"Alright!" Spencer glanced at the people in the room. Nobody seemed to be looking their way, but he felt eyes on him. It was moments like this that he longed for those kitchens that were hidden in the back away from the eyes of paying customers. Back there cooks could pull their knives on each other or lose a digit during prep and no dinner guests would ever know anything happened. Out in the dining room they were always under a microscope. "Gordo, back to your station!"

The side-towel was whipped out from the back of Gordie's apron. It cracked down against the butcher block table before he turned and stomped away.

Wylie looked in their direction from the bar. Spencer couldn't tell if anyone else heard over the sound of the exhaust fan above them or the din of conversation and music. The trouble with working in a kitchen was that the heat, the potential for danger and the high pressure of food getting out in time often made tempers boil. Even he could feel it growing inside him and not just at the new cook who couldn't get with the program, but he couldn't afford to have a Gordon Ramsay moment. He was pissed off at both of his cooks, Jonas for not getting it and Gordie for not controlling himself. He started plucking all of the shucked oysters from the rectangle plates and put them onto a folded towel. "What plate do oysters go on?"

"Order in, Chef." From behind him.

Jonas sighed. "Round ones. Look, I thought …"

"Jonas, I don't care." Spencer's father always told him to be a good leader you had to ride the line between encouraging and commanding. "I don't want you to think. I want you to plate my food the way you've been shown. Salads on the rectangles, oysters on the rounds. If you forget or don't know I'm right beside you, so ask."

Jonas smiled and nodded. He pulled out two round plates from under the table.

Spencer crossed to the sous chef and leaned in close. "Gordo, you've got to calm down man." He put a hand on the big man's shoulder. "We have to stay calm out here."

"He's a dink." Gordie tried to whisper as he reached with tongs to turn a steak on the grill. His whisper was never really that quiet. "When you were in the back he screwed up my mise." The last word came out "meez." It was short for the French phrase Mise en Place which translated as "put in place." It meant everything from prepped food bits needed for dishes, tongs, spoons, rags and whatever else they needed to get through a service. "You don't touch a man's mise, Spencer. You know that. You might as well grab his crotch while…"

"Just cook." Spencer went back to making his sauces. Jonas was what Spencer's father called a character. He never said it in a good way. The chef didn't want to fire him within his first week, but if things didn't start gelling soon it was going to happen.

"Spence." There were two openings into the kitchen – between hot and cold and at the end beside the fryer. Jessie stood there. "You have a phone call."

Spencer looked at the order chits on the butcher block counter. "Can you take a message? Jonas, you got those salads and oysters?"

The cold-side cook barked like a seal as he put the correct plates up on his pass.

"Soups up." Ranger said.

Like a shadow passing by, Dee slipped in and scooped up the plates for her table.

"New order." Spencer finally got to the new chit on the pass. "Two covers, order-fire. One dippings. Second course is shrimp taco and fish and chips." The calls came back to him that he was heard. It was a good night for a Monday. Better than the night before at least. He reached into the small fridge and took out a small ceramic dish the size of a soup bowl with handles on each side and put it in the oven.

Jessie suddenly appeared across the path. "The woman says she really needs to talk to you, you or Chrys."

He thought about it for a moment. "Get Chrys to talk to her then."

The niceness left Jessie's face and her eyes darkened. She looked at her boyfriend a second before turning and marching to where Chrys was chatting to a table of twenty-somethings.

"Tortilla chips, Chef." Ranger manoeuvered around Gordie and slid a stainless steel bowl of freshly fried chips onto the counter.

Spencer looked across the room as his sister was told about the phone call. She too lost her sweet demeanour. As the two of them walked in front of the pass, he received stony glances.

"Salsa, Spencer. Chef," Jonas corrected himself.

Spencer took the rectangle plate from the cold-side. It had a small bowl of fresh salsa on one side. The bubbling spinach dip came out of the oven and was placed on the opposite end of the plate with the tortilla chips between. He put the whole thing up on the pass and called for Dee.

"Spencer!" Chrys slapped her hands on the pass. Her thumb ring tinked. "I'm taking your truck."

"What? No you're not."

A look of panic flowed down over Chrys' face. "They found Luke. I have to go."

"Where did they find him?" Spencer looked down at the orders they still had to do. There were no new tables yet to order and only main plates to finish. It was almost 9:00 pm, so they probably wouldn't get many more customers and Gordie could handle just about anything that would come up as long as he didn't kill Jonas. He wanted to see how this whole thing was going to end. He was still betting on Luke and Luca being an item more than cousins.

"I don't fucking know. Can I take the truck or not?"

"I'll drive. Where are we going?"

"The hospital."

Chapter 11

Chrys stared across the hallway at the four people sitting there. She wanted to say something, but no coherent thoughts were surfacing. There was nothing she could say really. The moment she got the phone call she knew what they were walking into.

Her brother stood next to her leaning against the wall. He hadn't said anything at all to her since leaving the restaurant. He too knew what the phone call had meant.

Two men entered the hallway through a door. The one in the suit wore shoes that looked like they had been shined recently with scuffs on the edges. His hair was perfect. He didn't look happy, but he damn near scowled when he saw the siblings. The other man wore a white lab coat and actually looked cheery considering his occupation. Their attention settled on the others.

Anne Carol sat between Mrs. Staples and her husband gripping both their hands. Her eyes were bright red. Her husband stared at the men. Emma Weston sat a little off to the side. Her eyes focused on the men's knees. The foster mother still had hope. The birth mother knew the reality of the situation.

"Ms. Weston, Mr. and Mrs. Carol, this is Dr. North," the suited man said in a firm but caring tone. This wasn't his first time telling people someone they loved was dead. "He will take you to identify the remains." When Mrs. Staples rose with them he opened his mouth as if to protest. He didn't say a word, however. The look he got from all of them was that this wasn't one of those times where he had to enforce the rules. He motioned the others to follow the doctor through a door before turning to the brother and sister. "You two stay there." He stared at them a moment for effect then went through the same door.

"That was harsh." Chrys mumbled after the door closed.

"You should have gone to the police." Spencer still wore his white chef coat though it was unbuttoned. His arms were crossed in front of him. He rolled so that his shoulder was on the wall and he was facing his sister.

"With what?" Chrys stretched her legs out and folded one ankle over the other. "I didn't find anything."

"Just the fact that he was missing was enough. They never should have asked us for help in the first place. We should have just sent them to the cops."

"They did that. What do you care anyway? Not like you did anything."

"I only spent my whole morning at the Greenleaf." Spencer stepped away from the wall.

"What? Why? When?"

"This morning when you were wherever you were. What did you do today?"

Chrys pushed back in her chair. She nibbled one fingernail, removing some of the polish. "Did you find out anything?" She asked, avoiding his question.

Spencer unrolled the sleeves of the chef jacket covering the tattoos on his forearms. It was chilly down here in the basement of the hospital. His mouth opened. It snapped shut as the morgue door opened.

The man in the suit stepped through. As soon as the door closed, Constable Wright of the Middleton City Police Homicide Unit focused on the two of them. "What the hell are you two doing here?"

Spencer turned to his sister. She looked up at him.

"Forget it." Wright blasted. "I don't want to know. This is the second time you two have put your nose into something that you have no right doing."

Chrys made a noise. "We were just looking for the poor kid."

Wright glared down at her. His hazel eyes were piercing. He had the air of a military officer with strong posture and the aura of authority. "And that poor kid wound up dead. Sound familiar?"

"That's not fair." Spencer said.

Chrys got to her feet. "How did Luke die?"

Constable Wright stared at her. His lips made a tight thin line. It was a long silent moment before he said, "He was found in an alley in Cumberland behind a Greek restaurant apparently beaten to death. Did you two find out anything?" He focused his attention on one for a moment then his eyes turned to the other trying to force the information out of them. He was an intimidating man, filling out his suit with broad shoulders and a firm chest.

Spencer looked at his sister. He hoped some psychic message would pass between them telling him what he should do and say. He wanted to spill his guts about Luca, but his mouth didn't want to work. Chrys was shaking her head. The corner of her upper lip was between her teeth, so he knew she was lying. He had to say something.

The door opened. Mrs. Staples came out first with her arm around the sobbing birthmother of Luke Weston. Neither of them looked up. They simply turned and slowly walked down the hallway toward the exit. The Carols did basically the same except James gave them a silent nod as if he was telling him that the body they saw was indeed Luke. A silent parade of parents all for the same child. The brother and sister knew that foster families could feel the same pain and sorrow as the real family. Every time one of the kids went back to their real family or went to a different home a little bit of Spencer's mother went with them. Thankfully, she'd never had any of her foster kids die or be killed.

Constable Wright cleared something from his throat. "You two stay out of this. You almost got killed the last time and I don't need to give any more bad news."

"Do you have any leads?" Chrys touched his arm. As he looked at her hand it snapped back.

He stared at her for a moment. In his mind he was probably going over how much he could tell them without compromising himself. "Everything looks like this was a hate crime."

"Why do you sat it was a hate crime?" Spencer asked.

Wright sighed. He slipped his hands in his pant pockets. "Luke was found in a dress with a wig over his face and "kill all gays" was spray-painted on the wall above him."

"Luke wasn't gay." Chrys said.

Wright focused his eyes on her. "And you know this for certain?"

She looked from him to her brother whose confused expression wasn't any help. "I … I just have a feeling." Her voice died. Chrys sat back down and kept her eyes on her ankle boots. She rubbed her knees.

"Would this have anything to do with those bodies found outside the city?" Spencer asked. He didn't believe Chrys, though he wanted to get the attention away from her.

"Now what would make you say that?"

Spencer shrugged. "I've heard about it on the news. Men beaten and left in ditches, isn't it? I know this is different, but could it have something to do with it?"

"No." Wright checked his watch. "Different victim type. Different drop point. You, you shouldn't even think of any, ah, connection. I don't need you getting involved in that too."

Spencer looked at the constable. He didn't know the man to stutter. "We won't get involved with it any more. It was stupid of us."

Wright gazed back and forth between the two of them. It was a long minute before he spun on his heel and marched down the hallway, leaving them sitting outside the morgue doors.

~ * ~

Chrys brought her feet close to the truck seat. She bent over and rubbed her ankles sinking her fingers inside the Steve Madden ankle boots. Her hair rolled off her shoulders and fell alongside her face. She felt bad about not saying anything to the police officer, but not so bad that she was going to give him a call and tell him. What was going to happen when they found out all of Luke's belongings were gone? She pictured the police knocking on the door when they came for her. At the next intersection she sat up straight startling pedestrians waiting for the walk sign.

"Where are we?" she asked.

"Almost home." Spencer sounded angry.

"I'm sorry about this."

"It's not your fault." Spencer's mind was going crazy. It was a problem he knew they shouldn't be involved in, but he couldn't help himself from being intrigued. "Do you know anything about Luca?"

"Luca? Like from that fucking eighties song about child abuse? Who's Luca?"

"Some guys at the Greenleaf said a woman named Luca was staying in Luke's room. She said she was his cousin."

"No. Does he have a cousin Luca?" Chrys asked. All her brother did in return was shrug his shoulders, so she decided to share some of her information. "Did you hear anything about Ms. Kara's Pride? A friend of Luke's from his construction job said I should go there on Wednesday and talk to Ms. Kara about how she helped him to find himself or some crap."

"But you were pretty adamant that Luke wasn't gay."

"That's what I was …"

Three police cruisers were parked in front of The Alcrest. Two of them still had their lights flashing. The dashboard clock said it was 11:13 pm.

Spencer signalled and turned down a paved driveway going to the back parking lot. Jessie's car was still there. Chrys didn't speak. The two of them got out of the truck and walked to the back door under the stairs.

The dishpit was quiet. All the dishes had been cleaned and everything was organized. There were no staff back there.

Spencer heard voices coming from the dining room. He tossed his chef coat on the back table and headed down the small hallway past the bathrooms. He felt Chrys' hand gripping his t-shirt at the back. This couldn't be a good thing. *Was Jessie okay?* There were no ambulances out front. *Maybe they left already.* If another staff member was dead there would be no recovering at all.

Chrys didn't want to go to the dining room. The detectives could have been to the Greenleaf already and found out she had been there. What was it, obstruction of justice? Interfering with an investigation? Tampering with evidence? Either way she was too pretty to go to prison. She was glad Hanni wasn't working tonight because she would have turned her in without a second thought.

Two police officers stood by the front glass door. Two others sat at the first table with Jessie and Gordie. Wylie and Dee sat at another table eating pizza from a box in the middle. There were no customers left and they were still supposed to be open for another hour. The two cops at the table each had a cup of coffee. One was taking notes in a notepad. Everyone turned at the sound of Chrys' heels on the hardwood floor.

Jessie slipped from her chair and crossed to Spencer. Her eyes had that dark look to them. Her lips brushed his cheek.

"What's going on?" Spencer's voice shook. At least there was no burning smell.

Jessie's tongue slipped between taupe lips and stopped there looking like pink bubble gum. It remained there as she thought of what to say. Her head twitched flipping her bangs from her eyes. "I had to fire your new guy."

"Okay." He trusted her judgement, but felt confused.

"The boy lost his marbles and the sack he carried them in." Gordie stated. "He started plating his own way again. I told him we had a chain of command and if he didn't do things right I was going to get it and beat him with it." He looked at the officer beside him.

112

"I probably shouldn't have said that. He started pushing things off his table and tossing them at the floor on the hot-line. I yelled at him and then he started throwing salad leaves around. Jessie told him to cut it out and he came walking toward me with a chef's knife. He jammed the knife into the counter top. Then Jessie started yelling at him to get out or she would call the cops."

"He left." Jessie added.

After the police left saying they would file the report and to call if Jonas came around again Spencer stepped into the kitchen. A yellow handled 10 inch chef knife still stood straight up in the counter. The tip was a half inch deep into the butcher block. Green and purple leaves of spring-mix were sprinkled across the black mat on the floor. A stainless steel bowl was turned over and several utensils could be seen poking out from under the equipment. "Well this ends a long night." He looked up at his sister standing by the hostess stand.

Chrys rolled her eyes. "At least we're alive. That's more than Luke can say."

Chapter 12

"What did you say you were going to pay me?"

"What?" Chrys turned her body to look out every window of Hanni's car acting as though she hadn't heard her. They sat in the parking lot behind the hospital with the engine still running. Surprisingly good music came out of the speakers. Chrys expected Hanni to listen to … she really didn't know what she expected. She just didn't think she would like it. "Is this a CD? Who's the band?"

Hanni literally grunted with frustration. "Walk off the Earth and it's on my phone synced to the car. Who the hell buys CDs anymore?"

Chrys rolled her eyes. "They're Canadian right?"

There were only a few cars spread out around the staff parking lot, most were closer to the building. It was past 1:00 am and at that hour most of the night staff parked around the front in the patient parking lot where there was better lighting. Out back some of the lights on high lampposts had either died or been broken by kids throwing rock after rock into the air. Dark shadows crawled at different ends of the pavement. Chrys felt like she shouldn't be there. Maybe she shouldn't. Who was she anyway? She was a dancing waitress. There she was staring at the grey doors waiting to do something that characters did on night-time television dramas.

"How much Chrys?" Hanni screeched.

"I don't know. Isn't the gratitude of a co-worker enough?"

"You said you needed a ride to the hospital to visit a friend and would pay me for it. Now we're in the staff parking lot staring at a door. Oh, I better get paid. And don't think I won't cash in on that favor you owe me either."

"Like you had something better to be doing on a Monday night."

"How about sleeping? You better pay me."

"I will. Trust me."

"Pfft" was the only sound Hanni made as she picked up her cell phone. She quickly lost herself in the land of textology.

Chrys' brown eyes returned to the door. All she could think about were the faces on Luke Weston's parents. What must it be like to have to identify your child's body? What did they see and how would it taint their memories of Luke? Being a foster child she knew that you didn't have to physically give birth to a child to love him. Chrys had watched Rose Alcrest's heart break a little every time a temporary foster child was sent back to their parents or to another home. By the time Mr. Alcrest got sick, Rose didn't seem to have much of her heart left. Chrys didn't want to do that. Seeing her foster mom and the three parents of Luke Weston she was certain that she didn't want children.

"I thought you wanted to see a friend." Hanni didn't even raise her eyes from her phone when she asked the question.

"Meet a friend. I said, meet a fr…" The word caught in her throat. All she saw outside the window were the whites of someone's eyes.

"What?" Hanni turned. Her mouth dropped open.

One of Chrys' hands squeezed the cell phone she forgot she was holding. The other groped the air beside her leg. She saw a snow brush with a long handle on the floor when she got in. It could be a weapon. Was the door locked?

Teeth appeared beneath the eyes.

Chrys wondered if rapists smiled.

Hanni pictured a smiling clown with blood and spit dripping from white fangs.

"Chrys." a voice came through the window.

How did he know my name?

A knuckle rapped on the window glass. "Are you coming in?"

Marc. Chrys remembered to breathe. She started yelling as she rolled the side window down, "You fucking prick! You scared the crap out of us."

A face developed around the eyes and teeth. The sinister smile evolved into a friendly grin with warm

117

eyes set into a face the colour of iced tea. Chrys'
friend Marc leaned in through the window. "Sorry, but
I got tired of waiting for you. Are we going to do this
or not?"

Chrys nodded and turned to Hanni. "Wait here. I
won't be too long."

"After he just scared the hell out of me? I'm not
staying here by myself."

If the blond could have seen the brunette's eyes
they would have appeared white from the massive eye
roll. "Then let's go." Chrys got out of the car before
the blond had time to protest.

In seconds all three of them were speed-walking
toward the door the women had been watching. The
late night air was comfortably cool compared to the
day. The clicky-clack sound of Chrys' small heels and
Hanni's tall ones echoed down the hallway in the
hospital from the basement second they were inside.

"What are we doing?" Hanni asked from behind the
other two. She had been ready for bed when Chrys
called, so she'd just thrown on tight jeans and a blue
V-neck sweater.

"We only have a few minutes." Marc said to Chrys.
"There's only one attendant at night and he should be
going for his lunch break, if he's not gone already."

They turned down a hallway that Chrys recognized.
She had been here just a few hours earlier. The chairs
were still there outside the morgue doors where she
and Spencer had waited.

"Whoa." Hanni stopped walking. "Where are we
going? This is the morgue, Chrys."

Chrys stopped and turned around. Maybe it was
time to explain everything, not only to Hanni, but to

herself. She said, "Luke is in there and I have to see him. I was asked to find him and I failed. Now I have to see what happened to him. The police aren't going to tell me anything."

"You want to go look at a dead body?" Chrys never noticed how high pitched Hanni's voice could get.

"I don't want to. I'm going to."

"Chrys, come on." Marc tugged on her jacket like a little boy insisting they move on. His gaze went from one end of the hallway to the other. "We have to do this quickly. I don't know when Peter will be coming back."

"Okay, Hanni, you stay out here."

"And do what?"

Marc flashed a nervous smile. "If you see a guy in a white coat with bushy eyebrows, try to distract him."

Hanni's arms flew upwards. "How would you like me to do that?"

Chrys and Marc were already inside the morgue. Marc's job as an orderly gave him access to almost every room in the building. He even had keys to the morgue in case something, or someone, had to be delivered there and the attendant was not around. The inside was cooler than the air-conditioned hallway. There were two large windows on the far wall with doors beside each. Marc explained that they were autopsy rooms. The windows were for the identification to be made without the family members getting up close to the deceased and possibly compromising anything. Luke's parents had to gaze through one of those windows. Through them she saw large dark rooms that were clear in the center and lined with stainless steel tables, work stations and storage areas. Grocery store-type weigh scales (the ones you weighed your banana bunches in) hung by each station. Everything had a pristine shine to it. This outside room had a stainless steel table with large sinks in it beside a wall and more storage. There were two desks, each with a computer. On the side wall was a large door Chrys recognized from the restaurant. It was a sealed cooler door, probably a freezer. Her eyes locked on the red and white tape crossing the seam where the door met the wall with Middleton City Police printed on it.

"What does this mean?" Her fingers touched the tape. It was like when her brother put Scotch tape from his bedroom door to the doorframe above where she could reach so that he would know if she snuck in his room to steal any of his saved Halloween candy. The broom handle sealed it back quite nicely so that he never noticed.

"The police put it there when there is a body needing an autopsy." Marc said from behind her. "Luckily, I have this." He pulled a black garbage bag from one of the big sinks. It had yellow tape wrapped around it closing the end.

"What's that?"

"Mr. Carter's amputated foot."

Chrys stepped back. "Fuck! There's a foot in there?"

Marc looked at the main door. "Do you want to see the body or not? If a limb gets amputated at night I have to put it the cold room with the bodies for disposal in the morning. I waited until Peter left, stashed this in the sink and came to get you. Without this I can't break the police seal. Now I can. I just have to document it. Are you sure you want to do this?"

Chrys agreed with a nod.

"Put these on." He handed her blue latex gloves before putting on his own pair.

Chrys stretched the gloves over her hands. She watched as the orderly took out a knife and cut a thin line down the police tape along the seam of the door. The thought of what was in the man's hand left her thoughts. She held her breath as Marc pulled the door open. She expected the smell of rolling death, but got a blast of cool freshness on her face. The inside was immaculate. It was just one large room. There were metal drawers along one wall. She counted three gurneys all covered in sheets and one with black plastic body-bags on it. Chrys stayed at the door. Marc put the bag he carried on a small table just inside the door and quickly read the name tags on each gurney.

"Luke Weston, right? That's this one. You better hurry up." He took out his knife again. "They sealed it with a zip-tie, but I know where they keep them." He cut the black plastic holding the bag's zipper closed and returned to the outer room.

Chrys stared at the four bodies lying on gurneys. If one of them moved she'd pee her pants.

What the hell was she doing? She had been asked to find Luke. He was found. It wasn't the best result, certainly not the one she had hoped for, but he was found. That was all she was supposed to do. Spencer was going to officially put her in this room if he found out.

She had been told earlier that Luke's autopsy was not going to be done until the morning. Chrys' finger and thumb grasped the zipper. It was best to do it quick like pulling off a Band-Aid. She saw that in a movie.

She tugged the zipper. At first it held then gave way like a train on tracks suddenly gaining momentum. A cloud of internal gases and aromas hit Chrys in the senses. They touched her nose then were in her throat. Something hot came shooting up her esophagus she pressed her full lips together making them almost disappear. Her eyes slammed shut. A hand slapped against her closed mouth like a second barrier. She didn't have a choice. Chrys swallowed hard feeling the yellow heat go back down. The thought of it made her want to throw up again.

"Don't be such a fucking wuss." she growled at herself. "Fuck."

Chrys ran her hand along her jacket before taking her phone out and turning it into a camera. She wished she had brought her digital, but thought walking around the hospital looking like a tourist might have been suspicious. The thing inside the black plastic bag was not Luke Weston. It was, but it was something else altogether. The face was thinner than the picture she had been given and not just from death. His hair was longer. It was dirty and caked with dried blood, but Chrys would be willing to bet it was close to her chestnut colour. His face was beaten beyond imagination. It was as if he had been beaten after being beaten. His lips were an off red, almost pink shade. Chrys' hand moved forward. Her finger reached out. The tip brushed the dead man's lip. A little pink smudged off. Luke had been wearing make-up, that or someone had put it on him. Lipstick, eye liner, mascara, blush. It all looked like it was there and applied with skill. She snapped a few pictures of his face.

Chrys pulled the bag open a little more and took more photos. He had fist-sized bruises over his torso and welts that looked long and thin. A pipe, she thought. On the back of one hand was a faded ink stamp. It was two #2s with the second facing the opposite direction. The morgue workers had taken whatever clothing Luke had been wearing leaving him naked. He had amazing muscle tone beneath the mottled bruising and cuts. Something was off though. His chest didn't seem right. He had breasts. They were small, not yet the size of Jessie's tiny ones, but they were still physically formed breasts. With the right bra the boy would have nice cleavage. There were also things that Constable Wright didn't tell them about. There were two puncture wounds, one on each side of his chest. They were round. She wondered if they were bullet holes.

Chrys looked around quickly. There was nothing there she could use. She put her hands in her pockets. She found a pen in her inside jacket pocket. Her hand shook. She didn't want to do this, but she knew the police would. They'd probably use a different tool for the job though. She put her phone down and held her wrist with the other hand as she lowered the pen into the puncture wound. It finally came to a stop at the pocket clip. She took a picture.

"Chrys, we have to get going." Marc came back in with a plastic tie in his hand.

"Okay, okay." She started zipping the bag closed. Her eyes saw something. She took more pictures.

Marc grabbed the zipper and finished closing the bag. He rapidly attached the tie-wrap and made it look just as it had when they got there. "This is my job, Chrys. We have to get out of here."

"I'm done."

As soon as the cooler door was closed, Marc put tape over the police tape and signed his initials with the date and time. He wrote a note on a clipboard saying why he had to go into the cooler, then made sure everything was in place. He carefully opened the door to the hallway and looked outside.

Chrys heard Hanni's voice. "Seriously, you're the morgue guy? I'm so fascinated by death." Her words sounded sickly sweet.

Chrys put her phone in her pocket and unbuttoned her blouse until you could get a good look at her frilly bra. She nodded to her friend and, like in some television sitcom, he grabbed her arm and shoved her into the hallway. "I said you can't be in here," he said with a raised voice.

Chrys stumbled a little. "Hey, don't be so pushy, man."

"I told you, you can't. Hey, Pete." Before the other man had a chance to say anything, Marc added, "I had to drop something off and these two chicks followed me down here."

"Don't call us chicks." Chrys yelled with a slur to her words. She wrapped her arm around Hanni's and the two of them headed off down the hallway being certain to wiggle their behinds.

124

Ten minutes later she got Marc's text "*you owe me*."

Chapter 13

Every Tuesday at 5:00 am Spencer found himself at the docks when the commercial fishermen came in. They set up a small market for people, mostly chefs and those selling directly to restaurants, to get first shot at the mornings catch before the fish were shipped off to grocery stores and wholesalers. Some had little stands with chalkboard menus noting what the boat was bringing in that morning. Others had ice bins for their catch to be unloaded into, so that everyone could see, touch and smell the freshness. Other people wanted to cash in on this collection of chefs and restauranteurs all in one place. They set up farmers' market-style vegetable stands. A food truck was parked in the corner of the parking area selling fresh coffee and baking. It was quite an event so early in the morning. During the summer it was often a tourist attraction.

As Spencer gave a nod to the chef of a downtown high-end French restaurant he felt like an imposter. Sales were down fifteen percent from last year. Last night the psycho baker and police probably cost him some more customers. Luckily, from the story he was told, just about all the customers were gone before the craziness started. He didn't want to think about it, but laying off some of his staff was a big possibility. The bank was telling him to raise the prices. That was always their answer to a drop in sales. Raise the prices to make up for the loss of customers and alienate those you still have. He didn't want to lay anyone off, but he couldn't afford to piss off the loyal clientele. He wondered if he should talk to some of these chefs about hiring the staff he would have to let go.

The early morning air at the docks was chilled by a breeze from the water. He was glad for his cashmere coat. One breath of the sharp sea air made his throat feel like he'd just sucked in shards of ice. The food trucks sales were not down like his restaurant. Spencer bought a cup of coffee from it before walking amongst the vendors.

The halibut was nice, but too expensive when you factored in the time to break it down. He was going to have to make the cheaper fish taste like a million bucks for a while. Spencer liked fresh and didn't want to resort to freezing any fish. He knew the bank would probably tell him to start using breaded fish sticks or some crap.

"Mr. Alcrest, you look like you're in a trance." The English accent was instantly recognizable.

"Chef Aldrich, how are you?" Spencer extended his hand to shake that of the college culinary instructor. Spencer had taken a semester of classes at the community college in Middleton before deciding it was a joke and went to the Culinary Institute of Canada on the East coast to finish his education. The culinary program wasn't bad, but it wasn't what he had wanted at the time. It was more of a general cooking with management classes. He wanted a more in-depth cooking program.

"I'm good. School is over for the summer and I'm back to catering. How is The Alcrest?"

"Good." Spencer lied. Well, the restaurant wasn't really doing that bad either. It just wasn't doing as good as it should. "Had to let a baker go last night, but otherwise it's all good."

"You've been having bad luck with bakers. What was wrong with this one?" The two sipped their coffee over a bin of gutted salmon.

Spencer ran his fingers along the skin of a salmon. He could see how the fish would soar through the water. "He lied on his resume and couldn't do what was asked." He was pretty certain of the first part. Last time he hired someone without calling references.

"How do you feel about students?"

"They have their place." Spencer smiled.

"I have one in need of placement for the summer. She's good, methodical. Has a mild case of OCD, but that just means she works clean."

"I don't know." Spencer wasn't sure if he could afford to pay anyone else. Sacrificing sleep to get in some baking might be the way to go.

"You'll get subsidized so that you get back half of her wage."

That changed things. "Tell her to drop by," Spencer said.

"Only if you promise not to cook her." Chef Aldrich gave him an awkward laugh as he walked away. Yet another reminder of Spencer's unfortunate experience earlier that year. He flipped the bird at his former teachers back and thought that next time he'd be on the menu.

~ * ~

For a few minutes Spencer sat in his truck watching the gulls circle above the boats. On the floor in the back seat were two cases of oysters, a Styrofoam box holding two full salmon on ice and another with haddock. He sipped the last of his coffee. A year ago cooks came to him asking for jobs and now he had to hope for a lost culinary student. Life sure was changing. He had to do something right.

In ten minutes his truck was parked on the curb near the alley where Luke was found. It wasn't that far from the Greenleaf.

As Spencer stepped from his truck and headed across the street he shoved his hands in his coat pockets. There was a little wind breaking through the buildings. At this time of day the street was not too busy. By 9:00 am the stores would be open and teeming with people. The Greek restaurant had a busy lunch trade. This part of the city, The Clothes Line was named that because back in the day it had been home to the Chinese immigrants and an assortment of laundries and tailors. The people and the industries had changed many times over the years. Now it was a mix of apartments above a variety of stores. The southern end of The Clothes Line contained the R&R dockyards that Spencer knew were run by Liam O'Donnell, who had links to the Irish mafia. O'Donnell also had links to Spencer's father and claimed to know things about Chrys' mother. After the troubles with The Alcrest's ovens, O'Donnell bought them new ones, with "no strings attached." But Spencer was nervously waiting for one of those "strings" to show up. He knew a big portion of the city's gay community lived in The Clothes Line. If you were going to commit a hate crime, this was a good place to get noticed.

On the sidewalk at the entry to the alley, he found a collection of flowers and items. There were notes saying things like, "you will not be forgotten" and "hate is not an option." A teddy bear stuffed among the flowers reminded Spencer of Paddington Bear but without the rain hat. He wondered if any of the people who wrote, "We'll miss you," actually knew Luke Weston.

Yellow police tape was still strung across the entrance to the alley. From the street he could see the words about hate spray painted in white on a red brick wall. There was a dumpster and pile of wood pallets. It looked like a movie set. All it needed was a grubby homeless guy sleeping under old newspapers.

131

He knew the Greek restaurant. He had eaten there once. It was well known and had won many awards. The chef/owner often balanced tables on his chin and they featured traditional dancers come in. It was one of those Greek places where the customers were encouraged to smash plates on the floor. From what he knew it was busy every night and along the street there were other restaurants and bars. That didn't leave much time to beat someone in an open alley.

Spencer took out his phone and snapped a few pictures.

"Isn't that disrespectful?"

On his right a man stepped up to the make-shift memorial. He crouched down and placed another teddy bear and some blue flowers with the others. He was at least 6 feet tall and thin. His tan trench coat was tied around the waist. His short hair was slicked back.

"I didn't mean it to be," Spencer started. "I was just..."

"Being a looky-loo taking pictures to show to your homophobic buddies." The man stood up and crossed his arms in front of him. His face was thin with high cheekbones and he wore glasses with small rectangular lenses. Pale blue eyes, almost white, stared out from behind. Spencer guessed him to be in his thirties.

"That's not why..."

"I bet with those pretty looks and cute as a button dimples you've probably had to turn away a boy or two. You beat them up too?"

"What?" Spencer didn't feel too comfortable. He was caught in something he didn't want to be in. "I would never do that."

"Sure."

"Look, you don't even know me."

"I know people like you." The man turned and strutted off leaving Spencer alone.

For whatever reason Spencer had that "*I did something wrong*" feeling.

~ * ~

"This guy just bitched you out like that?"

"Pretty much." Spencer leaned against the pass on the dining room side. The hanging heat lamp warmed his shoulder. "I don't hate gays. I have a lesbian sister for Pete's sake."

"I'm not a fucking lesbian." Chrys threw her hands out. "I'm confused and unsure."

Spencer shrugged his shoulders. "I got a picture of the crime scene though." He passed his phone to his sister.

"Really Spence? This is your picture? If we're going to be investigating homicides much more you're going to have to get better at this."

"Investigating homicides? We're not ... Do you really think we're going to be doing this much?"

"What do you mean investigating homicides?" Jessie asked.

Chrys ignored her and shoved her phone in her brother's face. "These are good pictures. This is how it's done."

"What the hell? Are these Luke?" He took the cell phone from her. With one finger he flipped through the photos. Spencer couldn't really tell what he was seeing. The *person* barely resembled the man he was supposed to be. He had never seen anyone so bruised.

"Are those breasts? And what are …" He zoomed the picture in. "Is that a pen?"

"I put it in there to get perspective." Chrys said.

Beside them Jessie threw up her hands.

"What's this?" Spencer asked as he got to the last picture.

"Bite marks." Chrys said with excitement.

"Bite marks?" The picture showed two curved marks where teeth had broken the skin on the back of Luke's arm.

Chrys' eyes widened. "Human bite marks?"

"You guys have to leave it for the police." Jessie raised her voice.

"No!" Chrys looked at both of them. "I'm doing this. I have to for all the foster kids out there."

Jessie glared at her. "Seriously, Chrys?"

"What?"

Jessie just shook her head. "What are you even doing down here? You don't work today and you're still in your sleeping clothes."

"I can't come into my family's business? It's not like we're shit-ton busy." Her hand swept over the main dining area. There was a couple sitting near the door and Mr. O. by the window. Some conversation noises from the frame room could be heard. It was probably the early morning Magic crew, but they never spent much money. They played their card game, sometimes yelling at each other, and went on their way. "And for your information, Jessie, I had to put these clothes on to come down here."

Spencer didn't want to get between the two of them. If he did, he would mention how Jessie wasn't even scheduled to work, so she didn't have to be there either. He wasn't going to say that to his pregnant girlfriend, however.

"Watch your language," Jessie said.

"Don't be such a feneuter!" Chrys snatched her phone from her brothers hand and stomped off toward the back hallway.

The moment Chrys got upstairs to the apartment, Breeze zipped across the room yapping. Bullet waddled out of the kitchen area, then half-way across the living room he plopped onto his backside. After scooping Breeze in one hand, Chrys went to Bullet and scratched the wrinkles that made up his neck. Who the hell was Jessie to tell her to watch her language?

Chrys threw herself onto the small couch. The cushions were soft with the right amount of spring. Except the couch wasn't big enough to host much company. It had been a while since she had any special company though, but she liked having the option. Her last serious relationship was Dawn. After that whole mess six months ago the RCMP officer transferred to a northern community to further her career. Chrys went out a couple of times with Marc, but he was never "company." Maybe she should give him a chance.

Bullet waddled toward her and Chrys laughed. As the round beast walked his ass wiggled like that of a runway model. She loved the dog. She loved the restaurant and the apartment. However, she had to wonder if it was time for her to move on. She and her brother were fighting. She and his *whatever* were fighting. Perhaps moving out was a good plan. Finding another job might be an idea too. She already taught dance part-time and jumped around with other occasional jobs, so it wouldn't be much of a stretch. It might be difficult - such was life.

Spencer came through the door from the stairs. Chrys pushed up the volume a few more notches.

He sat in the green lounge chair that had been his father's. Bullet looked at him and raised a paw. A few feet was too far to go, but putting the message out there was enough. Breeze jumped up onto the couch and circled around before finding a spot at Chrys' feet.

"Did you have to be so rude to Jess?" Spencer asked after a few minutes of Tattoo Nightmares.

"Did she have to be so bitchy to me?"

"She's got some stuff going on in her life right now."

"We've all got shit going on, Spence."

"Well she's going to be in my life for a while. Can you please try and be civil?"

Something in what he said got Chrys' attention. "What do you mean she's going to be in your life for a while? You guys aren't getting married are you?"

"What? No. Just be nice to her. You guys should go out or something."

"Like a girls' night?"

Spencer thought his sister didn't have to sound so disgusted about the idea. He grunted in the affirmative and went to the kitchen. The only thing blocking the kitchen from the living room was a small island.

"Like clubbing or something? I'm not really in the mood."

"It doesn't have to be a club or anything. Just spend some time together." All Spencer found in the first cupboard was a can of pizza sauce, a couple of boxes of Kraft Macaroni and Cheese and canned vegetables. "Maybe the three of us could go out. Have you heard of Club 22?"

Chrys pushed the guide button on the remote. She grunted an answer. She had heard of it, just didn't know where. "Whatever." She flipped through the channels. She stopped suddenly and turned to her brother. "I get to pick the place."

Chapter 14

Spencer looked up just as a man with a bushy orange beard and bright red lips walked past the table. His eyes were lined in black. He wore a mesh shirt over a tube-top and extremely skinny jeans. Spencer dropped his eyes.

"You alright?" Jessie squeezed his tattooed forearm.

"I'm fine."

"You're being awfully quiet."

"Just stressed."

"We can tell Chrys we're going to go if you want." Jessie sounded hopeful.

"And go back to an empty restaurant where I can think about how much money I'm not making?" He tried to see how his sister was doing, but couldn't get a view of the bar through all the people. Based on her brother's advice, Chrys made Spencer and Jessie go with her to Ms. Kara's Pride. He didn't say she couldn't kill two birds with one stone.

"It's not that bad, Spence."

Spencer drummed his fingers on the small round table over a set of initials carved into the surface. "Jess, I had three paying customers between 5:00 pm and 9:00 pm. Even the crafting group cancelled. I didn't make enough today to pay for one staff member to be working. I'm willing to bet this month I'll be in the red. I've been teetering pretty close and now I'm going over the edge."

"But that …"

"I know, it's because of the barbeque and all that. It's just that since last year when all that happened, sales have taken a nose dive. And now I'm going to have this extra expense that I don't know how I'll pay for." He signaled with his hand toward her belly.

Jessie's hand slipped away from his arm. "An expense? What are you saying?"

"Expense isn't the right word. I don't know what is. The restaurant is in trouble. I haven't paid myself for over a month, Jess." Spencer looked up as his sister broke through the crowd. Her hands were loaded with drinks. He leaned in close to his girlfriend. "Chrys doesn't know any of this, so please don't say anything."

Jessie opened her mouth, but nothing came out.

Chrys put the drinks on the table. One splashed over the top of the glass. "I don't know why, but I thought drinks would be cheaper in a gay bar."

"How much were they?" Spencer took his Corona. As he looked at Jessie she turned away. *What did he say that got her so angry?*

"Are you sure you don't want a drink, Jess?" Chrys slid the glass of ice water toward her boss. "I mean a drink-drink."

Jessie's hand wrapped around the cold glass. The moisture seemed to seep through her fingers on contact. She stared at the cubes. "No thanks. I just can't."

"But Spence is driving. You won't get sloshed, right?"

"Why are we here, Chrys?" Spencer felt the need to change the subject. "Why this place?"

"Uncomfortable much?" She gave him a wicked smile. "I was told Luke came here by one of his co-workers."

"So he was gay then."

"The friend swears Luke wasn't."

"But if he came here then …" Spencer waved his hand to where two men were kissing.

"You're here." Chrys smirked.

Spencer shut up. He got the point.

As Chrys leaned back her chair creaked. She had chosen a pair of tight fitting jeans – they weren't her ass jeans but they did the job nicely – and a t-shirt. It had a spaceship on it with the words "I aim to misbehave" spread across her breasts which were outlined nicely by the form-fitting garment. She felt somewhat under-dressed. Most of the men in the room wore tight clothing, a lot of it seemed to sparkle, which left little to the imagination. Some had more eyeliner than she wore herself. The other women in the room seemed casual, nothing flashy.

Everyone seemed to be having a great time. Dance music pumped from a deejay booth and vibrated off the walls. A sunken dance floor was crowded with people moving to the vibrations. That myth that gay men knew how to dance was not entirely true. Chrys had to text Roy.

"Jessie, let's dance." Chrys pushed away from the table.

"You got over finding Luke's body quick?"

Chrys sneered at her brother. "I need to do something to get it off my mind. You're a stick in the mud. Come dance with me, Jess." She snatched the other woman's hand and jumped to her feet before there was any protesting.

In most bars Chrys had been in – there were quite a few – the dance floors were mostly women with a couple of men either dancing well and getting close to them or stepping side to side and calling it dancing. Thirty seconds after getting on a normal dance floor the two women would have had men dancing close to see if they had a chance. Neither of them were dressed provocatively. Jessie was in black slacks and a plaid shirt with the sleeves rolled up. The shirt was missing a button so you could see the edge of her baby-blue bra sometimes. Chrys guessed that could be provocative if Jessie had much of a chest. Nobody paid any real attention to them. Thirty more seconds and Chrys realized she missed the annoying attention. She grabbed Jessie's hips from the back, surged her ass out and arched her back. There was no real reaction except the surprised expression on her boss' face.

142

Spencer pushed the lime wedge that stuck out of his Corona bottle inside the neck. He left his finger in to block the hole and tipped the entire bottle upside down rocketing the wedge into the base of it. As he tipped the bottle back upright the lime settled in the golden liquid beneath the neck.

His aqua-marine eyes traveled the room, not really looking for anything. He was just observing. Something in his stomach churned and it seemed hard to breathe. The only word he could think of to describe how he felt was *uncomfortable*. It wasn't the place or the people inside it, but it was what the people inside the place were doing that made him uncomfortable. He had seen his sister with other women – saw them holding hands and kissing and heard them having sex on the other side of the bedroom wall (if Jessie wasn't staying over the last one often occupied his left hand), so why men doing most of the same things was peculiar to him he didn't know. He looked at his sister almost grinding his girlfriend and thought nothing of it. He looked to the right at a man with a moustache like the lead singer of Queen, Freddy Mercury, kiss another man and his stomach churned. Spencer really didn't like the feeling. He didn't want to be uncomfortable.

"Imagine finding you here."

Spencer looked up at the person behind him. He, Spencer was pretty sure it was a he, wore a long scarlet dress with slits on each side showing fishnet covered legs. The fabric was like a second skin over wide hips, a flat stomach and healthy breasts. His, her face was thin with a pointed chin. The lips were shiny pink and the make-up was dark around the eyes, not the vibrant colour Spencer expected. She, he had candy-apple red hair that shimmered different shades and highlights in the light of the club. That was something he expected. Except for the colour it looked real.

"Excuse me?" was all Spencer could say. He felt like he just joined a movie half-way through.

"You don't recognize me, do you?" Her voice was that of a husky woman. Jessie's had a similar tone. Maybe it was a woman.

Spencer looked for his girlfriend and sister as he tried working it all out. Did he know her? When and where would he have met a he/she? Was he a she or she a he? "I, um, I – should I?" He looked at the dance floor hoping the others were coming back.

She said, "I know people like you," and pivoted on a four-inch heel. She walked away whipping her hips to the side with each step like Jessica Rabbit. It took a moment for Spencer to realize he was watching her ass cheeks that seemed to be fighting with each other.

"Who was that?" Jessie slipped into her seat.

"I, I don't know." *I know people like you.* Where did he hear that before? He shook his head. Jessie had perspiration above her lip. "Are you having fun?"

She lifted an eyebrow and her eyes seemed to get dark. "Your sister's a freak. She might have been coming on to me."

"She always dances like that." Chrys was suddenly there with two drinks in her hands. "Jessie thinks you're coming on to her."

"You'd know if I was coming onto you." Chrys sat down, put her hand on Jessie's thigh and gave it a squeeze. "I brought you a drink, Jess. I know you said you weren't drinking, but drink up anyway."

144

"I told you I'm not…"

"Quiet! Show's starting."

The lights dimmed at first then spotlights started soaring all over the place, gaining everyone's attention. A deep male announcer's voice came from the speakers. Part of the evenings drag show was about to start. The music began to build. The woman in the red dress moved into the spotlight at the back of the stage. She walked seductively to a microphone stand which she grasped like she was about to make love to it. She sang the first two songs with loud cheers from the crowd before other performers arrived. By the third entertainer the three of them forgot what they were watching and just enjoyed what was happening - singers, some impersonators of famous female performers and a little comedy thrown in the mix.

Chrys bought more drinks and handed them all around. She had given up and passed Jessie another iced water. She now had enough evidence on that mystery.

A chair was pushed between the two women. Another woman circled around it and settled into the seat. Legs in thigh-high spiked heel boots made a display of being crossed. She wore a black mini-dress that didn't hide too much. Large garish sunglasses covered her eyes. Her long black hair had bangs and maroon highlights along the sides of her face. She had been part of the show singing a Katy Perry medley. She was very good. "What did you think?"

Her voice was the first indication Chrys had that she was a he. There was no way to hide his relaxed voice or the Adam's apple.

145

"It was great," Chrys said. "Do I know you?"

A smile erupted from his pink lips. He removed his sunglasses, revealing green eyes with dark winged eyeliner and silver shadows. Chrys didn't believe who it was. He pushed the wig back off of his short dark hair. "I thought I told you to come by on Wednesday."

"I couldn't wait that long." He stared into his eyes for a long moment. "Colby, this is my brother Spencer and his girlfriend Jessie. Colby was friends with Luke. Why did you say come Wednesday? Ms. Kara performed tonight."

Colby slipped his wig back on. The male all but vanished. He wore a fair bit of blush emphasising cheekbones. "I don't perform on Wednesdays. I was hoping to avoid this awkward meeting." He stuck his tongue out between his teeth.

"So your construction co-workers don't know you do this?"

"Hell no."

Chrys couldn't take her eyes off him. The transformation was amazing. "Do they know you're gay?"

Colby played with the black hair. He was a woman again. "I kind of lied about the whole gay thing."

"What?" Chrys turned her chair to face him head on.

"I'm not gay. I said that in case you did come here." He looked around the table at everyone staring back at him before slipping the sunglasses back on. "It's a lot easier to say I'm homosexual than to say I like dressing in drag and pretending to be a pop icon. Stay here and I'll go get Ms. Kara." As he walked away both siblings watched. One saw a woman and one saw a man.

Chrys backhanded her brother's shoulder.

"Ow, what the hell?"

"He's straight."

"He likes to wear women's clothing."

"I like to wear men's clothing." She sipped her drink. She had graduated from a Long-Island iced tea to an Electric Smurf. There was no surprise at all that they knew how to make it here.

After five minutes Colby came strutting back with Ms. Kara – the woman in the red dress – walking behind them. It was amazing watching them. Colby bounced like an over-exaggerated runway walk and interacted with the people around him, waving and blowing kisses. Ms. Kara had an air about her. All she had to do was walk and people parted. It was almost cold. As they got close to the table her pale eyes locked on Spencer. He felt uncomfortable and calm all at the same moment.

"I apologize for this morning." Ms. Kara was as elegant a lady as Spencer had ever seen. It was so much that it was over-the-top. "I've had to deal with many a friend's death and they are not always treated with respect. A year and a half ago another friend was found in that same alley. Colby told me you were friends of Luke."

"We're just trying to help." Chrys said. Colby returned to his seat between her and Jessie. Chrys rested one hand on her own thigh. She stretched out a finger and found it could touch his leg between the boot and skirt.

Spencer said, "I wanted to know what the crime scene looked like. We were asked to find Luke and now we need to see this through." He looked at his sister who was staring back at him.

"What can you tell us about Luke?" Chrys asked. Her finger kept moving beneath the table.

"I only knew Luke for a little while. Colby brought him in to talk to me because he was confused with who he really was. We spent hours talking."

"But you said you didn't know him that well. How can you talk to him for hours and not know him?"

Ms. Kara smiled. "I knew Luca."

"Who is Luca?" Spencer asked.

"Luca was Luke. She was his true self hidden away inside for eighteen years." She saw the confusion in the eyes around the table and continued. "Colby saw that Luke was conflicted. He brought Luke here to talk to me. After just a few minutes I knew that Luke was not meant to be a man. He was born with those parts, but inside he was someone else."

"So, he was Luca?"

Ms. Kara moved a hand through her red hair. "Exactly. Luca was trans-gender. She was born a boy named Luke, but had felt for a very long time that she was always meant to be a girl. She didn't know anyone who had ever dealt with that. I have, so talking to me was easier. I took her to see a doctor who got her in touch with a therapist and Luca decided to start making the change."

"How exactly does one do that?" Jessie asked.

"The transformation takes a long time. She was undergoing treatments to alter her estrogen and testosterone levels, but she wanted to see what it

148

would be like, so I helped her. I know how to make a man look and act like a sensual woman. We worked together to create Luca. I gave her a job and she came as her true self every day."

"That's when Luke quit the construction job." Colby said to Chrys.

"So he dressed as a woman every day?" Spencer asked.

Ms. Kara licked her lips while staring at the blond man. "Luca came to work as her true self, yes."

Spencer picked up his phone and scanned through his photos to the one sent to him by the guys at the hostel. "Is this Luke? Luca?"

"That's her. She went through a few different, um, evolutions of herself before finding this one."

"I don't think his parents knew anything about this." By this point Chrys didn't even realize she was rubbing Colby's leg.

Ms. Kara shook her head. "The common man is often afraid of people who go their own way. Luke was afraid nobody would understand. I do think he was planning on introducing them to Luca."

"Did you two have a relationship together?"

Ms. Kara's finger circled the rim of her glass. The pale blue eyes looked at him in a way that made Jessie nervous. "Spencer, I am a flamboyant homosexual, but Luke was not gay at all. He liked women."

Chrys slapped her brother's shoulder. "I told you." She smiled around the table, but no one was smiling back. Jessie was just staring at her hands. "I told you."

"Luke had a girlfriend when he first came here. They broke up a couple of weeks ago." Ms. Kara looked at Colby who nodded.

"His parents didn't say anything about that."

"I don't think he told them much. The Luke I knew was very private. For most of his life he felt like he had to hide everything. You don't know what it feels like to know something in your heart is right, but to have the world say you are wrong."

The brother and sister looked at each other. Even though Chrys dated women occasionally, she didn't know what it was like to be persecuted for it.

"What was his girlfriend's name?"

Ms. Kara shook her head. "I only knew her by Mary. She was a mousy thing, very quiet."

"Do you know if he had any problems with anyone?"

"She," emphasis on the *she*, "had the same amount of trouble as the rest of us."

Colby had his hands on the table playing with the arms of his sunglasses. "Sometimes there can be protestors outside or people going by yelling things. They'll damage our cars too. That's why I always take taxis. Sometimes people yell or throw things as they drive by."

"Have you made police reports?" Chrys asked.

"We have called the police," Ms. Kara started, "but there isn't much they can do. Or there isn't much they will do."

"So there's no way of knowing for sure if this was a hate crime or not."

"I can give you a list of protest groups," Ms. Kara said. "I don't remember Luca having any run-ins with them. She was quiet, but was starting to embrace herself. She was getting comfortable in the new skin she was creating. She would go out dressed as Luca and was talking to people. Here everyone accepted her. She wanted to see if she could be accepted as a woman out there. The last time I talked to her she was planning to go clubbing to see what would happen."

"What about here? Did he...she have any enemies?"

"I don't think so." Ms. Kara shook her head and looked at Colby.

He looked at her like he was trying to think of what he could say. "She worked as a server, so if a guy knew she was a guy he might touch her, but I don't think anything really happened. Men are men, even gay men."

Jessie leaned in with her lips close to Spencer's ear and whispered something. He nodded, then looked at Ms. Kara and said, "Thank you for your time. Chrys I'm going to take Jessie home. Are you coming?"

"I'll catch a cab." She flashed a wicked grin.

~ * ~

Almost two hours later Chrys opened the door to the apartment above The Alcrest. Breeze yelped and charged forward. Chrys scratched the dog around her head and shooed her in. Bullet rolled his fawn body off the couch. Her brother's truck was downstairs, so she knew he would have taken the dogs out. She slipped her boots off as soon as she was inside.

"Come on in," she whispered to the person behind her and giggled.

"Hold on. These boots ain't the easiest to get off." Colby closed the door. He was still dressed in drag from the thigh-high boots to the wig and make-up.

"Keep them on." Chrys grabbed his hand and pulled him forward. Her sock feet swished over the hardwood. Colby's spiked heels clicked with every step. Breeze leapt beside the clicking shoes as Bullet found his way back to the couch.

In the hallway she saw her brother's door was closed. She yanked the man in the mini-dress inside her bedroom and slammed the door behind him. The tiny Chihuahua scratched from the other side. Chrys pushed her full lips against Colby's and the two of them half fell against the door with a thud.

If anyone had been watching they would have seen two women kissing in one of the messiest bedrooms around. Clothes were scattered over the floor. A dozen painted ceramic masks, most of which Chrys had painted herself, stared down at them from every wall.

Chrys kissed down to Colby's throat. She pushed the black hair over his shoulder and felt his pulse quicken. She felt him swallow.

Colby slipped his hand to the back of Chrys' hair, his fingers mingled in the strands. He suddenly pulled her head back. Her mouth popped open. He put his lips to hers. Their tongues connected and twisted around each other.

Chrys tasted the man's lipstick. She felt his hand slide down the side of her body, his thumb caressing the edge of her breast, until it reached her hip. He pulled her in close making her gasp.

152

Chrys pulled her lips away. "Where have you been hiding that thing."

"Tuck and cover. Trade secret." They kissed again. Colby bit her bottom lip.

Chrys moved her hands over the body she was touching. There were "realistic" fake breasts and that thin stomach she had squeezed before. Her fingers latched onto the bottom of the black skirt and pulled it up. One hand grabbed what she had felt. Everything had been building since the bar. She knew she had probably had too much to drink and this may be something she'd think twice about later, but for the moment it was what she wanted.

She let go of him as he suddenly had her T-shirt up above her chest and his tongue traced circles around her own flat stomach. Oh yeah, she wanted this. As Colby pulled one breast out of her bra and latched his mouth around the nipple, her knees almost buckled. Yes, she might regret it, but Chrys always lived for the moment.

Chapter 15

Chrys ran her fingers over the latch of Luke Weston's smaller suitcase. She'd liberated some of her brother's clothes from their tiny laundry room for Colby to wear home after they were done the second time and walked him to the door.

"What are those?" He motioned toward the cases with the heeled boot in his hand. "You going somewhere?"

"Nope. Those were Luke's. When we couldn't find him I cleaned out his place." That was close enough to the truth.

Colby fixed how he was holding his bar clothes. Chrys bounced to the kitchen on the balls of her feet and came back with a shopping bag. "Thanks. Find anything interesting in the suitcases?"

Chrys scooped up Breeze and said, "I haven't really looked."

The moment Colby left to catch his taxi she wheeled the bag to the couch. She brought both feet onto the cushion and sat down. She wore turquoise, lacy boy-shorts and her shirt from last night. She put the case beside her and opened it up. All of the magazines and papers were there in a wild mess. She flipped through the magazines and found similar things in each one - articles on movie stars and the latest trends.

It was still so early Sandra wasn't down in the restaurant baking yet. Chrys hated the truly early hours. It was too quiet and calm. The only thing she heard was the refrigerator motor. She liked noise. She liked action. When it was too quiet she thought too much and her own voice in her head got loud. Bad people came out in the quiet hours.

On the back of a cellphone bill were a few handwritten lines.

"We never know what the world will hold. If I should go please dance and sing and celebrate."

Further down the envelope Luke or Luca (Chrys wasn't sure where one ended and the other began) had written, "Does anyone know what the future holds?"

Chrys opened her brother's laptop that always sat on the coffee table. She waited for it to boot up. Luke Weston had a cell phone bill, which meant he had a phone. She wondered if it had been found with the body. He was also an eighteen year old man/woman, so what were the chances he was on social media?

She tried Twitter first. There were a couple of profiles with the same name, but they weren't her Luke Weston.

Facebook was different, as she immediately found Luke Weston. It wasn't that secure. He had shared posts of joke sayings, a lot of Minions and other posts about bettering your life and being true to yourself. In his photos, there were a few pictures of wildlife and nature. The farther she got into the pics she found some of Luke. He always had a scowl or looked angry. She felt sorry for him. His profile picture was just white words on a dark background, "I'm a leaf on the wind." Under friends he had almost two hundred people. On her own profile she had over seven hundred and actually only talked to a few dozen, so Chrys knew it didn't mean much. She scrolled through all of the names until coming across a Mary - Mary Locke. Her profile was blocked, but her profile picture wasn't.

All of Luke's postings stopped about a month ago. That was around the time Luke became Luca full time.

Chrys typed Luca Weston into the search function. One profile came up. The profile picture showed Luca in a mirror holding a white backed phone as she took the selfie. Under photos were pictures of the new woman at Ms. Kara's Pride, with Ms. Kara, with Colby, some with Mary, Luca in different outfits. What Chrys noticed was that Luca was always smiling. She only had a smattering of friends. It looked like they were mostly people from the gay bar, people who knew Luca.

She was happy. How did she get into that alley? Someone, maybe more than one, beat her, bit her and who knows what else. She or he was helpless when they came at her.

"What are you doing?"

Chrys' heart leapt in her chest. Magazines fell to the floor. "Fuck! Fuck off Spence. Make some gorram noise or something."

"What are you doing?" he repeated. His voice was flat and annoyed.

"I'm looking through Luke's shit. What does it look like?" Her whole body tingled. She liked a good scare, but not when she didn't expect it.

Spencer expelled a breath. "Whatever. Jessie just texted and said she can't make it in. You're manager today." He spun around and walked back toward the bedroom. His bare feet padded on the floor.

Chrys stared at the words on the envelope still in her hand. "Wait," she looked up, "What?" Her brother had gone back to bed.

~ * ~

"Where's Jessie?" Chrys stood in the open doorway to the restaurants cooler with her hands on her hips. The cold recycled air on her face felt comforting, but thoughts of the morgue freezer gave her the willies.

Spencer didn't bother looking up from his clipboard. He was trying to come up with a prep list for the new girl to work on. "I told you, she called in sick."

"She didn't drink anything last night. How could she be sick?" Her brother shrugged his shoulders. "You knocked her up, didn't you? You little slut."

"Look who's talking."

"What's that supposed to mean?"

Spencer smiled at his sister as he stepped from the cooler into the dish-pit area and headed toward the dining room.

The sound of Chrys' shoes echoed on the walls. She was dressed almost the way Jessie usually was – dark slacks and matching jacket over a white tank-top. Okay, it was nothing like the front-of-house-manager's black shirt with rolled up sleeves, but it was more business-like than what she usually wore. Already this morning she had one server call in sick and today they were actually going to be busy. "What's that supposed to mean?" She yelled after her brother.

"You know what it means." Spencer side-stepped behind Ranger and Gordie. The new girl that the culinary teacher had sent over was at the cold-side table already doing some prep work. She had slid one foot out of a non-slip black clog and put the socked foot on top of the other. "Mallory, here's a prep list for salads and cold apps. Keep doing that through lunch and just try watching what goes on and helping as you can. For dinner we'll have you plating some of the dishes."

Mallory nodded and quietly said, "Yes Chef." She had organized the entire station lining things up on her tabletop in perfect order.

Chrys marched along the front of the pass and turned into the open space right beside the cold table. "Are you seriously calling me a slut?"

"You called me a slut." Spencer stepped past her and headed toward the back again.

Chrys gave the new girl a pleasant smile and followed him. "No, no, no I joked about you being a slut," she called out loud enough for everyone to hear. "You called me a slut. There's a difference."

"I didn't call you anything. I inferred it and you came up with our own conclusion," he said as he went into his office. Like always he didn't shut the door. He regretted it a few seconds later when his sister took it as an invitation to continue the conversation.

Chrys paused for a moment. She realized that meant she called herself a slut. Time to change the subject. "Are we going to talk about Luke and what we should do next?"

"What exactly do you want to talk about? We don't have any suspects. We don't even know the official cause of death."

"What about those round puncture wounds on his/her chest? Those were pretty deep and unique. That has to be something. And the mark on the back of his arm."

"It wasn't a mark, it was a bite. Somebody bit him." Spencer sat behind his desk. "Oh, but we're not cops."

"Are you going to bring that up every time?"

"I'm not having this conversation again, Chrys."

"Perfect. So we know it's not a hate crime."

"We don't know that." Spencer picked up a pen.

Chrys leaned her shoulder against the stand-up freezer. Inside were tubs of ice cream, a few desserts and cases of chicken breasts and lamb chops. In this world of television cooking shows emphasising the use of fresh, not frozen food, it was almost embracing to have so little meat in there. However, in the world of struggling restaurants it was not a reality. It wasn't a reality in any restaurant - no matter what Gordon Ramsay said.

"I don't think anyone would bite him if they thought he was gay."

Spencer shrugged. "The bite's on the back of the upper arm, so maybe Luke tried elbowing one of them like this and got him in the mouth?"

"What about the anti-gay groups Ms. Kara talked about then? We should go check them out."

"Chrys, we can't. The writer's group is in tonight. We have reservations. I have the new girl here and you're front-of-house manager today, so you're busy. We have a restaurant to run."

"Some things are more important than the restaurant, *Spencer*."

"Not this, *Chrysanthemum*."

Chrys groaned her frustration as she left the office.

~ * ~

Chrys rubbed her ear where the lobe had been ripped off. She used to love wearing earrings. Now she wore one on the other earlobe and had the top of her right ear pierced. She knew pain and fear, but probably nothing like what Luke had experienced. She had been a foster child and was in relationships with other women. What made her any different than a man who should have been or wanted to be a woman? Why would a hate group go after him and leave her alone? How possible was it that she could end up beaten and dead in an alley just like Luke?

161

Her phone vibrated inside her bra. She knew who was texting her before she even looked at it. Her brother must have noticed something missing. She slipped the phone out and scrolled through all the texts she hadn't read while she was driving. All of them were from him.

"Chrys, where are you?"

"Come downstairs."

"I need you at the restaurant."

The last one read, *"Jess called in sick. I need you at the restaurant. AND WHERE THE FUCK IS MY TRUCK?"*

Just the sound of her foot-falls echoing through the concrete parking structure gave Chrys a creepy feeling. Sunlight came in from all the open sides, but her Steve Maddens clomping on the ramp still bounced around and made it seem like someone was behind her. She had to park three levels up, so she quickly found the stairwell and ran down to the street.

She slipped her phone back into her bra without returning Spencer's texts. She should have asked before taking his truck, but he would have said no, so it was really her only choice to avoid that possibility. She had to know more about Luke. There had to be more to learn about him than what she got from a lonely room in a hostel and a gay bar.

It was a bright sunny day in Middleton, a change from the cold winds which had hit the last few days. She had decided to take full advantage of the warm weather by wearing a pleated skirt over grey tights and a loose silky blue-grey top with mid-length sleeves. It wasn't the most stylish or co-ordinated outfit she could have worn, but she felt good and that was most of the battle. She arranged her hair so that it fell down the sides of her face, covering her ears.

Behind the parking garage were a couple of eight-story office buildings, their occupants taking most of the parking spaces. Chrys knew there were some lawyers and government offices. She couldn't imagine what else was in there. There were office buildings all over the city with probably thousands of people in suits sitting at desks and Chrys didn't have a clue why. She couldn't imagine a reason to sit in an office all day. Whenever she went downtown among the skyscrapers she thought about going inside just to see what went on. The main street was more her style. Little shops were her thing.

She passed the bank and went into a store selling handbags and luggage. The manager and clerk didn't recognize Luke or Luca. It was the same at Lucy's Petite which sold dresses to only the thinnest of the population. Chrys fondled a couple of dresses but didn't feel right trying anything on while she was asking about Luke. She wasn't going to go into the lighting fixtures store, but did anyway. It was a bust. The clerk at the floral shop remembered Luke because he didn't have a clue what he wanted, just that it had to be nice and was for his two Moms. The smoke shop had beautiful glass-blown bongs that Gordie would have liked. Chrys wondered if he had ever been to it. The counter person with dreadlocks and a tattoo on her neck hadn't seen Luke or Luca. Every store seemed to be named after a person: Maureen's Cards & Gifts, C. Storm Gallery, Frix's Green Earth (earth friendly products where Chrys bought soaps that Luca apparently had as well) Beau's Antiques, Michel's

Munchies. The last was a bakery where the girl that talked to Chrys said she recognized both faces. However, the girl couldn't say when, she'd seen them.

Chrys purchased a cinnamon bun and sat on a bench outside the bakery. She tried to picture Luke and Luca walking up and down the street. She imagined him being uncomfortable and her being right at home. Two people in one body who felt different in the same skin.

A couple of young women exited Greenleaf Hostel and headed in the direction of the subway entrance, laughing at some private joke. The alley where Luke's body was found was only a few blocks in the same direction. What put him there? Where was he during the time no one heard from him? She couldn't find anyone that had seen Luke or Luca in the past weeks.

Through the large tan lenses of her sunglasses her brown eyes read all the store and business names across the street. The only door she had not gone through on that side was one with a frosted window. It had the name Canadian Traditional Family International written beside it. She didn't know what they were about or if Luke would have gone there.

"Can I help you?"

Chrys smiled at the woman behind the desk as she walked in. Her floral perfume filled the immaculate reception area. Delicate piano music came from speakers on the ceiling. There were framed awards on the walls and photographs of people she didn't know shaking hands with politicians and famous folks. On a bookshelf against the far wall were other awards stating the CTFI's dedication to community and the city.

"Hi, how are you?" Chrys flashed her best smile. "What do you do here?"

The lady folded her hands on her desk. "We are a non-profit organization which hopes to instill traditional family values into the Canadian household." She slipped a brochure across the desk.

What did that mean? Chrys wondered.

"Okay, can you tell me if you ever saw this man?" Chrys held out her cell phone with Luke's photo on the screen. The woman steadied Chrys' hand. She had perfectly manicured fingernails. The non-profit paid well. She shook her head then Chrys showed her Luca's photo. "What about her?"

"Nope. I don't think so."

A side door opened as a man walked into the room. He wore an expensive tailored suit. There was a crucifix pinned on his lapel. His salt and pepper hair was perfectly feathered. He smiled at Chrys with a mouthful of perfect teeth. "Patty, can you get the mayor's office on the phone for me?" He looked at Chrys. "Good afternoon."

"Yes, Dr. Frost."

Chrys stepped forward so the she would be noticed. From the corner of her eye she saw Patty dial the phone, but she was betting it was all show. "You're a doctor?"

He flashed his white teeth again. (There's no way those were natural) "Doctor in religious studies. How can I help you?"

"Have you seen either of these two people?" She showed him her phone and scrolled between the two pictures.

With his finger Dr. Frost took it on himself to flip back and forth. "Is this man and woman the same person?" He had been the only person all day to pick up on it. "That is disgusting. I've never seen this person before and we would never let them in this office. Transsexuals are unnatural."

"Luke was transgender."

Dr. Frost shook his head. "I really can't understand how people who are unhappy with their lives feel they have the right to defy God's plan. What is this about? Who are you?" He crossed his arms over his chest. His eyes glared at her.

Chrys pulled out her shirt as she slipped her phone in her bra. She watched the religious man's eyes flash to her cleavage for a quick look. This was probably one of those times where she should think before speaking. "I'm just a lesbian trying to find out who killed her friend."

He crossed to a rack just inside the door. He took a pamphlet and held it out. A smirk crossed his lips. "It may be too late, but we may be able to help you back to being normal."

"Normal?"

"It's not your fault. The media and modern society has programmed young men and women to believe having sexual relationships with members of the same sex to be natural." The way he said "natural" was as if it was the most foul-tasting word ever. "You can't blame yourself."

Chrys snatched the pamphlet. She saw the word reprogramming. "I have sex with both."

Dr. Frost flashed a polite smile. "Then there is still hope for you."

"What?" She felt a fire rising inside her chest. She had so much to say building up in her mind that Chrys couldn't focus on one thing.

"Read the pamphlet and when you come to the realization," Dr. Frost's voice was so soothing it made Chrys calmer. She hated that. "The CTFI will be here to help you come back."

~ * ~

Chrys looked at the facade of the fortune teller's building. The center of the window displayed a white hand with the palm lines drawn outward. The door advertised palm readings, numerology, tarot cards and supplies. A crescent moon flashed florescent blue. Inside the window were crimson drapes and leafy plants hiding what was beyond. Amid all of this was the phrase, "Know What the Future Holds."

The Canadian Traditional Family International hid hate behind religion and self-righteousness. What was hidden behind drapes and greenery?

A bell above the door rang as Chrys entered. A smoky scent greeted her. Book shelves lined the walls with sections for witches and wiccans, mythology, palm reading, basically every kind of fortune-telling option. A spinning rack held decks of tarot cards with an array of designs. On one wall she saw shelves of glass jars with labels like love, luck, blessings and fortune. In the middle of the room was a small round table draped in a maroon cloth and four wooden chairs.

A woman walked through hanging beads that blocked a doorway behind a small counter. The thin woman had a short shoulder-length blond hair died with a mixture of blue. She wore a tank-top and dark stretch pants. Her bare feet padded on the hardwood floor as she walked around the counter.

"Can I help you?" She asked.

"Yeah, I guess." Chrys slipped out her phone. "Are you the fortune teller?" In her head she'd already started referring to this woman as the Smurf. She knew a boy once who collected the little blue and white figurines.

"That's one way to put it. My name is Emma."

"I'm Chrys. Sorry, you're not what I expected. I pictured someone with wild gypsy hair and lots of jewelry and robes." Chrys laughed.

"I have these." She held up a wrist with a dozen elastic bracelets on it. "The wild-haired lady is my mother. She's a fortune-teller too. And we are descendants of gypsies. I'm guessing you came here for a reason."

Chrys squeezed the CTFI literature she had rolled up in her hand. "Are you guessing or predicting? I was wondering if you've ever seen my friend." She showed the woman the first picture.

"That's Luke. Something bad has happened to him," she stated. She stared at Chrys. It wasn't a question at all.

Chrys fought the urge to roll her eyes. "How often did he come here?" Her phone vibrated. She had turned the sound notifications off long ago and then stopped reading Spencer's texts.

The happiness seemed to fade from the woman. "He came here a few times. The first was for a reading and then he came for good-luck charms and potions. I told him I couldn't promise they would work, but he thought there was no harm in trying."

"Do you know this person?" Chrys showed the picture of Luca.

Emma nodded as she saw the picture and said, "That's Luke too. He came in dressed like that once. I guess it was the last time I saw him. At first I didn't know it was him until I heard his laugh. He said my predictions were right." She scooped her hair back with one hand. The blue strands fell through her fingers. She had a look on her face like she was challenging the woman across from her to question those predictions.

"What were your predictions?" Chrys slipped her phone in her bra.

"I told him things in his future would double as if there was two of everything. The number two was big on his chart. And that he would find contentment in himself."

Chrys' boob vibrated. She let out a frustrated grunt.

"An unwanted caller?" Emma asked.

"My brother."

"Can I see your hand?" Emma held out hers.

Here we go, Chrys thought. Somewhere deep, she wanted to believe in fortune telling and the sixth sense and spirits and all that, but growing up with Spencer, who liked to find a reason for everything made her somewhat cynical. There were times when they were younger that crazy things happened, but that was then. The older she got the more she saw things for what they were. She held her hand out. It wasn't helping that the fortune teller was still a Smurf in her mind. Emma Smurf took it and turned it palm up.

She traced her finger along a couple of lines. "You lead an often exciting life."

She could have gleaned that from the fact that Chrys was there asking questions.

Emma continued, "Is there something to do with flowers around you? A name maybe?"

"My first name is Chrysanthemum." Okay, that was a little odd.

"And I see someone around you. A small person. A child. Do you have any children?"

"Nope." Chrys took her hand back with a smile. She had her there. The Smurf wasn't that special any more.

"Have you ever been pregnant?"

Chrys pulled her phone out just so that her hands were busy. They were shaking. "What?" She stared at the woman.

"Did you ever have an abortion or miscarriage?"

"Um…" Her body was suddenly chilled. Nobody knew. How could anyone know about that? Even Spencer didn't know. It was years ago. She had been seventeen and was in a bad way. "How could you possibly…there's no way…"

"She's always with you."

Chrys stared at the woman for a long time. She really did not know what to say. She had thought about that moment many times over the past eight years. She had no regrets about it – she had not been in the right state to have a child then – but she still wondered if she was right.

Her phone vibrated again.

"I should get going." Chrys' mouth was dry. "Thank you for your time."

"I'm sorry about whatever happened to Luke. He was a nice person. You're welcome back any time."

As Chrys stepped out into the bright sunlight she suddenly forgot what the Smurf had said. Across the street was the Greenleaf. She saw the back of Constable Wright as he ran up the steps. The police were about to find out Luke Weston's room was empty. She didn't know if it would come back to her, however she knew Wright was a smart man. It was just a matter of time.

~ * ~

"Where the hell have you been?" Spencer barely looked up when Chrys walked through the front doors of The Alcrest. He had abandoned his white chef coat for a striped apron over an Alcrest t-shirt.

"What?" Chrys took her usual spot across the pass from her brother.

Spencer continued chopping onions. "Jessie called in sick. Then you steal my truck and run away." He grabbed another onion and sliced it in half with one swift chop. "The first time we have a busy lunch in a week and I'm short-handed."

Her thumb ring tapped against the hot tile beneath the hanging heat light. "You had Megan and Sam here. Was it really so busy you needed another server?"

He put the 10 inch blade down. Sweat shone on the tattoos of his lower arms. The other cooks, except the new girl, had traded in their coats as well. They were busy during lunch, busy enough to build up a sweat

171

anyway. "I did when Mrs. Staples walked in wanting to talk."

Chrys stood up straight. "What did she want?"

"She wanted to know if we can have a memorial for Luke here. I said, yes of course."

Chrys wanted to tell him what she had done earlier in the day, but she didn't know if she had found out anything. "So what do you want me to do?"

"You're manager tonight."

"I'm supposed to be serving tonight."

"If Jessie doesn't show up I need a manager hosting the night. Hanni and Izzy are booked to work." He let Gordie move around him with a plate holding a cheese burger and fries for a customer in the frame room.

Tap. Tap. "What's Jessie sick with? If it was…" her eyes flipped to the other cooks. "…you know, wouldn't she be fine by now?"

"I don't know." Spencer slid the chopped onion into an insert. He placed it into one of the holes at the back of the butchers-block table that opened into the lowboy fridges underneath. "She hasn't been answering my texts either. Maybe you should call somebody in, just in case. Wylie or Dee. We have a few reservations."

Chrys groaned before turning and storming down the hallway toward the back stairs. At the bottom she sent Dee a text. *We need you to work tonight.* By the top of the stairs she got a text back – *I was going to go out dancing tonight.*

Chrys scratched Breeze and Bullet all around their ears. She got them ready to go for a walk. Luke's suitcases were by the door. Should she hide them before the police came? She sent another text – *if you*

172

work tonight we will go out after. Ever hear of Club 22?

Chapter 16

Ranger dipped a metal scrubby into a bucket of soapy water with a capful of sanitizer and put it to the stove. He scrubbed off any bits and pieces that had fallen out of pans during service.

Spencer and Gordie took inserts and containers from the lowboys, pulled plastic-wrap over the tops and placed them onto sheet-pans. The busy night had been fast and furious. It started right at 5:00 pm but fizzled by 10:00 pm. Now it was almost 11:00 pm and they were about finished cleaning. Mallory had a couple of desserts for the last table, but basically the kitchen was done for the night.

"Spencer, I'm off the clock," Hanni stated. She leaned against the open entry to the kitchen waiting for everyone to notice her. She had changed out of her skin-tight black work clothes and into a skin-tight white mini-dress. As the chef looked at her she ran the back of her hand across her nose.

In one glance Spencer took in her pushed-up breasts and the fact that her crotch was barely hidden by the skirt. "I know. I told you guys I would finish."

Hanni had looks that could usually get whatever she wanted. She gave him one of those. "I just wanted to make it official."

Chrys stepped through the opening by the cold-side table. "I'm ready for those desserts now." Mallory nodded and went to work without a word.

"Where are Dee and Izzy?" Hanni asked.

Chrys looked down the small kitchen line around the three cooks. "They went home to get changed." She turned back to watch Mallory plating desserts and whispered, "Not all of us bring our whoring clothes to work." To her brother she said, "Spence, as soon as I deliver these I'm going upstairs to change."

Spencer slipped a sheet-pan of covered inserts off the table and headed for the back. It had been a good night. For over four hours they had been so busy in the kitchen that he forgot about the bills and the baby on the way. He had to keep jumping over to help the new girl, but she picked up on everything quickly. It had been fun. It had been a while since cooking was actually fun. Those days were few and far between now.

The night's dishwasher wiped his hands on a cloth folded over his apron strings and leapt for the walk-in cooler door. "Almost done, Chef?"

"Almost." Spencer slipped the pan into railings on a rack-n-roll inside the cooler. Next on his to-do list was a quick inventory of the cooler to make a prep list for the next morning and see if he needed to buy anything. "There'll be a few dessert plates and glasses, but I can handle those. If you want to look after the garbage you can hit it after."

"Cool. Jessie's in your office, by the way."

Spencer looked up. "How long has she been there?"

"Like an hour ago. I told her I'd get you. She said she wanted to wait."

"Thanks." He took a step to leave the cooler. They had to talk, but he wasn't sure he was ready. He grabbed a clipboard from the wall outside the door and went back inside the cooler.

They needed to make more of the honey-lime vinaigrette and Caesar dressing. Vegetables had to be cut for soup. Spencer tapped his pen against the prep list. He remembered his parents arguing about responsibilities and priorities. He was pretty sure the only reason his father agreed to foster children was to give his mom something to do. It was a way to stop her from complaining about him spending so much time at the pub. It was just a pub then. Spencer was doing the same thing with his gastropub. He always put it first and Jessie knew that. Before they were officially together, he put The Alcrest first. He was going to do the same thing when his child was here. His only excuse was that was the way the restaurant business worked.

Something had to suffer. Restaurants weren't like retail stores where you had a dozen people and if one called in sick you gave another a call. In the kitchen they had four people – that was it. If Ranger called in sick the only one to cover was Spencer. And cover was a loose term. Do both jobs was more like it. Each of the kitchen staff got a day off on one of the slow days, sometimes two, but Spencer was there every day. Something was not going to get the attention it required. When he was a kid his father went to maybe one or two of his school sporting events. Still, Spencer had to make a good life for his child. Was that his father's reasoning for missing everything in his kids' lives?

"Hey, how're you feeling?" Spencer looked at the woman sitting behind his desk. She had her jacket pulled around her.

Jessie didn't even look at him. "Fine." Her voice was flat.

"You didn't answer any of my texts or calls."

"I was…" She absently moved things on the desk. "I couldn't use my phone."

"What do you mean?" Spencer crossed his arms in front of him. He could have sat down on the other chair in the room, but some macho thing inside told him to remain standing.

"I was at a clinic half the day. I wasn't supposed to use my phone." She looked up at him. Her eyes were red and the skin around them puffy.

"Oh." He didn't get it. Why wouldn't she tell him she was in the clinic? "What about the rest of the day then?"

"Can you shut the door, Spencer?"

He didn't like her tone of voice; it was almost absent. That was the only way he could describe it.

Plus any time someone asked to have a door shut it was never a good thing. When he was sitting behind the desk and he had others shut the door it was usually to discipline them. He shut it and did not say a word.

Jessie looked at her hands. She was not the manicure type; in fact her nails had been chewed down. "I know," her voice was so low Spencer could barely hear it, "you have a lot of problems with the restaurant and all that. I don't want to be a burden on you. I know a baby would add to all of it."

"It would, but I'll figure it out. We'll figure it out."

"I know you think we will, but it would be more than we can imagine." Jessie drew a couple of lines on a sticky-note pad, then put the pen down. Her fingers started spinning her gold watch around her wrist. "You said yourself you didn't have enough money to pay peoples' wages. How are we going to afford anything?" A tear ran down her cheek.

Spencer felt his stomach churn. His knees were numb and he suddenly felt like there was a ring floating around his head. "What are you trying to say, Jess?" He knew what was coming. *How could it be coming?*

"I know you weren't happy with this whole ... this situation. I did what I thought was best."

"What was that?" He stared at the woman behind the desk. Anger pushed the numbness away.

~ * ~

Chrys inspected herself in her full-length mirror. After serving the desserts and taking payment at the table, she had bolted up the stairs for the fastest shower

179

she had taken since she was a kid. She wasn't planning on meeting anyone so she didn't need to go overboard on the smelling pretty stuff. A hairdryer was out of the question. She settled for standing naked in the bathroom and violently whipping her body and hair back and forth spraying water on the walls. In the mirror she saw a beautiful woman dressed in a black long sleeved top and black leather mini-skirt. The weather was finally warm and Chrys' legs really were her best feature, so why not show them off. All the dancing paid off, and her caramel skin really made them pop. The top didn't do anything to accentuate her small breasts, but the droop neckline gave the image that there was more there. A little make-up around the eyes, some lipstick and she was set.

She ran down the stairs with shoes in hand, stopped at the bottom to put on the black leather 4.5 inch heeled Pleasers (they were t-strap with a small wedge and mini-bondage rings down the front) and opened the office door. "Spence, I ..."

"Chrys, get out."

Chrys followed Spencer's gaze to his girlfriend sitting at the desk. Tears fell down her cheeks. One hand wiped some away only to have more fall in their place.

"I had an abortion," Jessie said. Her words could barely be heard over the running dishwashing machine in the room outside.

"What?" was Spencer's reaction. His face went blank. It was as though every emotion was trying to fight its way out. His eyes said anger. His body vibrated. "What did you just say?"

"You have too much going on." Jessie's voice rose in pitch. Her words were broken by sobs. A bubble of snot formed at one nostril. "You always complain about bills. This was one more thing. I didn't want this to be … I wasn't ready …"

"This is on me?" Spencer's hands were in tight fists. "You did this because of me?" Spit flew from his mouth.

"Spence," Chrys touched his arm and he spun on her. His face showed anger, fear and confusion all at once. His eyes glistened and in those she saw loss.

"What?"

"Calm down."

"Calm down?" All she saw in his glistening eyes now was rage. That emotion was winning. "You heard what she said, right?"

"You don't know what she was thinking at the time."

"She wasn't thinking. Not about me." Spencer bit down on his lip. "This isn't something you can go back and fix."

Jessie was having trouble breathing. She wiped more tears from her cheeks. "I was …" quick breaths.

"You were what?" Spencer snapped in his girlfriend's direction.

"Okay, okay," Chrys reached out and grabbed her brother's arm. This time he didn't move. "I think everyone needs to calm down a little." She stared into his eyes trying to get a telepathic message through to him. "Jessie, why don't you come with me?" Chrys put her hand out toward her manager while staring at Spencer. She mouthed the words, "Let her go." as she moved Jessie behind her and to the door. Before

Chrys left she whispered, "It'll be okay." to her brother.

"Come on in here," Chrys held the door to the woman's washroom open as she ushered Jessie in. "Over to the sink. We have to calm you down."

"Chrys, what did I do?" Jessie couldn't stop the tears any more. They flowed down her cheeks. Her body shook. "What if I made a mistake? Spencer hates me."

Chrys ran paper towel under the cold water and dabbed at her boss' face. "He doesn't hate you. Why don't you come out with the girls and me tonight?"

Jessie wiped her nose with a tissue. She said, "I'm not going drinking, Chrys. I still hurt and I'm on meds."

"You can sit at the table and guard our drinks. You shouldn't be alone. And you can be designated driver." There had to be some way of putting a positive twist on this. Any other time she would have bowed out of dancing and spent the night with Jess, but she wanted to see what Club 22 was all about. It was the last place she knew Luca went. It could be the key.

"No, Chrys, you don't know what kind of pain I'm feeling." She sniffed and rubbed her nose.

Chrys stared at her for a moment. It wasn't the place or time. "You're coming. Let's go."

The first thing Chrys saw as she left the hallway was Hanni standing by the hostess stand sneering in her direction. Then she saw the man by the door. The salt in his salt-and-pepper hair almost sparkled in the mood lighting. He looked official standing there checking his watch. His eyes locked on Chrys.

"Miss Alcrest, I think you have some explaining to do. Is something wrong?"

Chrys squeezed Jessie next to her. "It's a family thing."

Hanni jabbed a finger in her back as she walked behind the two.

"What about this?" Wright turned his hand like a magician revealing a hidden card and suddenly there was an Alcrest business card between his fingers.

"Shit. I forgot about that."

"I found this at the Greenleaf Hostel. Is there anything you want to tell me? Like why all of Luke's belongings are missing and the only thing in his room was your name?"

Chrys' dark eyes looked down the line. Izzy and Dee had returned and now stood by the bar with Hanni. They all watched what was going on. "I went there looking for Luke and saw that he hadn't been there for a while, so I took his things for safe-keeping."

"How did you get in his room?"

"It wasn't locked." Chrys squeezed Jessie and looked down. "I knocked. There was no answer, so I tried the door and it opened." It wasn't a lie.

Wright ran his fingers under his chin. "Is that so?"

Chrys nodded. "That's what happened."

"Miss Alcrest, we talked about you and your brother not…"

"This was before you found his body."

"Don't you think you should have told me then?" His eyes tried to pierce hers, so she looked away. "What about his cell phone? His parents say he had one, but we can't find it."

183

"It wasn't with the body? It wasn't in his room."

"Why do I think there's more you're not..."

"I hate to be a bitch, Constable," she waved the other women to come down, "but we were just going dancing. Spencer can tell you everything." Chrys liked interrupting him. She was certain Wright was used to being in charge, so she wanted to put a little chink in that. She also knew it was his goal to catch the killer, but that often sick little voice in her head wanted to beat him to the prize. Chrys wanted to catch the killer. One way or another.

~ * ~

"I wouldn't worry about Spence." Chrys had to lean in close to Jessie and almost yell to be heard over the pounding dance music. With one finger she absently spun the tiny food menu on the table. There had been a line-up outside Club 22, but as in most cases good-looking women got ushered to the front of the line and they were soon inside. It took thirty minutes before a small table was open. As soon as it was Jessie sat down and didn't move. The others took turns sitting with her, but she wouldn't say why Chrys had brought her along. "You know what he's like. He'll cool down tomorrow."

If Chrys were honest she knew he would probably cool down, but it was going to fester. Her brother could hold a grudge. He still complained about Shane Pratt getting him in trouble by throwing mud in elementary school. Sometime in the future this whole thing would blow up again.

"He was so mad though." Though Jessie had stopped crying her eyes were still red and her face puffy.

"Do you feel it was the right thing to do?" Chrys sipped her Screwdriver. She looked at the back of her hand where they had stamped it with ink when she came in. It was two #2's, but the second one was backward making a mirror image of the first. She had a picture of the same stamp that she had taken in the morgue.

Jessie dipped her finger into her glass of ice water. She stirred the cubes around before answering. "I think so. I don't know."

After taking a deep breath, Chrys said, "Jess, at some point you'll change your mind and think you were totally wrong." She ran a finger around her glass rim and plucked the slice of orange from it. It tasted better than the sample platter of food they had ordered. The small quesadillas were particularly bad. "Other days you'll be so glad you did it. Spence will feel that way too. She wanted to tell her how she had done the same, but shouting it over drinks at a club just didn't feel right.

"Hey." Dee was suddenly beside Chrys. Her black hair draped down as she reached for her drink. She asked if everything was okay before finishing off her Cosmopolitan.

"It's fine," Chrys said. She and Jessie didn't tell the others what the fight was about. Hanni was the only one who asked.

"Are my shoes still safe?" Dee looked under the table. Chrys had insisted that Jessie at least needed nice shoes to go to the club and the only extra ones were Dee's Christian Louboutins that she had in her trunk.

"Seriously?"

"Chrys, Loubies are nothing to play around with." Dee stared at both of them. She was extremely serious about her shoe collection. "My sister bought those for me."

"They're safe." Chrys stuck out her tongue.

"Fine. I'm going to dance with a friend." Dee was dancing before reaching her friend.

Chrys let her eyes roam the club. Bright lights flashed with the beat of thundering music. Lights like lasers crossed over top of everyone's heads. The center of the room was a large packed dance floor with a rail all around it. Breasts were being thrust out, hips and booties shook like jelly. Small tables were scattered around the outside forcing people to interact. On the side were rows of leather couches, each filled with people yelling at each other. There was a large raised deejay booth in the corner; everyone could see the guy dancing behind his machines. The bar covered the far wall and two smaller bars were located in the far corners. Above it all her brown eyes focused on a large window. At first she thought it was a mirror, but she was sure there were people on the other side watching what was going on. Just looking up she felt like eyes were on her. Chrys' entire body shook.

"Someone walked over your grave," Rose Alcrest would have said.

Maybe it was Luke.

The crowd inside the club was a fine mosaic display of every race and colour. The majority were young, well-dressed and good-looking. It didn't slip Chrys' attention that she and her work chums fit in that category. All young, all gorgeous.

"Look, I'm going to be right back. I have to go find something. You'll be okay for a few minutes?" Chrys was on her feet and walking away before Jessie could answer.

There were so many people in the club that she couldn't walk without bumping against others. In just a few steps she felt a hand graze her backside. She realized the benefits of the gay bar. There was no point in protesting. Nobody was going to admit to it and there were too many people to accuse.

When she first went for drinks Chrys had asked about a lost and found. She was told anything they had would be at the coat-check by the front doors.

A cardboard box was dropped on the countertop without a word from the woman. Chrys was disappointed. As had worked hard on her story. The coat-check room was between the outside doors and the club itself, so the music was still loud. There were guards dressed in black standing by both sets of doors. Chrys reached into the box. There was a pair of heels, some underwear, a purse, a couple of wallets and even a hair piece. At the bottom she found three phones. Only one had a white case like the one from Luca's Facebook photo. Could this really be Luke's? She held down the power button, but nothing happened.

There was clicking noise behind her, the sound of stilettos on the floor. From the corner of her eye Chrys saw the outside door open.

"Mr. O'Donnell."

Chrys froze. She held her breath and stared straight ahead into the coat-check room. She didn't want to move. She couldn't tell if it was fear or something else.

"It's good to see you again." the woman's voice continued. "Please follow me." The clicking started again.

Chrys checked over her left shoulder. She saw blond hair and then two men in dark suits walked through the door into the club. She thanked the coat-check woman and walked into the club. It took a moment for her eyes to adjust, but then she found the two men being escorted by a woman. She recognized both men. They had been in The Alcrest before. She kept her eyes on them until they disappeared through a door beneath the large window.

"What's wrong?" Jessie stared at her. Even in the bad lighting she could tell Chrys was pale.

Chrys put the white phone next to her glass before taking a healthy drink. "Nothing. It doesn't matter." Or maybe it did?

The only thought in her head was "what did Luke get himself into now?"

Chapter 17

"Chrys," Izzy squealed as she suddenly appeared beside the table. Chrys would swear the ginger's red dress had inched its way up her thighs a little. She drank her martini in one go. "Come dance with me."

"I'm talking. Where's Hanni?"

"I don't know. She went off with some guy." Izzy snatched a salmon roll from the platter on the table. After a nibble her face scrunched up with mild disgust and she put it back.

"What guy?" Chrys got to her feet to survey the room. It was like a video where the further her eyes went the more everyone went out of focus and blended into one dancing palette of colour. She couldn't see the blond or her white dress anywhere. "Did she know him?"

"I don't know. He was just some guy. They whispered to each other and then she went off with him, so I guess she knew him."

"And she just left you?" Chrys knew Hanni and was certain of her bad habits, one of which as thinking of herself first. She'd never really gone out with her before, so maybe this was a common thing for her. Her eyes turned up to the window. She could tell there was someone standing on the other side, but all she could see were fragments of an outline. Perhaps this wasn't the best place to go wandering off. Still, it was Hanni and she could handle herself, couldn't she?

"Chrys," Jessie sat up in her chair. She flexed her shoulders. She pushed her short sun-kissed brown hair back from her face. "You go dance. I'll keep an eye out for Hanni."

"I don't want to leave you alone." She still hadn't sat down.

"Go dance. I'm fine." Jessie tried smiling, but it was awkward.

"Alright. Can you put this in your pocket? I don't really have any." Chrys slid the white phone to Jessie.

Chrys let Izzy pull her onto the floor. Men and women gyrated around each other in different styles of dance. Chrys' formal training was in jazz, ballroom, ballet and hip-hop, however in a dance club she just liked to be free and do whatever moved her. In this case it was trying to get Izzy close to the door that led upstairs so that she could see what was happening there. Glow-stick necklaces of blue, red and green swung from almost everyone's necks. Some dancers had them tied to their wrists. She wondered if one was found on Luke's body. But then his death could have had nothing to do with this club. Club 22 might just have been a stop on his journey. She glanced at the big window.

Izzy didn't do any dance moves well, though she moved with the rhythm of the beat and her hips had a natural sway. She wasn't that good on heels though and had to catch herself a few times to stop from tumbling. She had her clutch purse under one arm while the other was up in the air. Her hand and fingers danced and twisted like they were in a mystical trance. She spun around and bounced her backside toward Chrys.

"Chrys." Izzy stood up straight. Her purse fell.

Chrys stopped dancing. "What?"

"That's the guy who hit me." Izzy pointed toward the VIP door. She bent down and grabbed her purse. As she rose, using Chrys' leg for balance, she stared at the man by the door. He was dressed in black and looked different from the man with the hoodie who burst out of Luke's hostel room.

"Are you sure?"

"That's him. I know it's him. What do we do? What if he sees us?"

"Let's go back to the table," Chrys said as she took her phone from her bra. She pushed Izzy ahead of her.

Izzy quickly sat down at their table and put her head down on the surface.

"I haven't seen Hanni." Jessie said. "What's going on?"

"I've texted Spencer to come meet us."

191

"What? Why? What's going on, Chrys?" There was that tone again.

Chrys was about to tell Jessie everything until she saw what was coming her way. A pink dress moved through the crowded table area. Then she saw the woman wearing it. The pink fabric was stuck to her body, not moving unless she moved. It started just below her knees and traced over strong thighs and hips cinching in at a thin waist. Her breasts, well more than a handful, were firm. If she looked close enough Chrys could see her nipples. She sure couldn't see any panty lines. Silken blond hair flowed over her shoulders like a gentle waterfall. People seemed to disintegrate in front of her as she walked. The moment she arrived at their table, she crossed one leg in front of the other. Her hand went to her hip. Her manicure and black polish was perfect. No nibbling there. There was a large ring on one finger. Bright green eyes checked over the three women until she locked onto her target.

"Miss Alcrest?" Her voice had an attitude to it. She was in charge and wanted everyone to know. Chrys knew that voice. It was the same one she heard in the front lobby talking to O'Donnell.

"That's me." Chrys said as she put her phone away. She felt it vibrate against her boob. "Who are you?"

The woman cocked a perfectly sculpted eyebrow. "One of our VIP guests requested this be delivered." She motioned for the server who had followed her to come forward. He placed a stand next to the table. It held a bucket of ice and a bottle of champagne. Four glasses were placed on the table. "He also requests, Miss Alcrest, that you accompany me to the executive room. Follow me please." She turned and strutted off without receiving any response.

Chrys wasn't going to follow her, but her curiosity was too enormous. As she began to follow she told Jessie to make sure Spencer came to the club.

The sea of people parted as the pink dress moved forward. Chrys followed close and the sea filled in behind them. She had no idea what trouble Luke and Luca got into, but she was sure that she was about to get into her own. Excitement began to swirl in the pit of her stomach.

She stared at the two men in black suits standing beside the VIP door. One was the man who hit Izzy and fought with them. She didn't recognize the other. Chrys didn't speak. Her heart raced. She held her breath. The swirl in her stomach tightened. As they got closer to the door she looked down.

The moment they were through the threshold and the door closed the sound of the music faded. The woman pushed the button for an elevator.

"You never gave me your name." Chrys felt her chest vibrating.

"No, I didn't." She inspected her fingernails.

Chrys fought the urge to swear at the woman and smack her. "Who wants to see me upstairs?"

The woman looked at her with thin lips and her eyebrow raised. Even with her six inch heels the woman was shorter than Chrys. "I'm sure you know."

The elevator door slid open.

"You're just full of fucking information."

"After you." The woman waited.

Chrys looked at the empty elevator. "What if I say no?"

"Please get into the elevator, Miss Alcrest." To this woman *please* was just a figure of speech.

Chrys stared at the woman. They wouldn't hurt her upstairs. The others knew where she was. It would be stupid if anything was done to her. Luca was probably alone where ever it happened. She took a breath and stepped into the elevator. The door closed behind her. Her phone vibrated. It was a text message from her brother, but she didn't read it. She went to her photo gallery instead.

"Did you ever see this girl?" She placed her phone in front of the woman's green eyes. She said nothing. "It might have been a week ago. She could have come in other times too."

The door opened and the woman stepped forward. "Follow me."

The upstairs area was quieter and darker than downstairs. The odor of cigars and cigarettes was evident. A dozen tables were spread apart with luxurious chairs around each. The large window was on the far wall and the party continued below. The patrons in the room were a mixture of men in suits and women wearing barely any clothing. Each woman seemed to be artificially augmented. The only table without women was close to the window. Two men sat there. One had his back to the room and the other his back to the window. Chrys recognized them both because they had been at The Alcrest. They were the men that she saw come in to the club earlier. The man facing the window was in the news every few months either for doing something great for a community or on suspicion of criminal activity. As the two women got close, he slid his chair to the side and stood.

"Chrysanthemum, you look lovely." The Irish was thick in his voice.

The man at the back of the table stood as well. He never looked once at the women as his eyes surveyed the room. It was too dark to see, but Chrys knew there was a bulge in his coat.

Liam O'Donnell's demeanour demanded respect. He wore an Armani suit with an open collar and no tie. Silver hair fell almost to his broad shoulders. The nails on the hand he extended to her were manicured, his skin soft. There was an elusive smile inside a goatee. Chrys' brother told her to never trust this man. She didn't want to, but did want to, all at the same time. He turned to the pink dress and said, "Thank you for accompanying her, Brandi."

This was the first time the woman smiled. "Nothing is off the menu, Mr. O'Donnell."

Chrys watched her walk away before whispering "intense woman" to herself.

"Brandi is good at her job." Liam O'Donnell sipped his drink. Chrys could smell the Scotch.

~ * ~

Spencer stared at the bouncer dressed in a black suit standing in front of the club. A second and similarly dressed men stood by the door. Both acted as though he wasn't there. They were the gods of the red rope. The one in front of him decided who got could enter Club 22 and the other backed him up. Both were muscle-bound lumps. They looked at the line-up of people hoping to get in ignoring the blond man before them.

"I have to get in there, man." Spencer tried to sound tough to the man who was taller and wider than he was. "My sister said she needs my help."

"There's security inside."

Oh that was comforting.

"Spencer," Dee came through the front door. Right away she put a hand on the guard's chest. "He's with me, okay?"

The guard grunted and opened the rope.

"What's going on?" Spencer yelled in Dee's ear the moment they were inside.

Dee grabbed his arm as they made their way through the maze of people. "Chrys is up in the VIP room, not sure where Hanni is and the guy who hit Izzy is here."

Spencer felt a headache stab behind his eyes and it wasn't from the pounding music. Izzy and Jessie sat at a table. Spencer couldn't raise his eyes to his girlfriend. He didn't want to be there.

"Chrys wanted you to come." Jessie said then lowered her eyes.

"Why did she want me here?" He took the bottle of champagne from the ice. It was open, but had not been drunk. "Why do you guys have a Louis-Roederer 2005? This is a $200 bottle of champagne." Spencer had never tasted it, even though there was a bottle in the basement at The Alcrest. A special customer sent it to him as a gift.

"The VIP hostess brought it when she asked Chrys to follow her. She said one of the guests sent it." Izzy always looked like a little kid playing dress-up.

"You don't know who?"

"Liam O'Donnell." Jessie said into her chest. When she looked up her eyes were dark with shadow. Spencer had no idea how that happened, but he both loved and hated it. "I recognized him when he came in. I didn't say anything to Chrys in case she didn't recognize him. I didn't want her ..."

"And now she's with him," he glared at Jessie. "Is that what you're saying?" He stared her down until she looked away. To the others he asked, "How do I get to where she is?"

Izzy pointed across the room. "That door. The bouncer on the right is the one who hit me."

"He was in Luke's apartment?" Now he knew why Chrys really wanted to be here. It all went back to finding out what happened to the foster kid. He remembered the woman taking down the Club 22 sign when he went to the hostel. Damn it! "Dee, are you good to drive?"

"I had two drinks earlier, then a lot of water. I'm good."

"Take these two home." Spencer didn't look at Jessie. "I'll get Chrys."

"What about Hanni?" Izzy wobbled in her shoes.

Spencer wasn't dressed for the nightclub scene. He had showered after service and dressed in tan pants and a white T-shirt with a pale blue shirt over top (unbuttoned and the sleeves rolled up almost to the elbows) after his sister texted. He was dressed for a corner bar rather than this dance place. "I'll look around for her. She probably found a date. Text me when you get home." He didn't direct the request at his girlfriend. As they headed off toward the front

197

door. Spencer started toward the door below the large window.

~ * ~

"Your brother is here." Liam nodded toward the window.

Chrys saw Spencer talking to the others at their table in the nightclub below. She felt better that he was here. She had been listening to the Irishman the whole time in the VIP lounge while trying to think of a way out. She felt safe for the most part, but she was uncomfortable. It was as though she was the kitten that got invited to the dog side of the pound for drinks. She didn't recognize anyone in the room. It was obvious that they all had money and bodyguards. Some spoke different languages. She saw a couple of men with the over endowed women on their arms disappear through doors. Yeah, she wanted to get the hell out of here.

"I think maybe it's time for you to go, Chrysanthemum."

"You said six months ago that you could tell me things about my mom." Another Screwdriver had been delivered to the table shortly after they had sat down. She still hadn't touched it.

Liam smiled at her. "Not the place or time, love."

"Do you really know something or are you just yanking my chain?"

He pushed himself to his feet. "I wanted to tell you about this place and now I have. I think it's time for you to go." He held out his hand.

Chrys took it and got to her feet. She began to walk with Liam toward the elevator. "You're sure you didn't see Luke or Luca?"

"I told you, I don't come here that often. The people and businesses around the docks listen to what I have to say and come to me with concerns. I came here a couple of times to make sure I knew what was going on." He pushed the elevator button. "This is not the place for a good girl to be."

"I'm not a girl. And who says I'm good?" Her eyes moved from O'Donnell to the view over his shoulder. The woman in pink stared at her.

The door opened and Chrys stepped through. This time she was alone in the elevator. She let out a breath she didn't know she was holding and felt her knees threaten to buckle the moment the door slid shut. She had heard stories about Liam O'Donnell. He was a killer. He paid people to kill others. Spencer told her that he could kill anyone with nothing more than a look. He looked and the man who accompanied him took care of the person. She didn't know if it was true, but some police officers she knew warned her of the same thing. She didn't think Middleton was that kind of city. It was something that happened in prime-time dramas that took place in New York and Boston.

From what Liam told her Luke/Luca was probably not the first person to disappear after going to Club 22. Worse things could have happened than what did. Yes, being beaten and killed was pretty bad, but having to live a life of unimaginable tortures and uses, to her, could be a greater hell. Chrys' body shook violently. Luke had been hurt in the most violent of ways; beaten, sodomized, stabbed, bitten – she couldn't imagine what could be worse. She didn't want to.

As the elevator door opened, she stumbled into the small hallway. How close did she come to the same fate? Where was Hanni?

~ * ~

For the second time tonight Spencer found himself talking to another man wearing a black suit and pretending he wasn't there. This one was at least more average in size. He was also the man who Izzy said hit her. "My sister went through this door."

"Please step back sir." This guy had been trained to be polite. He kept his hands together in front of him. He was nothing like what the ladies described.

Spencer wondered if these bouncers carried guns. He wished he hadn't thought that.

"I'm going in this door," Spencer replied.

A white teeth smile appeared in the dark skinned face. "No, you're not."

"Look..." Spencer stopped as the door opened. He stared at the face of his sister. She looked back. He said, "See," to the guard and grabbed Chrys' arm. "What the hell, Chrys? Are you okay?"

They started back through the table area. "Where is everyone?" She looked back over her shoulder. The bouncer stared after her.

"I sent them all home. What happened to you?"

"Hanni? Where's Hanni?"

"Don't know." Spencer held her close so they could hear each other.

Chrys looked behind them. "Spence!"

The black suit was following them. As Spencer turned he saw the man's hand rest inside his jacket. The guy wouldn't do anything in a crowded club would he? It happened in other places.

Spencer rapidly searched the room. There were black suits by the front door, more around the room. Patrons dancing were completely oblivious to what was happening. Spencer pulled his sister toward the front of the room. They weaved around people. A couple yelled at them as they brushed past. Every time they looked back the guard was closer.

"What are we doing Spencer?"

"We have to…" He stopped talking. Two other men in black suits appeared in front of them. The brother and sister stopped. Spencer looked over his shoulder. The smaller one was right there. "What do you want?"

"It's time for you to leave." The short bouncer said. His eyes were on Chrys.

Spencer pulled her closer so that the bouncer's eyes followed her and went to him. "We were just doing that."

"We'll take you the back way. It's faster."

Chrys yanked at her brother's shirt. She whispered in his ear that the two new guys were the others from Luke's room. She turned on the one who hit Izzy. "What's your fucking problem, Dick? You, Tom and Harry here better leave us alone." She screamed loud enough that people near them looked.

"Shut up." Dick flexed his arm. "Let's take a walk through the kitchen."

For a moment no one moved. Spencer squeezed Chrys' hand. They followed the guy she had called Tom.

To Chrys Spencer said, "Tom, Dick and Harry?"

"Yeah," Chrys took a breath. "This guy's obviously a dick for hitting women, the ugly one looks like a Harry, so the other one is Tom."

"Ugly one?" Spencer took a look over his shoulder. "Could you be more specific?" He stumbled after his shoulder was punched.

Tom led the way through a swinging door followed by Chrys, Spencer and the other black suits. Their eyes fought the bright lights. The aroma of cooked meat and burning oil filled their nostrils. Around a small pass where they could only "pass" one or two plates at a time was the kitchen line with a stainless steel prep table on the right side and the equipment on the left. They had three deep-fryers, a flat-top grill with a salamander on top to melt cheese, and a charbroiler. Two East Indian cooks looked up from their work as the five people entered. On the prep table was a large open jug of Frank's Red-hot sauce, a plastic cutting board, a chef's knife, a pineapple, steel bowls, aerosol cans of pan spray and other implements for cooking. More utensils and pots were located on the shelf just above. At the far end of the room, beyond a walk-in cooler and freezer, was the door leading outside. Spencer knew they wanted to get out of there, but he didn't want to go outside with these three. Spencer touched his sister's back.

They passed one cook who dropped a basket of wings into the fryer. As the wet wings touched hot oil the water inside the meat clashed and bubbled.

Chrys speared her heel into the back of Tom's calf. She actually felt the muscle fibres strain and break beneath the spiked heel. She heard his pant-leg tear open, or was it his flesh?

He turned and dropped to one knee. His mouth opened to scream.

Chrys' hand grabbed at the closest thing she could find. The red hot sauce poured down over Tom's face. His eyes opened wide before slamming shut. He spit out the liquid. The smell of the sauce made Chrys want to sneeze. She rammed his head against the table.

Spencer grabbed the green top of the pineapple and spun. The hard spiky surface slammed across Dick's face, tearing at his skin. Spencer rammed his shoulder against him. That was one of the few things he remembered from years of playing hockey.

Dick's feet slipped on the oily tile. He grabbed at what he could as he fell to the floor. One of the fryer baskets twirled through the air and crashed into the shelf above the table.

"What the hell?" The cook quickly jumped out of the way.

Harry surged forward and grabbed at Spencer.

Spencer seized his arms. His fingers clutched the fabric of the man's jacket. Kitchen objects suddenly flew over their heads. A box of salt hit his shoulder.

"Let…" Chrys snatched whatever was there and threw it. "Him…" A steel bowl frisbeed past the two men. "Go…" The can of pan spray soared through the air.

Spencer saw the yellow can deflect off of Harry's forehead. His eyes followed the aerosol can as it spun through the air. It bounced off of a fryer basket, summersaulted and landed in the hot oil. His eyes went wide. He had seen that happen once before. He tried pulling back. Dick was getting up behind Harry. Spencer remembered every fight scene he had ever watched in a movie and suddenly lunged forward. His head smashed into nose and mouth. He heard teeth crack, felt them embed into his forehead above the hair line. Harry's fingers lost grip. Spencer pushed him away and stumbled back. The room spun around him. Pain spider-webbed though his skull. He felt something hot run down his face. He could hear his sister, but couldn't make out what she was saying.

"Spence...let's..."

Dick pushed Harry away from him. He reached into his pocket.

"...fuck sakes!"

Chrys grabbed her brother's hands and pulled him toward the back door. Tom didn't make any move to stop them. Having a 4.5 inch heel rip into his calf muscle had taken any fight out of him.

Behind them the oil in the deep fryer began to bubble. One cook yelled to the other in Hindi. Neither of the Alcrests understood, but they were sure they knew what it meant.

Chrys pushed the cook aside and looked back. She saw the gleam of chrome. There was a flash of light as she heard the bullet break the air above their heads. Her hand hit the bar on the door. She pulled her brother out into the cool air.

At that moment the hot oil ate through the aerosol can and, with a thunderous boom, the pressurized can exploded. Oil erupted into the air. The can shot like a projectile through the side of the fryer. Boiling oil spewed out like water through a broken damn. Tom leapt away from the kitchen volcano. Dick screamed as the oil ran over his hand. Harry pulled Dick away as the lava rained down on them burning their flesh with spots of boiling cooking oil.

Chrys and Spencer heard the explosion. They didn't stop. They didn't know what it was, but someone had already shot at them. The cool air washed the dizziness from Spencer's head. Chrys ran, limping, as one of her heels had broken off her shoe. It was somewhere back in the kitchen still in Tom's pant leg - or maybe still in his leg.

Chapter 18

"Chrys, get up." Spencer reached into his sister's room and flicked the light switch without looking inside.

"What the hell? It's early," Chrys pulled her Scooby-Doo blanket over her head. By the time they got home from the club and calmed down enough to go to sleep it was almost 4:00 am.

"I told Constable Wright I'd have you and the others at the police station by nine. We leave in thirty minutes."

Chrys groaned. The last thing she wanted to do was hang out at a police station. Suddenly she sat up. The blanket dropped. "What did you say?"

"You should take a shower." Spencer shut the door louder than needed.

Twenty-five minutes later Chrys twirled her damp hair, twisted it into a bun and secured it at the back of her head with a pen she found in a cup holder in her brother's truck. She had walked outside with bare feet and threw her ankle boots onto the floor. She put her feet on the dash. The warmth of the morning sun felt good on her toes. After a quick shower she'd thrown on jeans and a T-shirt with a knit sweater over that.

Spencer came out of the restaurant dressed in black chef pants and a green shirt carrying two travel mugs and two fresh cranberry-orange muffins. His sister was too busy checking missed text messages and her friends' latest Facebook posts on her phone to take anything, so he climbed into the driver's seat. He glared at her feet on his dashboard. He had to pick his battles and this wasn't one of them. She wasn't going to stop any time soon, (especially not if he told her to) so there was no reason to make this a battle. He started the truck and drove away from the restaurant.

"Why are we going to the police station?" Chrys asked through a mouthful of muffin. She honestly didn't know where it came from, but was glad it was there.

Spencer shrugged his shoulders. "Last night I was in my office ready to punch something and Constable Wright knocked on the door because you sent him to me on your way out. I told him the truth about how you got the Luke's suitcases and he wants descriptions of the men who attacked you guys and whatever else we've found out. I texted Izzy and Hanni to meet us.

Izzy says she will. Hanni finally answered a text and said she is sick and would try to make it."

Chrys stuck out her tongue at the thought of Hanni. Yes, she wanted her to be safe, but that didn't mean she wanted to step foot into her cave. "What about last night?"

"I haven't heard anything about it on the news."

A droplet of cool water fell from Chrys' hair right where the sweater met her neck. "They're practically running a whore house for people like Liam O'Donnell upstairs. I'm sure nothing will be heard about it. They probably have the cops and the media on the payroll."

"We're in a 1940's gangster movie now are we?" Spencer sipped his coffee; it was bitter. He'd have to look into that when he got back. "Is that really what was going on up there?" His sister nodded. "That why you were invited up there?" Spencer smiled showing his dimples and he got a punch in the leg. One thing about his sister was that she sure didn't hit like a girl.

He wasn't really in the mood to smile. Jessie had tried texting and calling him already this morning. After he got a text from her last night saying she was home he only replied with "Ok." He would talk to her, but wanted to do that on his own time. At the moment he wanted to hurt her, so ignoring her and being indifferent was the best way he could think to do that.

Chrys finished her muffin and took a bite from her brother's. "Fuck you. Liam wanted to warn me about Club 22. He's actually a nice guy, you know." She saw her brother look over at her with a look that had nothing to do with his muffin. "He said the men upstairs were into a lot of criminal activities. I heard thick accents, so I think some were from overseas. And he said the hostess of the room was the worst. He didn't give any specifics, and I didn't ask, but he basically said she would get those men anything they wanted. She even said to him that nothing was off the menu."

"What does that mean?"

"I don't know, but maybe Luke was on the menu and somebody wanted to send him back."

Spencer looked at her like she'd just told a ridiculously bad joke.

"What?"

"Too many restaurant references," Spencer said. "Luke was a guy dressed as a woman. You really think these guys were into that?"

"Well something happened to Luke and I bet it was at the club. If you look down from that big window they have you can't tell who is what and Luca looked like a hot woman. He had the stamp on his hand, so he obviously didn't have time to wash it off. I think he went there as Luca and somebody told little miss panty-less to bring her upstairs. Or maybe someone danced with her or something then realized she was really a he and beat him to death."

"Look," Spencer showed her the back of his hand. The 22 was still there with the bottom corner rubbed away. "I tried washing it off in the shower this morning. What about the punctures and the bite mark?"

"I don't know, Spence. I'm not a cop."

"You only say that when it's convenient. How's the muffin?"

Chrys smiled as she munched. She said, "Good. You want some?"

He shook his head.

"You think this is the end of our investigation?"

"I don't know, I doubt it." Spencer hadn't really told Wright anything that he didn't need to know or didn't already have suspicions about. He told him about Chrys and the others going to the hostel and being confronted by men who tried to take Luke's belongings and about why he went down there the next day. He hadn't told him about Ms. Kara's and what they learned there. Spencer too was competitive. He knew he had to reveal it all, however, last night he was all caught up in it too. Ten minutes early, he pulled the truck into the parking lot across from the Middleton City Police Department.

"Should we get our stories straight?" Chrys slipped her phone into her bra.

"How about the truth? And can't that give you cancer?"

She rolled her eyes and retrieved her phone. Her brother wasn't sure at which comment she rolled her eyes.

~ * ~

"Miss Reid, you are free to go." Wright opened the door to the interview room Izzy exited. She gave the others a nervous wave. The room wasn't what Chrys or Spencer were expecting. It was warm. There was a window facing downtown but no two-way mirrors or video cameras with flashing red lights. There was a round table with chairs around it and another table in

211

front of the window with potted plants on it. The interview was just the Constable asking simple questions about what went on as if he already knew the answers. The siblings told him who Luke really was and about Luca. Before Wright closed the door he signaled someone to join them.

The man who walked in wore a crisp dark suit and carried a suitcase in his hand that he put on the table with emphasis. His brown hair was shaved short and dark-grey eyes took in everything in an instant. He took a moment to straighten his tie – or was it some attempt to show off his power watch?

"Regional Field Operative Lavallee, meet Spencer and Chrys Alcrest."

The man extended his hand and squeezed each of theirs in turn. "I've eaten at your restaurant. The crab risotto was amazing." His voice was deep.

"Thanks." Spencer said.

Chrys asked. "Who are you?"

Lavallee took a seat opposite them. "I'm a regional field operative…"

"Yeah, we got that part."

"…with CSIS, the Canadian Security Intelligence Service. We are the Canadian version of the CIA. We keep Canada safe from terrorists."

Chrys snorted. "And how's that going?"

Spencer put his hand on his sister's arm. "What do you have to do with Luke?"

"Not a damn thing. Last night the two of you were at Club 22. You, Chrys, were invited and went up to the VIP room. I hope I can call you by your first names. I like to be personal." His voice sounded nice enough, however he projected a sense of superiority.

For Chrys it was like talking to one of the rich-bitch moms at the dance studio.

"Whatever. And what if I went to the VIP room?" Chrys was getting ready to fight. She had no idea what was going on, but she didn't want to sit there and take it. "We went to the club to let off some steam. It's been a hard week."

Wright reached across the table and grabbed Chrys' hand. The stamp from 22 was still there. "Luke had the same mark. You just went there to blow off steam, eh?"

"How was I supposed to know that?" Chrys folded her arms across her chest and started nibbling on her bottom lip. She felt ambushed. It was like having her teacher and the school principal try to catch her in a lie. "I didn't see the body, remember?"

"I'd like to know how you knew to go there them." Constable Wright said as he stared at the young woman. He really had no idea.

"Constable, please." Lavallee clicked the latch on his briefcase. "The fact that Luke Weston might have been at the club is irrelevant."

Spencer ignored Chrys tapping her foot against his as he watched Wright's reaction to the way the other man said, Constable. It was as though he shushed the little boy who was fifteen years his senior.

Lavallee started again, "You were invited upstairs by Liam O'Donnell." He tossed a glossy photograph across the table. "This is you having cocktails with him. You look rather chummy. How do you know him?"

"Is that what this is about?" Spencer squeezed his sister's arm hoping she would stay quiet. "If you want

213

to know about Liam O'Donnell and the Alcrests you can ask Constable Wright. He probably knows more about it than either of us do. I thought we were here to talk about Luke Weston."

"You sound defensive, Spencer."

Spencer bit his tongue. He was getting defensive. He didn't know much about what happened with O'Donnell and Chrys, but he was pretty sure there was more to this man's question than just that meeting. Something went on between O'Donnell and Spencer's father years ago. It was one of those things he wanted to know more about and also didn't want to know. As far as his own dealings with O'Donnell it had all been good. The known criminal probably saved the restaurant six months ago, so why he hated him was rooted deep inside with all the questions and suspicions. It was something he would talk about – someday.

Chrys was trying her best not to say anything. If this were a cartoon her face would be a deep, unnatural red with wisps of smoke coming from her ears. She wasn't sure how long she could stay quiet.

Lavallee took another photograph from his case, but handed this one across. "Chrys, did you see this man there?"

Chrys held the picture up so that her face was blocked. Her brother leaned in to see. The face looking back from the photograph was long. He had chestnut hair falling over his shoulders and dark hair on his chin. The man's shirt was open a little exposing gold chains and more curls of hair. He had deep eyes and even though he was smiling there was something sinister about him. He wore gold jewelry and his clothes were obviously expensive. This picture was taken outside of Club 22. Chrys remembered him walking to the private rooms with a couple of busty women. She didn't say anything.

"Do you know who this is? This man is a suspected arms dealer. He is quite possibly responsible for hundreds of thousands of deaths around the world. Did you see him last night or not?"

Chrys shoved the picture across the table. "You obviously have spies there, so you know I did. Does this have anything to do with Luke or not?"

"What about this woman? I know you were in contact with her." A third photograph came from the case and was handed across the table. The brother and sister both recognized the blond woman frozen in motion as she was walking into the club. "Her name is Brandi Reynolds. At least that's what she's going by. She's said to be the hostess at the club, but actually she's the owner. She's popped up all over the world running different clubs in different cities for these multi-millionaire criminals to meet and enjoy themselves. When the heat gets too much the club closes overnight and she shows up a couple of weeks or months later in some other city in a different club. From what we're told people have disappeared from her clubs and shown up in an emergency room or in some other city far away without knowing how they got there. Her clubs are suspected of snatching women for the sex trade and who knows what else."

"So why aren't you arresting her?"

Lavallee looked right into Chrys' eyes. "Lack of proof and taking one for the team. As long as she is out there running her club we know where to find the big fish. The people in that VIP room are not people you want to deal with. Compared to them, Liam O'Donnell is nothing but a mugger in a back alley. Brandi Reynolds could eat him for breakfast without blinking."

"And what does this have to do with me?"

"CSIS has had Club 22 under surveillance for some time. We got word that Constable Wright's homicide case might cross our paths, so I came to talk to him and show him some photos of suspects. He recognized you and told me about your *vigilantism*. We thought it wise to tell you how dangerous this situation is and that you should avoid it. In doing so, everything you have been privy to today is strictly confidential. If you speak to anyone about this you can be arrested under felony charges for terrorism."

Constable Wright cleared his throat. He seemed uncomfortable about the situation. "If Luke Weston lost his life at this club or because of anyone in the club we will find out. I'm telling you two again to keep your noses out of this."

"If you've had Club 22 under surveillance then you should know whether or not Luke went into the club, right?" Chrys didn't mean to ignore Wright. "He would have been dressed as a woman. We can show you a picture of her. Do you have video tape or something of people going in? You've got to have something?" Chrys' voice continued to rise.

For the first time Lavallee lost his composure. "We don't make it a point of videotaping the common person going in there. We're looking for the big fish."

"So who gives a fuck about some transgender fag, is that right?"

"Chrys." Spencer put his hand on his sister's shoulder and squeezed. "We're free to go then?" He looked at the city police officer. As soon as the man nodded he was on his feet and pulling at his sister's arms.

"One last thing." Lavallee leaned back in his chair. "Do you know anything about an explosion in the kitchen at Club 22? Video surveillance shows you two running out moments before a small explosion is heard. You wouldn't have anything to do with that would you?"

"Nope. I thought you didn't have video surveillance."

Lavallee sneared and shoved the photographs back in his briefcase.

Spencer grabbed his sister's hand and headed out the door. Neither of them spoke until they were outside. "Holy crap, this is crazy."

Out of habit, Chrys checked her phone. She carried it in her hand instead of in her bra. "Do you think Liam knows who those men are?"

"Mr. Alcrest." Constable Wright caught up to them as they waited for the crosswalk light to change. "I want to emphasise that you two should not be looking into this anymore."

"Constable, one thing we don't like…"

Wright raised his hand. "You don't like being told what to do. I remember. Have you heard about the bodies found in the woods east of the city? Similar injuries to Luke Weston were found on those men."

"The puncture wounds or the bite?" Chrys blurted out.

217

"How do you know about those?" He glared at Chrys who shrugged her shoulders and looked away as she nibbled on her lip. Spencer quickly took over and asked if they were what killed Luke. Wright looked around to make sure no one was near. "No. He died due to strangulation before those punctures were even made and we don't know if they have anything to do with the other bodies. The poor guy had multiple injuries on his body and the medical examiner even said some wounds had started healing."

"Healing? How could that happen?"

Wright slipped his hands into his pockets. "Wherever Luke was for that week, he was healing. Anyway, I thank you both for coming and telling me about Luke's life. I'm asking you personally to stay out of this. There are things here that are too dangerous for you to be involved." He wiggled his finger at both of them before turning around and walking back to the station.

The siblings ran across the street making it to the other side before the light changed. They didn't speak to each other because too many things were going through their heads at the same time. Terrorists, arms dealers, possible serial killers…it was all too much. Their top priority was finding out what happened to Luke and now they were told not to get involved at all. They had to have faith in the police to do their job. Without having to say a word to each other they both agreed to stay away from trying to catch a killer. The fact that the killer might come to them was not something they could control.

Chapter 19

"The Illuminati are real, man. They've been around for forever. Secret societies, hidden treasures…hey Chrys."

Whenever Chrys walked through the front door of the restaurant she felt the internal warmth of being home. Whenever she walked in on one of Gordie's conversations she felt like she was walking into a stoner convention and forgot the snacks. She smelled tomato sauce and garlic the moment she stepped inside. It was home. It was safe.

Gordie and Ranger were behind the line.

Megan, the morning server, leaned against the small wall dividing kitchen and dining room waving her hands beneath the heat lamps. Today she had maroon streaks in a nest of black hair. She wore a pink flower above her ear. "Gordie, the Illuminati was founded in the late 1700's. And everything about them is up in the air. Nobody can truly say what is real and what is not. They were not around forever."

"Says you."

"I told you I'm taking a class on it. Don't try and school me on conspiracy theories. I know them all." She had a piercing through the side of her nose and a ring through her bottom lip. She was the server with the most eclectic tastes.

"Are we really that slow today?" Chrys asked.

"The bosses ain't here." Gordie returned his attention to the server. "Just because they weren't official until whenever don't mean they weren't around. They were involved way back to the pyramids, probably before that."

"Gordie, all I want to know is who is your dealer and is he taking new clients?"

Chrys touched Megan's shoulder. "Where's Jessie?"

"In the office, but she said she's not staying."

Gordie said, "I guess you're the boss today. I made a pot of tomato sauce and one of meat sauce. Mallory made French bread, so we are running a spaghetti and garlic toast lunch special. Is Spencer coming in after lunch?"

"I don't know. I have to change." After the police station Spencer said he had something to check on and dropped her off in front of The Alcrest without saying what it was. He didn't say much after leaving the station. Neither of them did. Chrys was worried he was going to find Liam O'Donnell and made him promise not to, but she didn't know if she trusted him. She hated how he always felt like he had to protect her when she was more than capable of taking care of herself. She got into trouble once in a while and he did pull her out, however, that was part of life. Walking into his office she realized she had to fight his battles too sometimes. "Hi," she said to Jessie who sat behind the desk with her coat wrapped tightly around her. "How are you feeling today?"

"Sore."

Chrys nodded. She didn't know what to say.

"Where is he?"

No flipping idea. "Out. He had some errands to run." She honestly didn't know what he was doing and for some reason she felt guilty.

Jessie's face was pale. Chrys wondered if she had gone to sleep at all. "He won't answer my calls or text me back."

"You have to give him some time, Jess. He's hurting right now." And we could both be getting stalked by terrorists who can make us disappear with the snap of a finger or possibly another serial killer, but I'm sure as hell not going to tell you about it. "I'll try talking to him later. I never told him about what I went through, so maybe this is the time to do it."

Jessie got to her feet. She dropped the sunglasses that sat on her head down to her eyes. "You don't have to do that Chrys. Just let him know if he doesn't want me to be here then he has to tell me. I can't afford to be out of work for too long, so I'll have to find something else."

"I'm sure it won't come to that." Chrys wasn't a fan of Jessie as a boss, then again she knew that if Jess left it would be up to her to fill the front-of-house-manager's position. Chrys could do it but that didn't mean she wanted to. She didn't like being stuck somewhere. She liked having her freedom. In the past two months she had worked part-time at the locksmiths down the street, modeled for a photographer, taught an engaged couple to waltz, walked dogs and stood in for a friend applying make-up on a couple of corpses in a funeral home. She enjoyed being a gypsy.

"I brought this for you." Jessie's handed her the white cell phone. She repeated her request for Spencer to call her then walked out the back door.

Chrys checked the phone. The magical power ferries hadn't shown up overnight to inject any juice in the small device. The hole for the power cable was bigger than the one for her own phone. Somehow she had to find the right power cable for this phone. First she had to walk the dogs and play hostess at lunch time. She was going to stretch her promise of staying out of police business just a little.

~ * ~

It would have driven Jessie nuts if she knew Spencer didn't have to ask for directions to get where he was going. He had been to the apartment building a few times before for different reasons. He even knew what floor to go to and the exact suite number. He didn't know if he cared about what his girlfriend thought any more. Did she care about what he thought? Did he still want to refer to her as his girlfriend? Maybe she had been right and he was overreacting. The abortion was for the best, right? Who was she to decide that? She should have talked to him about it before making the decision for both of them. That was it. Whether or not he could get over it was the real question.

As the door opened he wondered what Jessie would have thought knowing Hanni would answer her apartment door in what looked like just a plaid shirt. It was oversized, obviously a man's, and buttoned incorrectly.

"What are you doing here?" She held the door open and blocked entry with her body.

"You said you were sick, so I thought I'd check on you since you disappeared last night. Is that a bruise on your cheek?"

She turned the darkened cheek away from him. "I'm fine, Spencer."

He grabbed her chin and turned her face. There was a dark mark along the cheekbone beneath her eye. "You're obviously not fine. What happened to you last night?"

Hanni spun around and walked into her apartment leaving the door open. She walked on the balls of her bare feet with heels in the air. As she heard the door close behind her she turned to stare at her boss and said, "I guess I went off with the wrong guy."

"So this guy hit you?"

"I guess he wanted more than I was willing to give."

"Give for what? For drugs?" Spencer's watched her carefully. Besides her reaction he searched for other bruises and trauma. He could see most of her and didn't see any. When she sat down on the couch he saw that she wore panties underneath her shirt which was open enough at the top for him to see cleavage. Two fingernails were broken.

Hanni frowned as she looked down toward her feet. "Still playing detective?"

"Come on, Hanni, I'm not that stupid. None of us are. Either you're taking drugs or you've had the sniffles for a year now. I've been around enough to see the signs of an addict."

"I'm not an addict."

"But you do use drugs right? Is it cocaine? Did you get some last night?"

"Why are you even here?" Hanni stared up at him. He had never seen her eyes moist before. The blue glistened. "Your girlfriend sure was upset last night. Don't you have to go fix that first?"

"You're a friend. Last night you just vanished. Today we hear that women who go to that club show up in other cities as hookers or worse. I care about you." Spencer didn't know what to do with his hands.

"What the hell are you talking about?"

"I, I just wanted to make sure you were okay."

Hanni's face took on a wicked gaze as she said, "You're afraid of me."

He put his hands in his pants pockets. "I'm not afraid of you."

"Come sit with me then."

One voice in Spencer's head told him he should leave. He wanted to make sure Hanni was okay and she was. She was a little bruised and didn't want his help, so he should go. That voice kept talking until he was sitting beside her on the couch. Then it told him he was an idiot.

"I make you nervous," she said. She lightly placed her hand on his thigh.

"You're changing the subject." Spencer tightened his stomach.

"Yes I am." Hanni took his hand (without any resistance) and placed it on her thigh. All on his own, Spencer rubbed it back and forth on her soft bare skin.

Spencer had to swallow before he could speak. "We should talk about your drug problem." Her leg felt smooth and firm. Her hand squeezed his thigh. He felt himself growing.

"You don't really want to talk about that do you? I know you and Jessie are fighting." Her hand slipped upward. "Isn't that why you came here?" Her lips were close enough to his ear and neck that he could feel her hot breath. Tingles shot through his body.

He had to run. The voice in his head yelled at him to get up and go. "Hanni." In one swift movement he was on his feet and stepped away from the couch. He couldn't decide if this was something smart or extremely stupid.

~ * ~

Chrys filled a plastic dishwashing tray with glasses and pushed it into the machine. She took another tray from the floor and started putting plates in it before spraying them.

"Chrys," Megan appeared from the hallway and put a couple of large bowls and utensils next to the sink, "A man is asking for you."

"Be right there." Jessie couldn't work. Spencer was missing and not answering his phone. The

225

dishwasher called in sick. To top it off they were having a busy lunch. If somebody was trying to teach her a lesson they could go to hell. As she came out of the hallway she saw someone she wasn't expecting and really didn't want to deal with. "Mr. Carol. This is a surprise."

The older man lifted his head slightly. He looked like he was barely holding himself together. Even though he was mourning for a foster child he couldn't let the world see it. Mr. Alcrest had been the same way. "I wanted to come talk to you about tomorrow's memorial." He ran a hand around to the back of his neck and squeezed. "Anna and Emma are not ready for this."

"Would you like to sit down, Mr. Carol?" Chrys led the way to a close table. She had Megan bring them a pitcher of ice water. As soon as they were settled she asked if they were having flowers tomorrow.

"Faye…Mrs. Staples, is taking care of that. She will come by tomorrow morning to set up." Jim Carol sipped his ice water. "There's been a reporter asking questions and saying things about Luke."

Chrys looked at the door hoping her brother would walk in. She took a deep breath and sipped her own water. "How was Luke when he was younger? I know you guys didn't have him when he was really young, but how was he when he was with you?"

"He kept to himself. A lot of kids that come from troubled homes keep to themselves. We had some kids who just wanted to lay in their bed staring at the ceiling or swing by themselves on the swing set in the yard. Luke liked to read. At our house though we believe that kids need chores, so we try to get them to do things. Luke would still take his books with him when he was doing chores. I'm sure he spent more time reading than working." Mr. Carol smiled for just one moment.

"Mr. Carol, I'm going to tell you some things about Luke that you should probably know. You're going to have to tell your wife and his mom because some people will probably come tomorrow to show their respects and you will all find out about his life."

"We love him. Loved him." He nodded as if to secure his words.

Chrys sipped her water again and began telling Luke Weston's foster father about Luca Weston. He listened in silence. Once he nodded and another time he smiled. Chrys showed him the picture of Luca that she had on her phone. She told him about Ms. Kara's Pride and how happy Luca was there.

"Can you make sure his friends…I mean her friends are invited for tomorrow? I always thought there was something he wasn't telling us, but I thought it had to do with what happened to him when he was little. This is amazing. Was Luca really happy? He said he wanted to tell us all something. Was this it?"

"I'm told he was happy. I hope he was or she was. I will let Ms. Kara know that she and his other friends are welcome. I'm sure they can tell you more about Luca."

"Do you think Luke taking on this new life was the reason for his death?'

Chrys picked up her glass of ice water. The condensation on the outside of the glass cooled her fingers and seeped between them. She couldn't answer the man's question because she had no idea. She wished she could satisfy him with answers.

~ * ~

"Where have you been?" Chrys followed her brother into the office. She had basically been walking from the front of the restaurant to the back office every ten minutes in case her brother came in. This time she was lucky.

Spencer hung his coat up. "Have you walked the dogs lately?"

"What? No, I've been running a fucking restaurant." Chrys had one hand on the doorframe and the other flew around as she spoke. "I had no dishwasher, no manager, and no chef. I wasn't even scheduled for today you know. I should be out doing my own thing, not here doing your thing."

"You're not winning your argument. Excuse me." His sister moved as Spencer walked through the open door. He went into the stairwell leading to the apartment.

Chrys groaned and followed. "Plus I had Mr. Carol come here. That was an awkward conversation." Her brother took the stairs two at a time, so she had to run to keep up.

"Have the guys been able to do any of the prep for tomorrow?" As he opened the door Breeze yapped her joy at someone being there and flashed across the room. Bullet rolled off the couch and began his waddle. Halfway across the room he turned and headed for the outside door.

"Yeah they got some of it done." Some of Chrys' annoyance slipped from her voice. That pissed her off. "Where the hell have you been?"

Spencer was hoping to ignore the whole subject. "I was doing something." He was about to put the harness on Bullet when the chubby dog took that moment to roll onto his back exposing a white belly. "Come on dog."

"No way? You were doing something? Oh gee whiz I would have never thought that." Chrys attached a leash to Breeze's collar.

"A bit bitchy today, are we?"

"Oh bite me. You heard what I went through. I had to tell Luke's foster father about Luca. Now I get to go and invite drag queens to a memorial."

"Try not to sleep with any."

"Oh you're just so funny."

Spencer clicked the last clasp shut on the harness. "I'm taking the dogs for a walk. Are you coming?"

"Just tell me if you went to see Liam O'Donnell."

"Why would I go to see him?"

"I don't know." It sounded good when Chrys first thought of the possibility. She didn't say anything else until they reached the ground. "Maybe you went to bitch at him for talking to me or to ask him if he was involved. I don't know."

"Well I didn't. I went to see if Hanni was okay." They crossed the parking lot heading into the rows of houses. Clouds were coming in.

"How is she doing?"

"Good. She's good." Spencer kicked at a small rock on the sidewalk.

Chrys looked at her brother. His cheeks were flushed. He was staring at the ground and wouldn't look at her. She knew that look. She stopped walking. Breeze barked her annoyance. "Oh my God! You slept with her didn't you? The bitch finally got her claws into you," she screamed as her fists pumped. "Oh you are going to that special level of hell."

"I didn't sleep with her." Bullet sat on Spencer's foot. "She started something and I stopped it."

"Oh yeah, right. This from the guy who would eat a whole bag of chocolate chunk cookies in one sitting. You can't stop something once you get started, Spence."

Spencer tugged the bulldog's leash to get him moving again. She wasn't going to believe him. That was why he didn't want to say anything. When this got back to Jessie she would probably go with what the majority believed.

Chrys and Breeze stayed beside him. She really didn't want to say any more. She honestly didn't. "You have a girlfriend, Spence. She was pregnant with your child."

"That's right, she was. She *was* pregnant and she ended that pretty quickly."

"So you go out the next day and find some snatch? Get over yourself."

"I didn't do anything," Spencer yelled out. He lowered his voice and said it again.

"Then what were you doing there?"

"I went there to see if she was okay and then I," he closed his lips tight as he thought a moment, "I can't say what we talked about. It's personal to her."

After a few minutes Chrys asked, "Is that what Hanni's going to say?"

"You don't believe me. My own sister doesn't believe me."

"If I went to some guys place and he was always hot and horny for me, would you believe it?" Chrys flourished with her hand.

"There's a difference between you and me."

Chrys' eyes went wide. "Are you calling me a slut now?"

"Of course not." He was thinking it, but Spencer wasn't saying it. His sister was not known for having long relationships and often would not wait long to jump into bed.

"Well I don't want to be manager, so you better figure this out."

~ * ~

Chrys looked up the moment she felt the outside air as the front door to the restaurant opened. She had been sorting through the night's receipts getting ready for closing. It hadn't been a busy night, however they did make money. Most of the staff were gone except for Wylie in the bar, though he was reading one of his law books, and her brother in the back room.

The biggest surprise of the night was seeing what walked through the front door.

"I'd like to speak to the owner," the woman said.

"He's in the back room doing some prep work. I can get him." Chrys stared at her and didn't move. She hoped the woman didn't hear the shakiness in her voice that she felt was there.

The woman stared back with an intensity and pursed lips. She stepped forward. "I can find him. Down this hallway?" She didn't give Chrys a chance to respond.

For the memorial Spencer wanted finger food that wouldn't dirty anyone's hands. During the afternoon Ranger had sliced chicken breasts into strips and marinated them in a mixture that included onion, garlic, lemon grass and spices. They always had bamboo skewers soaking in water for use on the grill. Instead of making the guys skewer the chicken strips in the morning Spencer wore blue latex gloves and was doing the tedious job himself. Also on the menu was flatbread pizza, shrimp cocktail, dips with fresh tortilla chips and some pre-made items he bought after escaping Hanni's place. The problem was that they had no idea how many people were going to be attend.

"Excuse me." There was a sound like rings knocking on a doorframe. The scent of wildflowers seemed to circle him.

Spencer turned, but kept his hands above the chicken dripping with marinade. The woman in the doorway would have been short if not for the stiletto heels she wore. Her blond hair was perfectly straight falling over her shoulders. He'd seen her before in the fourth floor hallway at the Greenleaf and in an 8x10 photograph in a police station. Her hair was different, her clothes were different, but this was the infamous Brandi. Today she wore jeans that were practically painted on with a silken white blouse and a leather jacket. It was open enough to show off her cleavage. Raindrops glistened on the jacket and moistened her hair slightly. Her shoulders were back and her chin up. In her gaze he was afraid to speak.

"Are you the owner?" Her words were cold and flat.

Spencer nodded.

"My name is Brandi. I'm the owner of Club 22." The woman took a few steps into the dish-pit area. The heels clicked on tile. She looked around it like the room was disgusting. "You blew up my kitchen."

He felt his throat tighten. "I don't know what you're talking about. Have you gone to the police?"

"I have a security guard with third-degree burns in the hospital who says you were the one that did it. You and *her*." She flipped her head back toward the dining room exposing her long beautiful neck. "What are we going to do about this?"

Spencer carefully pulled one glove off and then the other. He noticed that she didn't say anything about going to the police. He was pretty sure with what was going on in the VIP room at Club 22 she couldn't risk calling the police. Perhaps there were other things going on. That meant he didn't have to admit to anything. "Like I said, I don't know what you're talking about."

Brandi's eyes became wide for just a moment before settling back into their stare. Something seemed to gleam in her face. "What's your name?" She was older than Spencer thought the first time he saw her. There were lines by her mouth and eyes that indicated she had witnessed life. Her eyes had a darkness that was more than colour.

"Spencer," he said it knowing damn well that she already knew. He was willing to bet her spies and information were superior to CSIS. He smiled showing his dimples.

"I have a problem, Spencer." The corners of her lips curled when she said his name. "I'm out a deep fryer and a couple of security guards. I need something to make me feel better. You say you didn't do it. I don't mean to offend, but I still think you did."

"It would take more than that to offend me." He had confidence when he needed it.

"You could always buy me a new deep fryer."

"I can't afford that."

"What about dinner?"

"I can't really afford that either." He flashed the cockiest smile he could muster. He didn't know if he should be afraid of her or if he should try to charm her.

Brandi ran a hand through her hair. Her fingers had a perfect French manicure and most of her fingers bore rings that sparkled. "You're having worse luck than I am. That girl," she motioned back down the hallway.

"My sister?"

"She was asking about someone at the club. I might be able to help with that." Her sculpted eyebrows seemed to flex.

Spencer hated being told what he was allowed to do. The police asking him to stay away from whatever happened to Luke bugged him. It was his sister's issue and was possibly life threatening. That just made it more interesting to him. He was screwing up his life, so he had to solve something. "I could always make you dinner."

"I work horrible hours," she said.

"So do I."

"Come by the club tomorrow afternoon." Brandi spun on the ball of her foot and marched down the hallway toward the dining room. The purpose of high heels was to accentuate the legs, buttocks and push out the breasts. Hers did all of that. Spencer didn't have a clue what had just happened. It seemed impossible.

The moment he saw his sister coming down the hallway he blinked and turned back to the chicken. She exclaimed, "you slut," and walked through the door to the stairwell.

Chapter 20

Spencer looked up as Jessie walked by the kitchen taking dirty plates to the back. She flashed a half-smile at him but it disappeared in an instant. Neither of them had really spoken since she came in to work the memorial service for Luke Weston. Spencer hadn't expected her to show up at all. He slipped a tray of sliced flatbread pizza under the heat-lamp.

Chrys suddenly appeared. "Thank you…slut."

"Cut it out!" He looked over his shoulder.

"Do you honestly think I'd call you that in front of her? I have more respect for her than you do."

Spencer glared at his sister. "Cut it out!"

As she walked away with the serving tray she took one last look over her shoulder and stuck out her tongue. Luke's memorial had brought in only a couple of dozen people. Most knew the Carols and didn't really know Luke. When they saw the photo Chrys had blown up and printed of Luca, taken from her Facebook account, their eyes dropped and they didn't know where to look or what to say. His three parents had stared at the photo a long time before taking their seats. Ms. Kara had come in dressed the way he was when he first met Spencer at Luke's murder scene and sat near the windows with Colby. He was tall, thin and still elegant. He moved like his female self; however, in a suit he reminded Chrys of an elegant Anne Rice vampire. When he first arrived he found Luke's parents and spoke about both Luke and Luca as he knew them. Colby was dressed more casually. When he arrived he squeezed Chrys' arm and sat down. She wasn't sure what she felt when she saw him as a man after being with him as a woman. She tried not to look in his direction as she crossed the room.

The conversation in the room was not about Luke. Sure, some would talk a little about him, but people at funerals rarely spoke about the reason they were there. A few words sufficed and then they went on with their own lives.

"Spencer made you some flatbread without onions," Chrys said as she slipped the tray onto the table where Mrs. Staples, the Carols and Emma Weston sat.

Mrs. Carol looked up with a curt smile. "Thank you so much. Please thank him."

"I will. Is everything else okay? Do you need anything?" They all nodded that they were okay.

"Excuse me." Chrys and the others looked at the woman who spoke. She was young, early twenties and

238

pretty in a humble way. She had round cheeks and chestnut hair surrounded her face. Her lips were naturally red. She wore a very plain long dress. She and Chrys looked like complete opposites. "I'm Mary," her voice shook. "I knew Luke."

"You were his girlfriend," Chrys stated. She so wanted to grab her arm and pull her into a private room.

"Just for a little while. I wanted to say how sorry I am. Luke was always nice to me."

Jim Carol smiled. "He mentioned you. He said you were sweet."

Mary smiled and stood there a moment before turning away. She scanned the room. Chrys thought her gaze turned to Colby and Ms. Kara, but she moved to stand near the end of the bar.

"I'm Chrys," she said as she slipped in beside Mary. "I'm sort of looking into what happened to Luke. Can I ask you some questions? I never knew him, so I don't know much about his life." Mary nodded, so Chrys went on asking when she'd last seen him.

"It had been a few weeks. We texted a little. I don't know what I can tell you." Mary looked down at her nails. With her thumb, she chipped polish from one.

There was a minimal crew today. Only Spencer and Ranger worked the kitchen. Jessie, Sue and Chrys served. Chrys asked Sue to get out from behind the bar so that she and Mary could be alone. "Well, can you remember anyone giving him a hard time about – about his life?"

"No. When he started going to Ms. Kara's I guess some people said things, but not anyone in his life. People would go there and yell at them, carry signs saying how being gay was against God and stuff. I know he had water thrown on him once." She rubbed a rough patch of skin on the back of her hand. Her complexion was blotchy indicating didn't do well in the sun.

"Have you ever heard of the Canadian Traditional Family International?"

She nodded. "They have an office across the street from where Luke lived. I know their signs were outside Ms. Kara's. Even when Luke was with me, people said things to him. When he changed and only went out as a woman things died down a bit, I guess."

"What did you think of his decision to change?" Chrys looked down the line and excitedly waved at her brother to join them.

Mary's shoulders shrugged. "I didn't care. I liked the person not the package. I would have stayed with him through the whole thing."

Chrys quickly introduced Spencer to Mary. "If you liked Luke why did you two break up?"

"I lost Luke when Luca showed up."

Spencer leaned on the bar. "What do you mean when Luca showed up? They were the same person."

Mary looked at him before her gaze drifted around the room. For a moment they weren't sure she was going to answer. "Luke was shy and private. Luca was confident and outgoing." Her eyes locked on Ms. Kara and Colby. "She was shown how to act and then she started getting attention. Luke didn't like men in *that way*, but Luca liked getting attention from them."

"It sounds like he had a split personality or something." Chrys had a confused look on her face.

Mary took a breath. "Do you know how you feel when you are dressed really nice and you just feel good and ready to take on whatever is coming? That's what Luca was like all the time. She could go up and talk to strangers. Luke made a far better-looking woman than I ever will." She had a sweet laugh. "Luca was popular where Luke was a shadow. She kept getting attention and I couldn't compete with that. I didn't want to compete with that. It was almost like Luca was Luke's drug of choice."

"Do you know anyone who would have wanted to hurt Luke?"

Her eyes locked on Ms. Kara's table again. "No, but I know people who wanted Luca to stay around. They liked Luca more than Luke."

Spencer felt a hand on his back. Jessie was there in the cramped space.

"Spence, we have a problem outside." She nodded toward the front doors. "There's a small mob."

"What?"

"They have anti-gay signs."

"What?" He repeated. At first he didn't believe her. He eyed the front glass doors and saw the people outside. There were probably more people outside with signs than there were mourners inside. "What the hell. Don't let the Carols and Emma see." Spencer threw his apron on the cold-side table and quickly crossed the restaurant floor. Others inside had noticed what was going on. Ms. Kara stood. The chef went out the door. The warmth of the day hit his face.

241

Warmth often riled up emotion. "Excuse me," he said as soon as he as outside. Nobody paid attention.

The small crowd was not yet organised. A dozen people were talking and nobody was hearing. One man in particular was giving orders.

"Hey fuckers!"

Spencer turned his head. Chrys ducked down behind his back. The people outside stopped talking and looked in the direction of the restaurant, only seeing the brother. They were a mismatch of ages, ethnicities, and statuses. A lot of the group looked to be families with small children in tow. A small blond boy held a blue sign with white writing that read, "Kids do best with Mom & Dad." Other signs said, "Traditional families are 1 man + 1 woman," and "Traditional families for a better Canada." None of them came right out and said what was behind the meaning of it all. A man in a nice-looking suit, the one who had been barking orders, broke from the crowd and stepped toward the restaurant door. The sun sparkled off crucifix on his lapel. In one hand he carried a leather bound Bible.

"There is no reason to use profanities," he said sternly. "We have children here."

Spencer stared at him for a moment. "Okay, and you are?"

The man thrust out his chest and extended his hand. "Dr. Frost of Canadian Traditional Family International."

"Spencer Alcrest." He reluctantly shook the man's hand. "I own this restaurant. We're having a private function inside and…"

"And we are doing nothing to stop that. We are exercising our right to assemble and our freedom to speak our mind." As the man smiled Spencer was sure he saw a glint of light flash like in cheesy television shows. He looked to his right and acknowledged a young woman wearing a camera with a bulky lens around her neck. The symbol on her jacket said she was with the city paper. "We have every right to be here."

"Show some respect." Chrys called out from behind her brother's back.

Spencer flung one arm back and hit his sister lightly on her forearm. He leaned in toward the man calling himself a doctor. "This is a funeral, okay? Surely God or whatever wouldn't want you to make a mockery of..."

"I assure you, son, this is not...."

"Don't call me son!"

Dr. Frost stared into the chef's eyes. His lips formed into a wicked smile. The next words he spoke were more for his audience, both behind him and in the restaurant, than for the Alcrests. "God would not be bothered with what we are here to do today. Homosexuality is a sin." There were a few voices of agreement.

Chrys stepped from behind her brother. Right away she saw the recognition in the man's eyes. "He was transgender you gorram prick!"

"Even better. God has a plan for all of us. You can't play with that plan like it is some child's toy with mismatching parts. We are here to speak of the traditional families and traditional values. We are here..."

243

Spencer turned around and pulled his sister back into the restaurant. The man's voice faded as the door closed, but he didn't stop preaching. Spencer asked Jessie and Sue to pull down the blinds on the front windows. The only blinds they couldn't cover were those around the door. He stood for a few minutes watching what was happening outside. Dr. Frost spoked to his crowd, his words muffled by the door. The people marched back and forth in front of The Alcrest bouncing their signs up and down. A few car horns blasted. He didn't know if they were in support of the group or against it.

"Should we call the police?" Jessie asked as she, Chrys and Spencer gathered at the host stand.

"They won't do anything. The guy's right. They aren't doing anything illegal. The sidewalk is city property, so as long as they stay on that they can protest what they want."

Chrys slapped the stand. "That's bull." She lowered her voice but it was sharper. "They're protesting me, my lifestyle, not just Luke's. Look at me, I'm shaking." She held out her vibrating hand.

Spencer rubbed his sister's back. He was never more worried about the way she lived her life than he was at that moment. She had dated both men and women as the mood hit her.

~ * ~

"Table twelve – second course fired. Two New York medium, one Alfredo, one salmon."

"Two medium, one salmon, heard." Gordie already had the steaks ready. With tongs he snatched an oily rag from a small insert and seasoned the grill on the hot side. He took the steaks from the turned-off edge of the grill and put them on the oil. He then seasoned another section for the grilled salmon.

Ranger dropped a couple handfuls of shoestring potatoes into the fryer to accompany steaks as a garnish.

Spencer had the chicken Alfredo sauce (made of leek, garlic, chicken and heavy cream) in a pan at the back of the stove. He brought it onto a front element and turned the gas burner higher. He dropped a handful of pasta into one of the inset strainers (they looked like four Trivial Pursuit wedges) that were in a large pot of boiling, slightly-oiled and seasoned water. For Friday night's menu he went with easy dishes. They didn't have as much time to prepare after the memorial as they would normally have. Grilled meats with sauces and simple pastas; no one had complained yet.

"Order in chef," Wylie slid an order chit across the pass. Hanni had called in sick, so instead of the tall man working behind the bar he was out on the floor and everyone had to get their own drinks.

Spencer spun around and grabbed the small paper. "Don't go too far. Twelve is up in five." He turned to the kitchen crew. "New order. Two covers, table fourteen. First course, Alcrest salad and mussels. Second course, New York rare and chicken." The other cooks announced that they had heard their parts." Spencer nodded at Mallory to show he had confidence in her. In an instant he had two pans on high flame. The chicken breast had already been pounded a little during prep and breaded. He poured oil in the pan and it began to smoke almost instantly. The dance between chef and sous chef was perfect because at the moment Spencer was turning and going down to grab a chicken breast and an order of mussels from the lowboy fridge under the butcher's block table Gordie was coming up with his new steak. He wouldn't even put it on the grill until the second course was ready to be fired. The chicken breast went into the oil. The mussels went into the other pan. He spun on the ball of his foot, snatched a handful of chopped onion from one of the sunken inserts at the back of the table and a quarter cup of stewed tomatoes and spun again to add them to the black shellfish before taking another pan down and placing it atop upside-down to create a lid. His finger hooked tongs from the oven door handle and used them to turn the chicken breast to expose the golden breading. Then he used the tongs again to grasp the pan and place it inside the oven. One more dance move had plates out of the right oven (which was turned off but still warm from the residual heat of the left) and on the tabletop for them to plate up table twelve's main course.

Ranger started those with potatoes and vegetables. Tonight they went simple with those too - garlic mashed potato and a ragout of zucchini, mushrooms, tomato and onion seasoned with oregano, cracked black pepper and sea salt.

Spencer smiled at Jessie as she accompanied a couple to the front corner near the door. The two of them still hadn't talked but he had put his hand on the small of her back earlier and that was something.

After brushing them with a barbeque sauce made that afternoon, Gordie placed the steaks on their plates.

The salmon went on its plate with the same sauce. Spencer drained the pasta before turning it into the pan and giving it a quick toss in the creamy sauce.

Suddenly, the pan slipped from his hand and crashed down to the stove top. Tongs hit the honeycomb matt under his feet and skidded beneath the fridge. The shattering noise behind him sent Gordie and Ranger ducking. Mallory screamed. A metal salad bowl fell to the ground. Someone else screamed. The sound of glass shards hitting tables and tile floor was like hearing hail on the car window, a tink-tink noise that almost sounded pretty.

Spencer spun to see the glass raining down on both Jessie and the couple sitting at the table. Jessie had her head down, arms covering the sides of her face. The couple dove for cover. For a moment every sound seemed to stop except for the tink-tinkle-tink of raining glass.

"Holy fu…" Gordie

"Everyone …" Spencer

"Oh my God!" Female customer

"… back." Spencer

"Don't move." Wylie

"… broom and dust …" Chrys

"Claire, are you …" Male customer

Spencer saw a paint can on the floor. Sky blue paint oozed out onto the floor.

"Hold still." Wylie

"Jessie, you're …" Chrys

Spencer opened the door and stepped out into the cool night air.

"… bleeding." Chrys

"Mallory, can you get me some gloves?" Wylie

"Careful, careful." Chrys

Broken shards and bits of glass rained down again as the customers at the table slowly rose to their feet. They fell into the glass of wine and tinked off a bread plate. The pieces bounced off the table and continued to the floor. Some landed in the growing pool of paint.

There was no one outside. Spencer turned in all directions. There were automobiles parked along the curb on both sides of the street, but there were no people about. Whoever threw the paint can through the window was gone.

As he walked back into The Alcrest Jessie and the two people who had been sitting at the table were standing, bent over at the waist shaking out their clothes. Chrys wore blue kitchen gloves and was carefully trying to brush glass out of the woman's hair. Spencer walked between the wall and table. His kitchen shoes crunched on glass as he righted the paint can.

"Is everyone okay? Jessie, are you ..."

"What the hell was that, Spence?" Chrys interrupted.

"I'm fine," Jessie said. She had small cuts on her arm where the sharp points of window had chipped at her skin.

"Chrys, can you take these two to the private room? Jessie, you go too." Spencer slipped his phone from his back pocket. "Wylie, can you get everyone a drink on the house. Dee, can you get the first-aid kit from the back and take it to Chrys then help Wylie. Ranger, in the basement are a couple of tarps. Can you get them and some nails?"

"Where are they?"

"On the shelving with the summer catering gear." Spencer raised his voice and faced the diners still looking in shock at what was going on. "Everything is okay. Sorry for, ah, whatever this was. Wylie and Dee are going to bring everyone a drink on the house." As he turned to face the open window he dialled 9-1-1 and finally took a breath. One bad thing seemed to follow another. There was no way this week could get worse.

Chapter 21

"Are you staying down here all night?" Chrys stood in the archway between the main restaurant and the hallway wearing wore pink pajama pants with horses on them, the cuffs rolled up to her knees, an Elizabeth Frances Dance Studio hooded sweatshirt and on her head a grey knit beanie slouched on the crown of her head like a dirty backward Smurf hat. Pulled to her body were a laptop computer, a phone in each hand and a collection of electrical cords.

"Do I have a choice?" Spencer pointed the chef's knife he was sharpening on a wet-stone at the blue tarp covering the window. They nailed one on the outside and another on the inside after the police left. "I can't get a window until morning. What are you doing down here?"

"Keeping my big brother company. Are you planning to sit at this table all night?" Chrys put her collection onto the next table as his was covered with the kitchen's collection of chef knives. "What about sleep?"

"I'll get a few hours in the morning after someone gets here." He had cookbooks piled on one of the chairs - chef porn. Instead of his usual kitchen clothes, he wore surfer-shorts with blue flowers on a white background and a T-shirt with a zombie on the front. One bare foot up on another chair. "What are you doing?"

Chrys stretched the laptop cord to an outlet in the wall. "When I was getting Luke's pictures enlarged I bought a charger for his phone. It's been charging all day. I haven't had a chance to go through it though. Thought I'd keep you company for a while and we could both see what's there."

"Chrys, give it to the cops. Give it to Wright." He sounded tired.

"I will once I check it out."

"That's not the way it works, Chrys. This is evidence."

She nodded almost violently. "That's right, it is. This might be the only way to find Luke's killer, so I'm going to take a look."

"Or it might just be a phone."

"Pooper," Chrys said and pouted. She turned on the computer and got ready to plug the phone into a USB port.

"What's with the toque? It's not that cold down here."

Chrys touched her hat. "It's a beanie, not a toque."

"It's a wool frigging toque. A beanie has a propeller on the top."

"You just don't know style, Spence." Chrys fingered the mouse pad and clicked on a file.

"You might want to wait on that." Spencer jumped to his feet. Lights of a car pulling up to the front curb swept through the horizontal blinds of the other windows, casting shadows across the room. "That terrorist guy, Agent Lavallee, called to say he was dropping by."

"What the fuck for?" Chrys snatched her hat off and dropped it on the phone. Her hair was instantly static and wild. The only reason she wore the hat was to avoid taking a shower until morning.

"Sorry for calling so late," Lavallee said as he came in. He was probably wearing a clean suit, but it looked to be the exact type he was wearing the last time they'd him. The smell of men's cologne followed him through the door. It had a manly aquatic scent that instantly made Chrys think, "Yummy." Then she wanted to slap herself.

"No problem. It's been a long night for us," Spencer raised his hand to the tarp that moved and snapped every time the wind blew. "I'm not going to sleep any time soon."

"I heard about your problem." Lavallee stepped closer to the window. After the police had come to take their photographs and get statements from all of the witnesses the shattered glass had been swept and the tables cleared. Bits of glass had travelled all the way to the stage at the far side of the room. The paint had been scooped up with a dustpan and the floor had been mopped twice. You could still see the stain where the puddle had been. Lavallee tugged on the inner tarp to look inside.

"How did you hear about it?" Chrys asked as she patted at the static in her hair.

Lavallee shrugged his shoulders. "My job is intelligence. I heard. Any idea who did it? Was it an accident?"

"No idea. I went outside right after it happened and didn't see anyone. The cops haven't come back to tell me anything different, so I don't know. Can I get you a drink?"

"Do you have any coffee brewed?"

Whenever the man wasn't looking, Chrys carefully gathered the white charge cord for Luke's cell phone under her hat. "It was probably the protestors from this afternoon."

"Protestors? I heard about that too. You think one of these ignorant pricks came back hours later to throw a paint can through the window?" Lavallee stirred sugar and cream into a cup of coffee.

"I don't know. Why not?"

Lavallee leaned his back against the short wall blocking off the kitchen and faced Chrys who was still sitting. "Did anything happen today when they were protesting? From what I'm told the whole thing was peaceful. They didn't even say anything when people left the memorial. Why would someone come back, Miss Alcrest?"

"You seem to know a lot, Agent."

"Regional Field Operative, Mr. Alcrest. RFO if you prefer. Like I said, intelligence is my business. What about Club 22? Could this be retaliation for that?" He sipped his coffee all the while keeping his eyes on them. He was fishing.

Spencer returned to his seat. "You obviously know more than we do, so why don't you just tell us. I'm too tired to deal with stupid games."

Lavallee took a moment to stare at the chef for some sort of effect. The chef just stared back. "The police arrested a man about an hour ago for breaking your window. Do you know him?" He handed a photograph across the table. There was Jonas as he approached the building with a paint can in hand. "His plan was to throw paint on the window, but he panicked and threw the whole can resulting in your shattered window."

"And you just happen to have a picture of him outside The Alcrest?"

"We have your place of business under surveillance in case there is any retaliation towards you for what happened at Club 22. Considering Brandi Reynolds was seen here last night I'd say it was a good decision. Do you want to tell me what that was about?"

"Not really," Spencer said.

"How did she know to find you here?" Lavallee put his coffee onto the table.

Spencer shrugged his shoulders. His eyes dropped to the floor. "I guess her job is intelligence too." He raised his head and stared back at the RFO.

A thickness seemed to float between them as their eyes glared at each other. Chrys looked on from where she sat. Her fingers twitched on her beanie tugging at the wool. She wanted to get into the phone and see what was there.

Lavallee's eyes never wavered. As he bent his arm back to put his cup on the pass he never lost Spencer's gaze. "I should be going. Be safe." He slipped his hands in his pockets and headed toward the front door. The chef got to his feet and followed him. "Oh, I almost forgot." The smirk on Lavallee's lips made Spencer think of a cat peering at a cornered mouse. One hand came from his pocket with a USB memory stick between two fingers. "I had surveillance go over videos of the club. They found your friend, the one who was killed, in a couple of shots. I had them put them together for you." He dropped the stick onto the table next to the door. "Have a good night."

As Spencer locked first the outer door then the inside one, the scent of the other man's cologne lingered in the air. Even a little cologne was too much for him. His general rule in the kitchen was avoid wearing colognes or deodorants so that he could smell the food and cooking process. He picked up the memory stick as he walked back to his seat and placed it in his sister's palm. He fell into his chair. For a moment he didn't want to do anything. The whole restaurant thing was getting tiresome. Earlier customers who had not been near the window and the shattered glass quickly left the restaurant once they'd had their free drinks and discounted meals. He did his best to apologize to them, but in the food industry that really didn't mean much. People remembered the bad things. One person talking about a window exploding often erased twenty people talking about good food and service. The bad stuff was more interesting.

Chrys reached around the laptop and slipped the memory stick into a USB port in the back. In a few seconds a file folder popped up on the screen. "Do you want to see this?"

"Give it to Wright." Spencer took up his favorite knife, wet the stone and started gliding the blade across it. The restaurant business was a strain, but cooking was his bliss.

"Fine then." Chrys clicked on the file. There was only one video clip inside it.

The video opened on the monitor. For a second it was black then her brown eyes saw a view of the front of Club 22 taken from across the street, likely from the second or third floor. It was night and there was a queue of people hoping to get in, much like when she was there. A black sedan pulled up and two men exited the back. Chrys couldn't be certain, but she was pretty sure one of them was Liam O'Donnell. The other could have been his guard. The two men walked past the line-up and through the front door. At the front of the line stood a woman with long brown hair and wearing a green dress. It could have been Luca. The quality of focus was not great. It had to be her. Did that mean O'Donnell did see her? Perhaps he saw her, he had the Brandi bitch bring her upstairs and he had her killed when he found Luke underneath. Most men would find it hard to handle. It wouldn't be out of the realm of possibility if everything she had ever heard about O'Donnell was true.

Chrys looked up to say something to her brother. He was testing the sharpness of a blade with his thumb and not paying any attention to her. He would tell her to take it to the police and stay out of it.

The video went black before coming back to the same view. The time stamp said it was at 1:30 am. There was still a line out front, though it was shorter. Chrys stared at the screen. She was afraid to blink in case she missed what she was supposed to see. A taxi pulled up, but. No one got out of it. It wasn't dropping off, it was picking up. Two people came from the alley beside the building (the same one she and Spencer had run through after the explosion) and headed for the yellow cab. One had brown wavy hair and wore the green dress she knew to be Luca's. It was the same dress Luca/Luke's body was wearing when she was found. She was certain now that had been Luca at the front of the line. She wasn't walking properly, but not like someone who was drunk. This was different. She leaned to one side, leaned on someone else. They both got into the taxi and it pulled away from the curb. As the vehicle left the frame, the video ended. Someone had been with Luca. It was a woman, a woman with black hair. Or perhaps because of the shadows, she really had light hair. Maybe it was that blondy Brandi getting the evidence out of there.

Who was she?

Chrys stared at the blank screen for a long moment. She heard the scraping of blade on stone, the air conditioning kicked on and the tarp snapped making her jump. She watched the video again and realized that was the last time anyone saw Luke or Luca Weston alive. Where was he for the next week? What happened to him? Who was the other woman?

She closed the video. Her finger moved over the mouse pad until she clicked on the file for the phone. The file popped up. She picked the photo gallery first.

There were over five hundred photos on his phone. She wanted to know about his life before everything happened. For some reason, she cared about this guy and wished she had known who he was - both him and Luca.

The tarp snapped.

Chrys grabbed the edge of the table with both hands. "Holy elephant sucker!" Her heart raced.

Spencer looked up. "What?"

"What? It scared me. Can't you get that tighter or something?"

"Then go upstairs and go to bed. You don't need to be down here."

"I'm fine." Chrys calmed down as she clicked on the last pictures on the phone. The date stamp was for the same night that Luke had gone as Luca to Club 22 and got caught on the CSIS video. There were a couple of crowd photos and a selfie of Luca. She must have been holding the phone out at the full length of her arm when she took it. It was Luca smiling with a lot of people behind her. Maybe she took a picture of someone going up to the VIP room that she shouldn't have. Chrys zoomed in and moved the picture around so that she could see the people in the background. She slid her finger across the mouse pad. There was a woman with black hair looking directly at Luca. She was out of focus, so it was hard to tell exactly who it was. Chrys had an idea, but that didn't seem right.

"What's wrong?" Spencer was now sharpening a paring knife.

"Do you really care?" Chrys raised one eyebrow.

"Tell me or don't tell me." He put the knife down. "You know what? No, I don't care. My own life is a mess. We were asked to find the kid and we did. It's not our fault how we found him. Give everything to Wright. Let him do his job."

"Why are you such a dick? Just because you are all fucked up about Jessie and whatever you're doing with these other women doesn't mean you have to take it out on me." Chrys settled back in her chair. All the emotions she felt when they first heard about Luke Weston and how her brother wanted nothing to do with it were coming back.

"How am I being a dick?" Spencer really didn't get it. He had been nice to Jessie when she was at the restaurant. He didn't talk to her much, but he wasn't really an asshole to her either. And he cared when she got cut up. "My girlfriend killed my child, so I was a little pissed off. I think I had the right."

Chrys closed the laptop so she had a clear view of him. "Your girlfriend made the decision she knew you wouldn't have had the balls to make. You two are so off and on again that she did what she thought was right. Think about it for a while, Spence. And it wasn't your child. It's not like it had a name and little shoes and your nose or anything. It was a peanut. A sperm with an excellent sense of direction had a good map and found his way." Why did her brother have to be so stupid sometimes? She wanted to jump across the table and slap him upside the head until he figured it all out.

"What do you know about it?" Spencer pushed away from the table. He was trying to decide if it was time to have a drink.

"Because I've had to do it." She didn't mean to say that.

Spencer didn't even make it to the bar. He turned around and looked at her. His body sagged. What she was saying instantly registered in his head. They had been around each other for many years, but still there was so much about her he didn't know.

Chrys felt her eyes swell with tears. "I was seventeen and dating Kyle Horton. He was an ass and I as too young, so I ended it." The tears broke free and ran down her caramel cheeks. She didn't bother swiping them away.

Spencer couldn't move. He didn't know what to do? "Why didn't you tell me?"

"You were off apprenticing and I didn't want you to go after Kyle or try talking me out of it." A touch of liquid formed in one nostril.

"Does Mom know?"

"She took me," she whispered.

The brother leaned back against the bar. The sister continued to cry for a while. Spencer wanted to go to her and tell her it was all good and that she made the right choice, but he wasn't sure he could be that convincing. He didn't think it was right. Maybe they could have helped find a way. Maybe there really was no choice in any of it.

Chrys slapped her beanie back onto her head. She wrapped the charger chord around Luke's phone. She'd never wanted to tell her brother what she had done. She didn't want him to think differently of her. Of course it was only one of many things she had hoped to never tell him. Others could turn him into a killer. She had the urge to find Bullet and Breeze and cuddle with them on her bed until the bad feeling went away. She remembered what the fortune teller told her about the little girl on her shoulder. How dare she say that? She sniffed as more tears fell.

Her brother's hand appeared in front of her holding a side-towel he had taken from a cubby hole behind the pass.

Chapter 22

"Miss Alcrest, how can I help you?" Constable Wright looked more unhappy than Chrys had seen him before – and she had seen him pretty unhappy.

Chrys woke early then waited in her bedroom until she heard Spencer come upstairs after the morning crew arrived. She waited until she was certain he was asleep then liberated his truck keys and drove downtown.

The plan was to get Constable Wright to talk to her about Luke. She had some ideas about the whole thing and the only way to get them sorted out was to make him talk to her. She was doing it as business-like as possible. She was dressed in a navy blazer with a white blouse and slacks. Her hair was straight and her lips glistened with a soft pink lipstick. She didn't wear too much perfume, but enough to be subtle. She was the essence of a business woman who was also willing to hold her breath until she got what she wanted. She didn't understand Wright's Bermuda shorts, Hawaiian shirt and leather sandals.

Chrys shook off his appearance and got to her feet. She had been rather boisterous about wanting to speak with Wright and wouldn't settle down until they said they would call him. Maybe that wasn't so business-like. While waiting for him, she sat watching all the happenings at the police station. There seemed to be a lot less in-your-face crime than on TV. It was a room full of desks and cubicles. She thought it looked more like a TV newsroom than police station. "I wanted to talk to you about Luke's case," she started, "I have some ideas."

Wright sighed and his head leaned to the side like her dad's used to when she did something stupid. "Miss Alcrest, this is my day off. We have people…"

"Day off?" People glanced in her direction to see what the screech was about.

"Yes, I was enjoying the Farmers' Market with my family until I got a call about a crazy woman demanding I come in."

"Oh that's nice. What about Luke?"

Wright checked his watch. "We're not getting anywhere on his case at the moment. I'm allowed a day off you know."

"Didn't you see the tape of Luca at the club?"

The man actually looked like steam would come out of his ears. He said, "Come with me," and marched through the room of desks. Nothing more was said until they were inside an office with the door closed. It was a very plain room with a desk, chairs on both sides and a computer. "What the hell did Lavallee say to you?"

Chrys felt the anger inside her rising. "He showed me a video of the day Luke went missing and you're not…"

"I've seen the video, Miss Alcrest." Wright circled the desk and lowered himself to the seat behind it. He didn't speak again until Chrys reluctantly sunk into the other chair. "We have people looking into the identity of the woman with Luke Weston and we're trying to find the taxi driver. I assure you, even though I have the day off, people are still doing the job of bringing this boy's killer to justice." It sounded like *be a good girl and play with your dolls*. "This is the last time I will ask you to let us do our jobs. Any more of this and I will charge you with obstruction."

Chrys stared at a mark on the front of the desk. It was a stain or an imperfection or a rubber mark where someone kicked it. It meant nothing, but she couldn't stop staring at it. Thoughts twisted in her head. Luke was just another person to them. To them he was as insignificant as a scuff mark on a desk. "I want to see the Medical Examiner's report."

"Excuse me?"

"I demand it!" Chrys shot her foot out and kicked the desk right where the mark was.

The Constable's hands hit the top of the desk. The frustrated parental face was replaced by a pissed off one. He was in charge. This was his show. "Who the hell do you think you are? You don't get to come in here and throw a hissy fit. Do you want to be the one put in jail?" By this time he was standing and leaning over the desk with his arms planted on top. Even wearing the surfer shirt he was intimidating. "The last time you did this your friend was killed and the same thing nearly happened to you and your brother." He settled back in his chair. His whole demeanour seemed to calm. "I like you, Chrys. I don't want to see you get hurt."

"I'm not going…"

"I also don't want you getting in the way of an investigation and possibly screwing it up."

She felt like she was disappointing him in some way. Whenever she did something crazy as a kid her foster dad knew better than to yell. Instead he got a sad look on his face and said how upset he was with her. That made Chrys feel ten times worse. "That's why I came to see you. I have a thought, but I need more information to be sure." Chrys didn't know if what she was thinking was right; she hoped it wasn't. She didn't understand how it would be possible.

"What's your thought?"

Something in Chrys told her not to tell him everything. She wanted to leave a little something for herself. She had to be like Lavallee last night and keep information hidden until it was time to divulge it. "I want to know about Luke's injuries."

"No you don't, Miss Alcrest. It was a brutal crime of which you don't need to know the details."

"Were any of them healing?" She took a guess. In the man's eyes she knew she was right. "They were, weren't they? Someone was taking care of him before he was killed."

266

"I don't know if we can say that." The Constable's eyes seemed to search hers.

Chrys didn't feel uncomfortable under his gaze. For some strange reason she felt safe. She took a photograph from her pocket and held it out to the police officer. It was a screen shot from the video showing Luca being helped to a taxi.

Wright looked at it quickly before tossing it on the desk. "Yes, I saw the video three days ago. I told you we have people looking for her."

"Three days ago?" That was Chrys' *what-the-fuck* voice. Lavallee had held back sharing with her.

"You shouldn't have seen the video at all, Miss Alcrest."

"I know who the guy is."

Constable Wright ran a hand over his white hair. "What guy?"

"The one who put Luca in the taxi."

"A woman did."

"Are you sure?" Chrys waited a moment until she saw the realization show in his eyes. "His name is Colby. He was a friend of Luke's and he's a cross-dresser." She felt her cheeks get warm and hoped the constable didn't notice. She'd had sex with the man who she now thought may have killed Luke.

Wright stared at her for a long moment before growling and grabbing the phone from its cradle. He punched in numbers like he was mad at the machine.

"Who are you calling?" Chrys was half worried he was calling someone to come take her away. She was even more worried that he was calling her brother.

The look he gave her said it was none of her business and he blamed her for it. "My wife," he said.

"I have to tell her I'm working the rest of the day. I have to find this Colby."

Chrys almost leapt onto the table. "I'm coming with you."

"No you're not. Hi honey, hold on." His hand covered the mouthpiece. "You are not coming with me."

"Fine, I'll find him myself." She sat back and crossed her arms in front of her. Her dark eyes took on one of the bitchy-attitude looks she'd perfected in her teen years. It used to result in at least one of her parents throwing up their arms and yelling, "Do whatever the hell you want." She wasn't fond of remembering what she referred to as her "dark years," but some interesting things had come from it.

Constable Wright pointed the phone at her. Sweat had broken from the pores on his forehead. "You stay away from this guy. You've gotten yourself in enough trouble."

"The only way to stop me is to take me with you."

~ * ~

It was strange walking into Ms. Kara's Pride during early daylight hours. No colourful lights flashed and there was no music. Everything looked plain compared to its sparkle at night. Chairs were up on the tables. An older man dipped a mop in a yellow bucket and ran it across the floor without squeezing out the access. There was a plop and splash as the water hit the tile. The air smelled like lemon-scented dampness. The only other noises were a radio playing softly across the room and the sound of bottles tinking against each other as they were moved. A tall thin man was behind the bar playing with the liquor bottles and making notes on a clipboard.

The old man looked up from his mop as the young woman and mature man came through the door, but he didn't stop.

The room didn't feel the same as the other night. In the daylight there was nothing special about the place. Except for disco balls and decorations it really could have been any old bar anywhere. It was sad.

As they were half-way across the room the man behind the bar turned around. Whether he was Thomas or Ms. Kara he was a striking individual.

"Chrys," he put his clipboard down, "what are you doing here?"

She quickly introduced the two men. "Constable Wright is working on Luke's case."

"Yes, we've spoken. How can I help you?" He looked from one to the other.

"Do you know where we can find Colby?" Chrys asked.

Thomas shrugged. On this thin tall man it seemed like a strong gesture. "Could be at the shop where he fixes bikes - Middleton Customs on 103 West. Why do you want him?" He looked past the young woman to the man really in charge.

"What is Colby's last name?" Wright asked flatly.

"Tucker."

"How was Mr. Tucker with Luke?"

"Friendly. He helped Luke admit who he was."

"How was Mr. Tucker around Luca?"

269

Thomas kept his eyes on the police officer for a quiet moment. "You do understand that they were the same person?"

"Were they?" Chrys pushed a hair away from her face. "You told me Luke acted different when he was Luca. You are obviously different when you're Ms. Kara. It stands to reason that people would treat both sides of Luke differently."

Thomas's lips pursed together. Without the drag make-up he'd aged nearly twenty years. Chrys wondered how long he could keep up his drag persona. At some point he was going to be too old, right? "I suppose he stayed close to her. Colby was very protective. He might have cared for Luca too much." He took a breath as he nodded.

"Define too much."

"Enough that Luca talked to me about it. I don't know how far it went, but Colby would argue with Luca when she said she wanted to go out more. He tried to discourage it."

"And what did Mr. Weston think about that?"

"Luca was discovering herself. Luke was finally free to be who she really was and wanted to be free to do that," Thomas said. "She didn't need someone holding her back."

"Do you think Colby could ever be violent?" Chrys wanted to know more for herself than anything.

"I saw him grab Luca once. He does have a record."

~ * ~

Before they were in the car Wright dialed the police station and got someone to run Colby Tucker through their computer system. When he finished the call he put his phone down, but hooked a Bluetooth device over his ear. He waited a couple of turns before addressing his partner for the day. "Is there anything you want to share with me, Miss Alcrest?"

"About what?" Chrys did a quick check of her phone. She had texts, but none from her brother.

"Was there anything going on between you and Mr. Tucker?"

Chrys looked at him. The guy was more observant than she gave him credit for. "We, ah, had a one-night fling. That was it." She slipped her phone into her bra.

"That'll give you cancer, you know."

Chrys pulled her phone back out without a word and rested it on her thigh.

"Do you think he could have tortured and killed Luke?"

"Shit, I hope not." Chrys watched the city go by, trying to keep thoughts of her night with Colby out of her head. As far as she could tell from Mary and Thomas, Colby had an obsession for Luca and she knew what could happen when people had obsessions. She knew too well.

Middleton Customs was a warehouse with big garage doors in back. The two of them walked into a front display area. A few bikes, about as fancy as they could be, were on display. One was stretched out to have a chassis twice as long as any other bike and another had an amazing paint job of sky blues and

271

clouds. The third bike was half old and rusted and the other fixed up like a before and after.

Constable Wright asked a salesman where they could find their man. He directed them through the display area to the garage in the back. The first section of the garage had several work areas. Another had thick plastic hanging from the ceiling with a number of exhaust fans in place.

"What's this about?" Colby wiped his hands on a rag. Three other men were in the garage working on different stages of bike repair. None of them paid the new-comer any attention. The bike Colby was working on was just a bunch of scattered engine parts on a table.

"Miss Alcrest was telling me about your relationship with Luke Weston."

Colby looked in the direction of the others. A radio blasted rock music and they were all involved in their own jobs, but still he lowered his voice. "I helped him out a bit."

"What about Luca?" The Constable had his notebook in his hand but he didn't write anything.

"What do you mean?" Colby slipped his fingers into the pockets of his jeans. There was sweat on his brow.

"What did you do to Luca?" Chrys blurted out. The two of them looked in the direction of the other mechanics before staring at each other.

Wright held a hand in front of the young woman and glared. "She means what was your relationship with Luca?"

Chrys fought the urge to slap his hand away; that wasn't what she meant at all.

Colby took a long moment before answering through grinding teeth. "I didn't have a relationship with Luca. There really wasn't a Luca. It was all Luke. I'm not into guys. Tell him, Chrys. He looked at her with desperation. His body twitched like a kid in an itchy sweater. Nobody here knows about what I do. Can we do this some other time?"

"Not really, Mr. Tucker. We can always go down to the police station."

"Is this you?" From her back pocket, Chrys flashed the picture she'd had printed. She pointed a finger at the dark-haired woman helping Luca to the taxi.

He stared at the photo for a long time. The noise went on around the garage, but he was silent. They could almost see his thoughts churning inside his brain. What would be the right answer?

"Is there a place we can talk in private?"

Colby looked at the Constable as if it were the first time and he was suddenly aware he was a police officer. He led the way out a side door. His hands snatched a package of cigarettes from his back pocket; he pulled one out and lit it. His hands shook uncontrollably. A drag on the cigarette seemed to help. "That's me in the picture. I was at Club 22."

"Were you there with Luca, Mr. Tucker?"

Colby took a long drag on his cigarette. "I knew she was going there and I wanted to check on things. I kept an eye on her."

"Okay, we have to go in to the police station."

"Just wait a second," Chrys raised her hand. "Colby, what happened?"

Constable Wright growled, but didn't say a word.

"I, I didn't say anything …"

"I don't give a fuck, Colby. Tell me what happened." Chrys glared at him.

"I watched Luca dancing."

"From a distance?"

Colby nodded. "Lots of guys were trying to pick her up. She kept shaking her head until a blond woman talked to her. The two of them crossed the dance floor and went through a door."

"The one under the big window?" Chrys had a lump in her throat.

Colby nodded. He stomped out his cigarette. "Over an hour later she came down with two men dressed in black. They took her through a door leading into a kitchen. I tried to go after them, but they stopped me. I went outside and ran around to the back. The guys were beating her calling her names, tearing her down. They knew she was a man." His eyes rapidly flipped back and forth

"Did you help him?" Chrys squeezed her cell phone in her hand. If they knew Luca was really a man, how did they find out? Was it a situation where she revealed herself or did something happen? And what did Colby think happened?

He pulled out another cigarette. He had to strike his lighter five times before it flamed. As soon as the cigarette was lit, he whispered, "No. I was dressed as a woman. They would have done the same to me."

"So you just let them beat the shit out of your friend?"

"I yelled out." Colby stared at the ground as he told his story. A tear fell from one eye and disappeared in the dust at his feet. "They threw Luke down and went back inside. I went to her…him right away and helped him up and got him out of there."

"When did you kill Luke?"

Colby looked up. "I didn't. I didn't kill him. I loved Luca. I wanted to save her." His body was shaking. "I took Luca to my place and cleaned her up."

"You loved Luke?" Chrys' hands flew out. "You're gay, you're not gay, now you're gay again." The anger was growing inside her enough that the others could see it.

"I'm not," Colby looked around them, "gay."

"You just said …"

"I loved Luca, not Luke. Luke was my friend. I wanted Luca to be more. She was fun to be around. She was confident. She was gorgeous."

"She wasn't a SHE yet, Colby." Chrys screamed. She forgot all about the police officer standing beside her. "Why did you kill her if you loved her?"

"I didn't." He looked at Wright and repeated himself. "I took care of her. I cleaned her wounds. I gave her pain medication. She slept for almost two days straight. I didn't do anything to her. I thought about taking her to the police, but," his eyes were moist as if overwhelmed with tears, "I was enjoying taking care of her. Then Luke said … he said it was a mistake. He didn't want to be a woman any more. It was too hard. People weren't accepting. He thought it would happen overnight, but it didn't. He was always going to be different. He said Luca was dead."

After a moment of silence Constable Wright said, "You need to come to the station with me, Mr. Tucker. We need to talk about this further." He put his hand on the young man's arm. Colby tensed and the officer squeezed. "Don't make this any worse."

Colby's eyes were wide. "I didn't kill her. Chrys, I didn't. When Luke said Luca was dead I told him to get out. He killed Luca."

"And then you killed Luke." Chrys walked behind the two of them around the building toward the police car.

"No, I didn't," Colby looked back over his shoulder. "I told him to leave and he left. He dressed, fixed himself halfway to look like Luca, looked for his phone and then I screamed at him to leave and he did. I don't know where he went, but he was alive when he left."

Chrys wanted to believe him, but her heart was dark. She put her hands in her pockets and let her hair fall along the sides of her face as she watched the ground directly in front of her feet. They were almost at the car when she felt a tear fall down her cheek.

Chapter 23

"Oh fuck," Chrys turned her brother's truck into the parking lot behind The Alcrest. Spencer had both dogs on the far corner of the lot sniffing at some grass along the edge. He didn't even look up. That was how Chrys knew he was mad. She parked beneath the stairs and watched him through the side mirror. She had hoped to get back before he woke up.

"How did you sleep?" Chrys asked after slowly walking over to her brother. Breeze tried to jump up her leg.

"Fine. I had a dream that someone stole my truck."

"Sorry. Police business."

Spencer turned to her with an are-you-serious look on his face. He would make a great dad someday.

Chrys actually took a step back. "I was with Constable Wright. We might have Luke's killer. Colby was the person who put Luke in the cab outside Club 22. Wright's questioning him right now."

"Colby, the Katy Perry wannabe?" Spencer tugged on Bullet's leash and got no response from the bulldog. "The one you banged?"

"Yes, that one."

Chrys could tell by the tone of her brother's voice and the way he held himself that he was angrier than he would admit. It was moments like this when she felt the most awkward. Her confidence waned. He wasn't a father figure or someone with authority as far as she was concerned, but he was her older brother. She had always looked up to him. She would follow him no matter where he wanted her to go and she hated when he was upset with her the same way she hated his Dad being upset with her. The only person she could blame was herself, however. Spencer would get over it. She held out his truck keys.

"So, he's your killer?" Spencer gave the leash a firmer tug. He heard his sister jingle his keys. She could hang onto them a bit longer. It would make her feel worse.

"It looks that way."

"Good." Spencer barely tapped the bulldog's rump with the toe of his shoe and the animal took off running for the stairs. Spencer snatched his keys from his sister's hand. "Maybe now you can stop committing grand theft auto and get to work."

"What do you need me to do? Jessie's here, isn't she?" The yellow Volkswagen bug sat in the parking lot farther away from Spencer's parking spot than

278

usual. Lunch rush (Chrys hadn't seen many vehicles when she pulled in) should have barely been finished. All that was left was to clean and get ready for the evening.

"Take the dogs." He put the leashes in his sister's hands. "I'm going out."

Chrys took both leashes as her brother crossed toward his truck. "I show up and you take off? What the fuck?"

Spencer spun around to face her. His shoe scraped the pavement. "I wasn't going to go unless my truck showed up. It's here, I still have time, so I'm going." His lips curved upward, but it wasn't exactly a smile. "I should be back before five."

Breeze circled Chrys' legs. "What the hell, Spence? Where are you going?" She should have guessed he was going somewhere when she saw him in a dress shirt. He never wore dress shirts.

Spencer waved his hand in the air as he climbed into his truck. No fingers were curled under, but he may as well have been saluting with one.

Chrys watched the truck drive away. She wondered if her brother leaving was just to get back at her. She thought he should have been more interested in Luke's killer being caught.

~ * ~

"Server. I need a server. Hanni." Gordie put three plates of food beneath the hanging heat lamps. He turned back to the mess of pans and tongs behind him.

279

"This isn't my table, Chef," Hanni said "Chef" with attitude and waved the order sheet around making the paper crack.

"I'm in the shit here," Gordie called out over his shoulder not caring how loud he was. "Just take it."

"Where's Chrys? This is her table."

Gordie turned around and glared at her. The cheeks behind his beard were bright red from the heat. "Quit being a bitch and just take the food. The table number is right there."

"I'm not being a bitch."

"Take the food!"

Hanni stared back at him. Over the kitchen and restaurant sounds you could hear her teeth grinding behind pursed lips. Her bruises were still there beneath her make-up, hard to see in the dim lighting, but they made her look evil.

"I'm here," Chrys stated as she slipped between the blond and the pass. Her gaze jumped between the two of them? "What's going on, Chef? Ho?"

Gordie turned back to the stove.

"What did you call me?" Hanni's fingers rolled into fists. Her rings reflected light.

Chrys took the plates in her hands, one on her forearm. "I know what you and Spence did, so if the shoe fits..." She headed to her table.

Hanni emitted some kind of growl and stomped off toward the back.

It was after 6:00 pm and there was no sign of Spencer. This was by no means their busiest Saturday night ever, but there were still many order chits sitting on the butcher block. The three cooks were doing their best. Their chef had done much of the prep work while he sat up through the night guarding the smashed window. All that meant was that they had less work during the day. Now they were quite literally "in the weeds."

"New order, Chef," Izzy timidly slipped a new order chit under the heat lamp.

Gordie snatched the paper and put it at the end of the row of orders without a word to the redhead.

Chrys delivered her plates and returned to the hostess stand. Jessie crossed off names on the reservation book. There were still three more tables to arrive. Who knew how many walk-ins would also show? "Have you heard from him yet?"

Jessie put her pen down. "Nope. I don't think he would call me."

"Who else is he going to call?" Chrys retorted and right away followed Jessie's gaze toward Hanni as she walked the length of the restaurant. Did she know something? Chrys hadn't said anything to her, but her brother's girlfriend had always had her suspicions.

The front door opened. Lavallee marched in dressed in a dark suit with a long black trench coat like a TV detective would wear. He looked around the room quickly. His eyes locked on the Aboriginal woman. "Where the hell is your brother?" He yelled before taking a step. Customers turned in his direction. Servers stopped for a moment. The only people who didn't pay him any attention were the kitchen crew. Lavallee stepped up to the hostess stand and repeated his question.

"I wish I fucking knew," Chrys blurted. "Look at this place. Wait, why do you care where he is?"

Lavallee took a few deep breaths. "At 1:30pm today your brother parked his truck outside Club 22. He went inside and ten minutes later my surveillance team witnessed him leave with Brandi Grave Reynolds, get into a Mercedes with her and drive away. She hasn't been back since, so where is Spencer Alcrest and where is that woman?"

Chrys looked at Jessie who was staring down at the reservation book. Her face was blank, but her face muscles were flexing. Chrys looked back to the CSIS officer. "Don't you have people following her?"

Lavallee looked over his shoulder as though someone might be listening. "She's not our fish."

Chrys looked at the customers watching and straining to hear what was going on. The two of them were no more than a roadside accident. She grabbed his arm and pulled until the man followed. They walked through the hallway. A female customer came from the bathroom and gave the man a once over before heading on. In the dish-pit the two teenaged workers occupied the only area in the restaurant that wasn't out of control. Chrys slammed the office door behind them. "What the bloody hell are you talking about?"

Lavallee crossed his arms. He pushed his shoulders back and revealed his height over the woman. "She's not high on the terror watch list, so no we don't have anyone following her. That doesn't mean she's not dangerous. This woman is suspected of killing several men in several countries. Did you hear about the body found by Tulloch Park?"

"And you let Spencer leave with her?" Chrys didn't know what to think.

"She's not our priority."

"She's not…what does that mean? If she's a killer and you know it why would you let my brother go with her? Is this some part of a game?"

"The surveillance team has their orders. As far as we knew Spencer was meeting her for an afternoon delight."

"He wouldn't do that," Chrys stated. Would he do that?

Lavallee almost chuckled, but his face twisted. "I saw the picture. She wasn't dressed for a walk in the park. She was dressed for seduction right down to the red and black stiletto heels."

"Stilettos?" Chrys thought of Jessie and wondered if her brother could be that much of an ass. Of course she still didn't know about him and Hanni. "He wouldn't do that. And what do you care? She's not a priority, right, so what are you doing here?"

"Curtesy."

"Bullshit."

He shook his head. "Fine. Word is she's closing shop. By this time tomorrow there won't be a Club 22. I want to know if your brother sold us out or if Miss Brandi had some other source of divine intervention."

"You think my brother's a snitch?"

Lavallee rolled his eyes. "Where is he then?"

An overwhelming feeling of dread entered her mind. Chrys reached a hand behind her and leaned against the stand-up freezer. Her brother was out there somewhere. Now she knew how he felt six months ago when she went missing. When she met Brandi she felt something wrong about her. There was something in her eyes. It was something she had never seen before.

"I have people trying to find them," Lavallee said with a soft voice.

Chrys snorted. "So he's screwed then. Did this woman kill Luke Weston?"

Lavallee's eyes dropped, then moved back up and caught her gaze. "No, I don't think so. I heard that Wright had a suspect."

Chrys gave a quick nod. "How much trouble is Spencer in?"

The man checked his watch. He put a hand on the door handle. "I'm sure he will turn up. Maybe they lost track of time. I'll keep you informed if I find out anything." With that he was gone.

Chrys looked around her brother's office. Everything was in place – just the way he liked it. Everything but him.

Chapter 24

"What are you talking about, Chrys?" Hanni mixed drinks for one of her tables.

Chrys stood beside her behind the bar with the glasses out for the drinks she needed, but hadn't started pouring anything. "The secret agent guy said Spencer went off with the blond hostess from the club. Nobody knows where they went and he said she's dangerous."

"Ah, yeah. My…the guy I was with…the one at the club - he pointed her out to me and said to keep away from her."

"Liam O'Donnell told me to stay away from there. A fucking drug dealer and a mobster are scared of this chick and my brother's who knows where with her."

Chrys scooped ice from the machine and rammed it into each glass. Three cubes fell onto the rubber matt beneath them. She voiced some profanity and dumped two of the glasses. They didn't need ice. "I can't do this. I can't. He said she's killed people."

"Seriously?"

"He said she was suspected of murders in different countries. Something about stilettos...I don't know." Chrys scanned the room around her and everything seemed to melt together. It had been thirty minutes since the man from CSIS had been there and all of the sights and sounds and images were blending into a mess. Every time alcohol in a sauté pan exploded with a ball of flame she caught her breath. Her brother should have been there in front of the stove. Every minute he wasn't there he got farther away. "I can't...I have to go find him. He came to find me, I have to find him."

Hanni grabbed her arm. "What are you going to do? You go to Club 22 and who knows what will happen. You don't know where to look."

"I know someone I can ask." With a crazed expression, Chrys looked at the blond. "I need your car."

"No way." Hanni added garnish to her drinks. Gordie called her name to get food.

"Then come with me." The truck was at the club. Chrys needed a ride by any means possible. "If your drug dealer said she's dangerous then I can use back-up."

"We can't just leave." Hanni ignored her comment. "We're busy. What about Jessie?"

"I haven't told her anything. I told her there were no problems."

Hanni hoisted her tray of drinks. "Can it wait until we're not so busy?"

Spencer had left around 2:00 pm. He would have arrived at the club shortly after that and was seen getting into that woman's car. Nobody had seen or heard from him in over four hours. Anything could happen in for hours. "I can't wait," Chrys said. "I have to do something."

"Maybe Spencer just wanted to get some." Hanni squeezed her way from behind the bar. Before walking away she leaned over the bar staring at Chrys. "Like you said, he turned me down, so maybe he went and got it somewhere else." She spun around and strutted off toward her table shaking what was under her black skirt.

Chrys made the drinks she needed. Wylie was supposed to be bartending, but he was sick. Short staffed, short chefed and all she wanted to do was get out of there.

"Jessie, I need your car." After delivering the drinks Chrys marched to the hostess stand ignoring everyone in the room.

"Excuse me." Jessie didn't even look up from the reservation book on the table.

"Spencer's in trouble. I need your car."

Jessie looked up. There must have been something in her eyes because Jessie reached under the stand and passed over her car keys.

~ * ~

287

Chrys dialed a phone number on her cell phone. She pushed the button to put it on speaker, perched it in her bra between her breasts and put her hands back on the steering wheel as she maneuvered through traffic.

"Miss Alcrest," was how Wright answered his phone.

"Did Lavallee talk to you?"

"About what?"

"Spencer. Spencer being missing. Did he talk to you?"

"Yes, and let the authorities handle it," came Wright's voice from her chest.

"What are you doing about it?"

The Constable groaned in frustration. "Everyone is looking for her car. We will find them."

"Before or after he has a stiletto heel in the throat?" Chrys snatched her phone and pushed the hang-up button then tossed it to the passenger seat. The one thing she hated about mobile phones was the inability to slam the receiver down like on the wired house phone her family had. Dad loved slamming it down when it had to do with employees or the business.

She had to get her thoughts in order. She often went off and reacted before thinking. One of her former girlfriends called it her worst feature. This couldn't be one of those times. She had to think about what she was doing before she put her life in danger as well.

Chrys drove south through the city. The yellow bug was not exactly a stealth vehicle. Her first thought was to drive right through the front door of Club 22. But, luckily she was thinking this time.

As she drove down the street she saw her brother's truck parked across from the nightclub.

Chrys knew only one person who might be able to help. He told her once to come to him if she wanted to know anything about her mother who'd disappeared when she was three years old. This wasn't that; however, he knew the world in which Brandi lived. Still, driving down to the docks and looking for the O'Donnell Shipping sign Chrys knew what Indiana Jones must have felt like being lowered into the pit of snakes. She wasn't even sure if he would be there as it was after 7:00 pm. Even suspected killers and crime lords had to go home at some time.

She saw the sign at the end of a street near the docks. She didn't know the extent of his business down here. All she knew was that he was extremely influential with the workers and unions. O'Donnell was once arrested on charges that were dropped due to lack of evidence, and most of the dock workers stopped showing up for work until he was released. The sign on the three story building was more modern than anything else around. It wasn't faded and weathered like signs on the other businesses in the neighborhood. Next to his name was a fancy trident with a shamrock where all the prongs met, a bit of his Irish roots holding everything together. There were cameras on the corners of the building, another at the door and Chrys was certain she saw some on other buildings directed at O'Donnells. A lot of security for just a businessman.

There was a black SUV sitting at the base of the stairs. As Chrys pulled behind it three men exited of the building, one of them O'Donnell himself.

Chrys opened her door and stood on the seat so she as higher. "Mr. O'Donnell," she yelled out. "I need to talk to you."

The other two men were in dark jackets with their hands in pockets. O'Donnell was dressed in a tailored suit. He sported a pocket square that matched his tie.

"Chrysanthemum." At the bottom of the stairs he took a few steps so as to be on the opposite side of the Bug, "This is a pleasure."

The two bodyguards (Chrys knew one of them) took a stance behind the man. Their eyes moved up and down the street while remaining on both Liam and Chrys.

"I need your help with something."

"I'm late for a charity dinner I'm afraid. You're welcome to accompany me if you wish. We can stop somewhere and get you a gown." He smiled inside his trimmed goatee. He was a handsome older man and had something in his eyes that said he had other interests.

"Spencer's missing," she said boldly.

"Missing?" His smile vanished.

Chrys tried her best to tell him what happened, though all of her words seemed to escape her lips at a rapid pace. She wasn't even certain anyone could understand her.

"Calm down, Chrysanthemum. What do you want me to do?"

What did she want him to do? That had to be the stupidest question she had ever been asked. "Find him. Find her. You always say you're there for him for whatever fucked up reason. Is that real or all bullshit?" Chrys saw the main bodyguard reach inside his jacket.

"Chrysanthemum…"

"Don't fucking call me that," she screeched.

O'Donnell put his hands with palms facing her. Chrys didn't know if it was to get her to stop or to signal the boys not to shoot. "Calm down. I'm just a businessman. I don't know what you expect from me."

Her hand slammed down on the roof of the car. The guard moved forward and the Irish mobster stopped him with a sideways glance.

"I know what you are." Chrys' body shook. She felt a pain in her chest. Anger pulsed through her entire body. They were wasting time, damn it. "I don't care about you right now. The feds said they saw Spencer drive off with that woman. He was supposed to be at The Alcrest by 5:00 pm and he wasn't. He's not answering his phone. We don't know where the hell he is. Are you going to help or is everything you've said just bull?"

O'Donnell puffed up his chest. "If you know so much then you know I can't get involved with federal police. I think your brother is on his own."

"So you're full of crap then." Chrys dropped to the ground.

He adjusted his suit jacket. "Sometimes you have to think about yourself. I can't have my nose out there."

"Sire, we have to get going," one of the others said.

"I will pray for Spencer." O'Donnell nodded and walked to the SUV. One of his men opened the back door for him while the other circled to the driver's side.

Chrys screamed something as the SUV drove away. For a moment she stood there staring at it. That was it. That was her big idea.

She had no clue where to find Brandi and, from the looks of things neither did anyone else. O'Donnell had a dinner party, Wright was "looking into it" and the CSIS people were observers. She was the only one doing anything. The question was, what was she going to do next?

~ * ~

Chrys parked the car as close to Club 22 as she could and marched down the street. As she got close her eyes moved in the direction she thought the CSIS people would be hiding. Part of her wanted to blow their cover right there and screw everything up for them since they didn't bother doing anything for her. But they probably wouldn't do anything then either.

There was already a line-up of people waiting to get in and probably just as many inside. It was a big party with special guest performers. One last big blow-out?

"Hey," Chrys called out when she reached the front of the line. The security guards didn't pay any attention to her. One stared down the cue of waiting party-goers. The other kept his eyes on a clipboard that he tapped with a pen. Rumblings came from the people in line about the bitch trying to cut in. "Hey you."

"Back of the line please." The guard with the clipboard didn't even look at her.

People in line cheered. One guy said something about how he'd let her jump the line with him if she did something special. On a normal night Chrys would probably have kicked him in the nuts. She didn't know what she was doing. Spencer's truck was still there. The club lights reflected off its paint job. It even had a parking ticket under the wiper. Did Wright even care or was he home with his family?

Chrys let go with a shrill whistle. At least the guard twitched in her direction.

"Hey Sweetie," a pretty boy twelve people back in the line motioned toward her. "I'll give you something to blow."

Chrys flipped him the bird as she yelled for the guard again. "I need to see Brandi. I have to talk to Brandi."

The clipboard lowered and his eyes took in the woman's face. This was not one of the guys from Luke's apartment or in the kitchen the other night.

"I need to see Brandi," she frantically repeated.

The guard looked at her for a long moment before returning to the clipboard. "She's busy."

"Busy? So she's here?"

"End of the line please."

"I need to get in there to talk to her."

The guard shook his head. "Not dressed like that. You can go to the end of the line, but I still won't let you in wearing those clothes."

"But I need to talk to…"

"She's busy." The guard stared down at her.

After a few minutes Chrys turned away. She began walking toward Jessie's car. She glanced at her brother's truck. She was there. Brandi was at the club, so where was Spencer? Was he in the club? Was Lavallee bullshitting her the whole time? If Spencer was in that club partying like the rock star all chefs think they are she was…she was...well she'd call Mom and tell on him.

She had to get into that club.

Chapter 25

Spencer opened his eyes again. How long had he been unconscious this time? So much of his body ached that he couldn't tell what hurt. A cool chill fell against his body. It was the kind of chill that said he was naked. His arms were still above his head as if he were at the start of a Village People's song and his legs were wide apart leaving his body in an X. The bindings holding him bit into his skin. He could feel the blood dry on his arms.

A chill? Why was there a chill?

He heard a door close and blinked as hard as he could to make himself focus. Spencer first saw her pedicured toes peeking through the peep-holes of black and red stilettos. His eyes moved up perfectly-formed bare legs that flexed on the high heels. Next he saw black lacy panties, then her belly button where the bottom of the man's dress shirt she wore was open. The next few buttons were fastened then it opened again showing the dark cleavage line. That was his shirt. What was she doing wearing his shirt? Her hands rested on her hips. White tipped nails drummed against her flesh. Blond hair cascaded over her shoulders like golden waterfalls. Her eyes were peaceful orbs. She was gorgeous.

Spencer's head continued to spin as if the whole room was turning around. He had to focus on anything that he could. There was music playing somewhere, but it was muffled as if it was coming through the walls or ceiling. And there was an odor. Something musty.

It hurt to lift his head hurt to lift, so he kept his eyes on the woman's smooth legs. He had seen this woman in long dresses before and had wondered what her legs were like. He thought they would be more tanned. Either way, she was good-looking and he'd had enough of her.

The woman screamed. Spencer flinched but couldn't move. She leapt forward. In four steps she was across the room. Her hand lashed out as fingernails ripped into his thigh.

"Fuck," slipped from Spencer's mouth. He felt the heat of torn skin and the wetness of blood start to trickle down his leg and switch direction with each hair. "Why?"

"Why?" She put her face so close to his that he felt the warmth of her breath on his upper lip. He could smell her shampoo. She was a hot vibrant woman.

This whole situation was insane. "Why, why, why?" she suddenly screeched. Spit splashed Spencer's lips. "That's what I used to ask. Do you know what their answer was? Do you?"

The heel of her hand connected with his lower jaw. Her palm and fingers spread out across his cheek. One nail caught the corner of his eye. Pain shot through his skull like several lightning strikes wrapping around his brain.

Spencer stretched his jaw. His eyes were open wide now. He had been hit harder before, but everything was adding up. Hit once he could handle, but being hit over and over took its toll. At least she took breaks between the hitting.

He watched Brandi pace the room. Her heels clicked on the floor. She shook the hand that had slapped his face as though to get the feeling back. Three fingernails had red stains over the white tips - his blood.

Having to hold up most of his body weight, his shoulders were numb. They tingled as all the fibers stretched inside. He didn't know what he was tied to or how he got up there. It was hard and cold against his bare back. He was certain there were slivers in his ass cheek, however Spencer couldn't tell one pain from the next. In a different life and a "fifty-shades" kind of way this could have been kinky; however he was feeling none of that.

The room was plain as though no one occupied it. Next to a wooden table, was an unmade bed and a chair facing him. During his time here Brandi had already lain seductively on the bed and sat in the chair staring at him for long minutes. Now she walked around the room mumbling to herself, her body shaking.

Spencer had been in and out of consciousness even before arriving at this place. The details in his memory seemed as though he was looking at them through water. His brain couldn't focus on one thing. When he arrived at Club 22, Brandi suggested a drive around the city. She told him she didn't know where many things were and wanted him to give her a tour. He remembered getting into the passenger side of her car. They talked. There was movement. He saw movement out of the corner of his eye, then felt something slam against his leg. No, it went into his leg. It was a sharp pain and then the gush of something beneath his skin. After that were thoughts he was certain were not real: Chrys handing him a wine glass of chocolate pudding, Bullet telling him he was in trouble. Then there was more movement, muffled voices and his body moving against its own will. He felt pain in his wrists and arms. Things went from colour to darkness then nothingness.

When everything cleared he was tied in this room. Brandi was there but no one else. Then the torture started. On the rectangular table sat what the woman called her toys. The stun-gun she had already used on him, a bullwhip was coiled up like a snake waiting to strike, a hammer, a wine bottle and there was a black roll-bag that he was sure contained knives. She hadn't opened it yet, but he had one of his own back in the restaurant.

Spencer knew that if he said anything this woman was going to do something that would cause him pain. He also knew that if he didn't say anything she was going to cause him pain. In the words of his sister, fuck it.

"Who would hit you?" He asked. He always heard it was best to get people talking to make them feeling like you were human.

Brandi stopped moving. On one foot the only thing touching the floor was the heel of her shoe. The toe swayed back and forth as if it was the decider of which way she would go.

Spencer tensed his body. He didn't know with what she would strike next. Blood dripped from his jaw to his chest. He had been shocked and hit, but the cut on his thigh was the first real bleeder. He didn't like the way she looked at it.

"You want me to tell you a story?" Brandi said oozing seduction.

"Please." He tried to remain calm, but could feel the fear taking over. She had already slapped him for asking why.

Brandi walked to the table. One time when Spencer became conscious for a few minutes she told him that she liked being comfortable during play time. Her body wasn't as perfect as he had thought when he saw her in the long dresses. She had scars. Her nails ticked on the table top as her fingers walked between the toys.

Spencer stared at her hand. He didn't want to feel the stun-gun again, but there were worse things on that table.

"Want me to tell you a story?" Brandi's voice was back to the calm sexy voice he had heard in his office. "You ever wonder what happens to those young girls who disappear?" Her eyes were on the table. Her

299

fingertips caressed the whip. "They get taken away to who knows where and told nobody is looking for them and then are beaten over and over again. They are made to have sex with smelly men." Her other hand moved as she rolled out and unzipped the mystery bag. "Then they are sold off like trading cards. They either give up and turn into ghosts or survive and ever-so-slowly thrive." She flipped open the top of the bag. Her eyes twitched. "Maybe they eventually run the show getting the powerful men whatever they want, making others satisfy the smelly bastards."

Spencer saw light gleam from a half dozen knife blades and other metal implements. He suddenly longed for the stun-gun. He watched her trace each handle with a now red-tipped nail. It was probably in his head, but he was certain he could hear her fingernail scrape against the stainless steel. His heart was racing. The sweat was cold over his body. "What does this have to do with me? I never did that to anyone." He heard the strain in his voice.

With her head down Brandi's eyes looked up at him. The corners of her lips slowly crept upward in a Joker's grin. "Not a thing. Do you know what a stiletto is, Spencer?"

"A shoe?"

Through closed lips she made a noise, almost a laugh. "It was first a small knife in medieval times, almost like a needle, that was able to go through chainmail and armor. Assassins used it." She pulled a tiny knife from its holder and circled the blade in front of her eyes, they seemed to lust after it. "Now it is the name for a woman's shoe. Why do you think that is?" She looked over at him and waited for the chef to shake his head. "A smart woman uses her shoes to lift her buttocks and make her legs longer to seduce a man. Our sexuality is our weapon." Her hands moved again across the collection of blades. Her fingers delicately took hold of one handle. The knife she chose made the distinct sound of honed metal against fabric as she slipped it from the case. She wasn't playing around. It was a 10" chef knife which looked too comfortable in her hand. Dull or razor sharp it was going to hurt.

Spencer tugged on the chain holding his wrist. It clinked, but didn't give way. He wasn't going anywhere. Whatever was going to happen was just going to happen. He had a pretty high pain tolerance, in a kitchen you had to with cuts and burns, but enough was enough. Whatever she was planning was going to test it.

"You don't have to do this, you know."

"You're such a silly boy." The woman turned the knife around in her hands. It looked delicate. Spencer loved the feeling of a chef's knife in his hand. It was an extension of his arm. It was part of the machine. With Brandi's fingers wrapped around the handle, the white tipped nails of her other hand running along the blade her knife appeared almost elegant. Beautiful metal and plastic handle, a tool, a weapon.

She gazed at him with sultry green eyes which now had a double shot of crazy. "The last one lasted three days." She started to walk toward him. Each foot was placed in front of the other as though she were slowly making her way to her lover.

The last one? "Luke?"

She smiled in a way that would make a man both lust and fear at the same time. "That who your sister was looking for? No, he was just a fun distraction who came through the wrong door and had to be disposed of." The hand with the knife dropped to her side. The other went to her neck and unfastened the snap. Her hand started at her collar and traced the shirt down to the buttons bellow her breasts then, with nimble fingers, she slowly undid them. The shirt covered her bare breasts, held there only by her flesh, and swayed over a flat stomach.

"What are you doing?" Spencer knew this was no time to be aroused, however he couldn't control his body's reaction.

"What are you doing," she repeated like a bratty child. "Have you ever killed anything Spencer? Ever feel the hot blood on your bare skin? It's sexual." She was smiling brightly. Her hand came up quickly. There was a flash of light on metal. The tip of the blade slashed the skin on Spencer's chest.

He gritted his teeth. The cut was no more than skin deep though his nipple was soon covered in his own crimson.

"Oh," Brandi tipped her head to the side. Her lips popped out in a pout. "Does that hurt?"

Chapter 26

Chrys smiled at the guards outside of Club 22 as she was ushered through the velvet rope. She made a point of looking over her shoulder and up at the building across the street as if to say "hi" to the CSIS officers. Jessie stayed back at The Alcrest, but Chrys had Hanni with her and they had called Dee and Sue to meet them outside the club – the addition of the other servers was probably what got them to zip right through the line.

Chrys sent out a quick text the moment they were inside. She held her phone firmly in one hand, so she could feel the vibration of anyone responding. Tonight she was dressed in tight pants and a dark blouse with a plunging neckline. It was both sexy and functional;

she could look like she belonged while trying to find her brother and wouldn't have a tight skirt in her way. She checked her phone the second it vibrated. "My back-up is here," she yelled into Hanni's ear.

"What back-up?"

"Derby girls." On her way back to The Alcrest Chrys had called the captain of her roller-derby team. A massive text was sent out to the rest of the team and even women on opposing teams in the city. She'd seen a few of them in the line outside waiting to get in and a few inside since arriving inside. She counted eight in total. There may have been more she hadn't seen. They might have enough to make a splash.

"So you do have a plan then?" As soon as Hanni said it she saw in Chrys' eyes that there was no plan.

"I have an idea," Chrys yelled back.

The blond woman stared at her for a long moment. "I need a drink." Hanni motioned to the others (all dressed in tight skirts and blouses that didn't leave much to the imagination) to head for the bar. Dee had left her expensive shoes at home, but the ones she wore were still amazing.

"We're not here to drink." Chrys' eyes turned up to the large window with the VIP room behind it. Spencer had to be up there. She let her eyes drop to the two guards standing at the door beneath the window. It opened and one of the servers came through carrying a tray of food. The kitchen wasn't through there. When she turned back she noticed Hanni was doing her own scoping of the club. "What are you doing?"

Hanni hesitated before saying, "Looking for Spencer."

"Bullshit." When she looked back at the door again she saw another server approach. The guards stepped out of the way, she reached for the door handle and with a turn she opened the door and went through. The guards stepped back into place on either side of the VIP door keeping their steely gaze on the crowd. Chrys stared at the door for a long moment – she didn't have to unlock the door. All she had to do was get past the men in black. "Give me ten minutes then make a hell of a lot of noise."

"What does that mean?"

"I need to get through that door." She nodded to the door beneath the window where two guards kept watch. Spencer may not be upstairs with the rich and infamous, but he had to be somewhere through that door. With the deejay pumping dance tunes there was no way anyone would hear if he was screaming. If he was upstairs enjoying a steak, dinner Chrys was about to get herself and her friends in a heap of trouble.

Hanni pulled her in close so she didn't have to yell. "I thought the secret agent man said they drove off. What makes you think Spencer's in there?"

"He's not a secret agent. The guy is barely a rung above a little old lady spying on the neighborhood. He's a glorified peeping Tom. Secondly…I don't have anywhere else to look." Her eyes connected with her co-workers and with that she conveyed her desperation. This was all she had. "Give me ten minutes and then make a scene." Chrys sent a group text telling her friends to start the noise countdown before heading into the crowd. She hoped they got the point.

The club seemed busier than the other night. Chrys weaved her way across the dance floor toward the guarded door and was bumping into one person or another the whole way. She felt a hand squeeze her ass once, but ignored it. The dance beat pounded in her ears. She could feel her heart racing. This was literally going into the lion's den.

The ten minutes came and went. Chrys was close enough to the VIP door that while she pretended to dance with people she could monitor the guards. They weren't moving. A server came through the door carrying a tray. It looked like an order of wings and their tropical burger with the grilled pineapple. Perhaps because of what happened with their deep fryer they had to find an alternative way to cook food. The men didn't seem concerned about anything. Their eyes surveyed the crowd. Where was her distraction?

One guy lifted a finger to his ear piece. That was when Chrys could tell something was happening. There was a rumbling of voices in the crowd. She didn't turn her head, but knew something was happening behind her. Some of the people around her seemed to lose the beat from the music as they tried to see what was happening. There were cheers that she could barely hear over the crowd. One guard got up on his toes to look beyond the people. That wasn't good enough. She needed both of them to leave the door. Of course everything was going to be screwed if the door was locked with one of them holding the key.

Two men walked along the wall and came face-to-face with the guards. A few words were spoken before one of the men in black smiled at the newcomers. He turned and opened the door for them, ushering them inside with a wave. He didn't have to unlock the door.

Maybe Chrys' luck was changing … if she could just get to it.

Somewhere across the club, a woman screamed, followed quickly by another. One guard touched his ear piece again. He said something to the other guard and they both headed into the crowd.

"Holy fuck." Chrys ran through the rest of the people. She bounced off one and got a nasty word in return that she ignored. She put her hand on the door handle. This was all for nothing if the door was locked. The handle dropped, the door opened and Chrys slipped inside.

The sound of the club was instantly muffled as she quietly closed the door and rested her back against it. Chrys closed her eyes and expelled out the breath she didn't realize she was holding.

"Going up?" The voice was thick with a French accent.

Chrys opened her eyes. The men she had seen go through the door minutes before stood in front of her. The one who spoke held the elevator door open. He was relatively good-looking with a great head of hair. She didn't say anything; she wasn't sure if she could. All she did was shake her head. He gave her a polite smile and stepped back keeping his eyes on her until the door slipped closed. In one way it made her feel flattered, but it also creeped her out.

The room was small with only three ways out: the door she had just come through, the elevator, and the door she was facing. She didn't know the next time a "crime lord" (or whatever they were called) was going to enter from the club or when someone was going to come down the elevator, so she didn't have much time to waste. The Frenchman with the feathery hair could be telling someone right now that he'd seen her down here. She had to continue.

She crossed to the other door and pushed it open. On the other side was a short hallway with another door at the end. Why so many doors? It was like the start of a maze or some horror movie where the girl goes through door after door and never gets any farther away from the bad guy or closer to the exit. Spencer could be down here somewhere instead of upstairs. She was suddenly aware of how clean the air smelled. Disinfected would be a better word. The scent of bleach lingered. The music sounds all but disappeared as the second door closed. New sounds appeared. She could hear something mechanical that was familiar in a way.

Her heart raced. Fear took over her body over. She couldn't go back. The guards were probably back at the door anyway. Her brother needed her. She put her hand on the door handle, took a breath and charged through with one fist raised.

It was a kitchen. This was smaller than other kitchen Chrys had seen, here but it was a kitchen. There was a charbroil grill and a small stove top with an oven underneath. On a table were two small fryers. The baskets were down, steam wafted up from the oil. There were a few burger paddies on the charbroiler. The exhaust fan above the machinery rumbled on in that familiar sound she knew so well. Another sound came from a space around a corner. She couldn't see what was there, but she had heard the sound before. It was something metallic. Where did she hear? It was an old memory. And there were voices. Chrys stepped forward one step at a time. She looked around for what she could grab if she needed to. There was a knife on the table ahead of her. She counted each step.

One. Two. She should go back before anyone sees her. Three. Spencer could be right there. Four.

Three men stood in the alcove. The metallic sound came from a spinning saw. Chrys remembered that sound from when her father took her down the street to the butcher's to watch him cut steaks. It was a meat saw. What bar would cut their own steaks? They weren't that fancy and didn't do enough food service. Something was hanging beyond them. It swung from a hook on the ceiling. There was a chain around whatever it was and that was attached to the hook. It wasn't meat. It was a foot. Two feet. The toes had nail polish.

Chrys held her breath. The men were doing something to the hanging person and hadn't turned around yet. She backed away counting each step again. In a thick stream liquid hit the floor beneath the men's feet. It was red.

Chrys turned and ran. She didn't care about noise any more. She had to get out of there. There were voices behind her. The men knew she was there. She reached out and grabbed one of the fryer baskets. She heard liquid hit the ground again and the fryer bang against something. Her hand pounded the door. The small hallway seemed longer than when she had walked through it.

She pushed through the door to where the elevator located was and was across the room in two steps. The door to the club opened and someone stepped through. Chrys screamed. Her feet slipped on the floor.

The man stepped back. Chrys planted her hand against his chest as she pushed through the door. Flashing lights spun around. The music pounded. The people were dancing again. She didn't notice the guards back at their posts, but heard one of them yell something as she sprinted onto the dance floor. Her hands pushed people aside as she weaved her way through them. The human wave seemed to swarm around her.

A hand grabbed her shoulder. All air left her body. This was it.

"Chrys!" She knew that voice. "Are you okay? What is it?"

Chrys stared up at the eyes of Jason Lavallee, the CSIS guy. What was he doing there? "Spencer," was all she said.

"Where is he?"

"Dead. He's dead."

Chapter 27

There were still flashing lights at Club 22, but now they were outside on police cars. Chrys stared at them like she was intoxicated by the alternating red and blue. She wasn't sure how long she had been leaning against her brother's truck. At first the metal had been cold against her bum, now she was just numb. Someone's had wrapped a coat around her. The night was cool, but she couldn't really feel it and the sun was starting to creep up over the mountains. Right now it seemed that everything around her was covered in a smoky haze. Her world had a yellow tint and she couldn't quite see all the way to the edges. The Alcrest girls were around her. Dee and Sue had cried for a long time then became silent. They sat on the truck's open tailgate. Hanni stood beside Chrys and mumbled continuously about how Spencer couldn't be in there. Chrys had stopped listening to them. Most of the derby girls were gone. All the other people from the club had been corralled and were being questioned before being sent home. She watched the goings on as though she were unattached from the event. She was just a spectator on a strange crazy movie set.

The security guards who didn't disappear when the police and Royal Canadian Mounted Police raided the club just minutes after Lavallee had grabbed her had been taken away in police cars.

It all happened so fast she wasn't sure what went on. She remembered the CSIS agent grabbing her and pulling her toward the door. The moment they exited the front door, the police entered the club in a giant wave with guns raised. They swept through the building as quickly as they could before anyone escaped. Chrys was told later that they had other officers come through the kitchen door and somehow into the VIP room.

Chrys' eyes focused on the two men walking toward her with purpose in their gait. One was in a suit with a bullet proof vest under his jacket. The initials MPD were across his chest. The other was in a dark suit. Neither looked happy.

Constable Wright started, "Miss Alcrest, are you …"

"Do you know what you did?" Lavallee finished. "Do you know how long we've been getting information on these people? You show up half-cocked with your posse of bimbos," His eyes shut down any protest Hanni was about to make, "And I have to call in the task force to save you and clean up your mess. Now half our suspects are in the wind and …"

Chrys stopped listening to him too. She stared at the man's lips moving, however didn't care what he had to say. She thought about her last conversation with her brother. What was she going to say to Jessie? What was she going to tell his mother? The woman had become her mother too, so how could she tell her about this?

"Are you listening to me, Chrys? What were you thinking?"

What was she thinking? She licked her lips as everything boiled up inside her. "You asshole! I did something. All you did was sit there watching what was happening. My brother went missing and nobody damn well wanted to help. I thought he was in there, so I went looking. I don't give a royal monkey shit about what you were doing." She shoved Lavallee making him stumble a step backward. "Did you know what was going on in there? Did you know and do nothing?" She was screaming now and gaining attention.

Lavallee shook his head. He tried taking a firm stance again. "That's not what we were looking for."

"Oh of course. Not your fish. Not your priority." Chrys flinched off Hanni's arm the moment she tried touching her. "My brother is my priority and now he's … he's …" She ground her teeth together. This time she let Hanni take hold of her arm. She had already cried enough to make her eyes dry and sore, still more tears streaked down her cheeks. She turned to Wright. "What about you? Did you know?"

Wright looked at the CSIS officer. "No, I didn't. We wouldn't have let this happen if we had known. Of course we wouldn't."

"I'm done," Lavallee said. "You want those who're protecting our nation to be the ones to blame – go ahead." He spun on his heel and marched back toward Club 22.

"You let people get butchered!" Chrys screamed after him for a long time, even after he was inside and out of sight. If those men up in the VIP room had actually been terrorists perhaps her brother's life was worth stopping them. The thought didn't make it any easier. She needed to know what happened to him.

"You know," Wright put his hands in his pockets, "he can charge you with assault."

Chrys wiped her eye with the back of a hand. "He comes near me again he'll have to charge me with more." She nodded toward the club.

A woman walked out dressed pretty much like Wright. She had been introduced to Chrys as Detective Washburn. Wright walked over to her. There were police officers all over with dozens of vehicles plus ambulances. Outside the perimeter, hordes of people watched. It was a movie crime scene and Chrys didn't want to be there. She wanted to be back in her apartment cuddling with the dogs and getting annoyed at the sound of her brother snoring in the next room. She watched as the Constable and Detective talked to each other, occasionally glancing in her direction.

Chrys held her breath as she saw ambulance attendants exit from of the club. On rolling gurneys, they carried large black body bags between them on rolling stretchers. There were three full-sized body bags and a few black garbage bags that had been tied off. She pushed herself away from the truck and started walking toward the police officers. She heard the other women following behind her.

"Which one is he?" Chrys heard herself say. Her only thought was that she felt like it should be raining, raining and grey, not a magenta sunrise.

Constable Wright faced her and said, "None. Wash says they were all female."

"What?"

"They found three dead women inside there. Neither of them or the other … parts were Spencer." Wright's voice soft, caring. The women beside and around Chrys all caught their breath.

"What do you mean parts?" Hanni asked.

Wright looked around to see who was listening. The detective had gone back inside. Reporters had started to arrive, but they were being kept out away from the immediate area. "This stays between us for now." He waiting until each of them nodded. "It's, ah, starting to look as if they were serving human, human steaks to the VIP's."

Dee gagged and quickly covered her mouth. Sue squeezed Chrys' arm. Hanni uttered the two words that were on all their minds. Chrys said the only thing she could think of, "Where's Spencer?" She felt a tug on her arm.

"I know where he is," Hanni said. Her face was pale. She stared at the screen of her cell phone.

Chapter 28

Chrys stood in the doorway of the hospital room staring at the lifeless body on the bed. Machines made noise and monitors showed life signs. Her brother lay there covered by a loose sheet, though it didn't really seem like him. He wasn't lively and demanding like he could be in the kitchen. He was lifeless and sad. A white bandage covered one cheek and his right eye looked swollen. Chrys wondered if it could open.

She breathed the moment she saw his stomach move on its own. It had been a crazy twenty-four hours complete with a rollercoaster ride of emotions. She thought they found the killer, that her brother was missing and then that he was dead. Being told Spencer was in the hospital had given her a moment of happiness until she realized she didn't know his condition. Seeing Spencer in a bed with oxygen flowing into his nostrils through a tube and a heart monitor brought back all of her worry and pain in a flood of emotion that almost knocked her over.

One of Spencer's arms was outside the blankets. The knuckles on that hand were red. Gauze was wrapped around the forearm covering his pig tattoo. There were marks around his wrists that were starting to go green.

"What happened to him?"

Chrys jumped. She had forgotten Hanni had come into the room with her. The other two Alcrest women were told to stay in the waiting room.

"I don't know," Chrys said. All she was told upon arriving was that he was found outside the ambulance bay. He didn't say anything after being brought in, except for asking for his phone. She stared down at him. As she stepped closer she touched his hand.

Spencer's eyes opened. "How's it going?"

"What the fuck, Spence?" Chrys smacked his shoulder. Her brother moaned. "Sorry, sorry. I thought you were unconscious, you prick. What happened to you?"

Spencer winced as he struggled to raise himself into a sitting position. The blanket slipped down showing bandages on his shoulders and chest. He quickly pulled it back before it could slip any lower. He sucked in air through closed teeth. "I don't know."

"What do you mean you don't know?" Hanni moved between the siblings completely ignoring Chrys. "Spencer, babe, look at you. You have to know what happened to you."

"I don't. Maybe it was an accident. I don't really remember."

"What about Brandi?" Chrys was worried about her brother, but wondered what was with Hanni calling him babe. She wanted to get her out of the room then make her brother tell her what happened to him.

All Spencer said was, "She wasn't there."

"What are you talking about? You left with her. What happened to her?"

Spencer took in a breath that seemed to catch in his throat. He had an IV attached to his arm. His skin didn't seem to have any colour almost as though he didn't have enough blood in his body to give his skin any tint. "I don't know. Look, I'm really tired."

Hanni leaned down and planted her lips on the chef's cheek. Chrys thought she kept them there way too long. As the blond stood she gave the brunette an evil look before turning and marching out of the room. The happy partnership was over.

Chrys dragged the chair, making its legs scrape the floor, so she was close to his head.

"You should go too Chrys. You look like shit." Spencer twitched his neck.

"What the hell is that?" Chrys grabbed his chin and turned his head. He groaned. On the side of his neck were two marks that looked like small red burns. "That's no car accident." She grabbed the sheet and yanked it down. Different sizes of bandages were stuck over his body. There were five alone on his upper torso. All over his chest were discoloured bruises. Some of them looked like they were bruises on top of other bruises. "Tell me what happened to you, please."

"Chrys, let it go. It's over."

Chrys sat in the chair and leaned back. The room smelled of disinfectant. The sound of the heart monitor seemed to echo in her ears. It mixed with the sounds of people walking and talking in the hallway. She checked her phone and returned a text to Jessie saying Spencer was alive. She turned to him and started telling him everything that had happened. He asked about how busy the restaurant had been and if the kitchen crew handled it well. When she told him about Club 22 he listened quietly. She told about the women that had been killed and everything that happened after. For a moment Spencer was quiet then Chrys realized he had drifted to sleep.

When she was done her eyes felt heavy. The twenty-four hours she'd been awake was catching up. She couldn't stop herself. Her eyes continued to droop. Her brother would make a noise and her head would pop back up, but soon she too was asleep.

~ * ~

"Mr. Alcrest."

Chrys opened her eyes. Constable Wright stood beside her chair. He wasn't wearing his bullet-proof vest anymore and looked like he needed as much sleep as Chrys did.

Spencer tried to focus his eyes. He still felt so weak that he could barely stay conscious. With large eyes, he stared at the police officer trying to figure out who he was and how he knew him. "Constable," he said eventually.

"We have to talk, Mr. Alcrest."

320

Spencer licked his lips. His mouth felt pasty and his tongue was dry. "I talked to the police already."

"Well, you're going to talk to me now."

"I'm tired."

"So am I. Your sister has been making a mess of everything."

"Hey," Chrys sat up in her chair. She wiped drool from her chin.

Her brother cleared his throat. "It was an accident. I fell."

Wright pulled the blanket down. "You fell on the knife rack?"

Spencer said, "We don't use a knife rack."

"Come on, Alcrest. I really don't have the time or patience for this. Where have you been?"

"I don't know." That was at least the truth.

"Where's the woman?"

"She wasn't part of the accident." Spencer didn't look at him as he answered the questions. Instead he kept his eyes on the droopy eyes of his sister.

Wright rubbed a hand over his forehead. "She wasn't there. Where did she go?"

"I don't really know what happened. I was in an accident, then I was in the hospital."

"Just like that? No idea how you got here?" Spencer shook his head, so Wright continued, "What about you, Miss Alcrest? No, of course not. So then neither of you have any idea why the guy you burned at Club 22 was found in his hospital room last night with a broken nose and indentations in his burn the size of fingers?"

Chrys tried to sit up. "I have no idea. How would I know?" Her brother said nothing, but his eyes dropped. "I, I was busy trying to find Spencer. I never even thought of going to that guy. Damn it. That was a good idea."

Constable Wright crossed his arms over his chest and leaned over her. "Oh was it? Someone basically tortured this guy and he's so scared now he won't say a word to anyone and even yells at the nurses to leave him alone when they just want to change his bedpan. One of you knows who did this."

Chrys shook her head. Her hair bounced around on her shoulders. Spencer stared down at the blankets.

"Great." Wright stroked his beard. "This isn't going to be the end of this conversation. Get some rest, Mr. Alcrest, I'll be back to see you this afternoon and we'll talk about how you got all these knife cuts on your body." He turned and marched out scratching his head as he went.

Chrys listened to the police officer's shoes on the tile floor until the sound disappeared then she got up and adjusted the blankets over her brother. On his stomach she saw burn mark like the one on his neck. He pulled the blanket up and closed his eyes. She stood there a few moments then sat back down on the chair and let her own exhaustion overtake her.

~ * ~

The next time Spencer opened his eyes for any length of time the television mounted in the corner was on with the volume down low enough that he could barely hear it. This wasn't the same room he had been in before. Chrys sat in an orange chair with her feet lodged against one arm rest. She was too involved in

322

her cellphone to be paying attention to the TV. There was no heart monitor beeping anymore and the oxygen tube was no longer in his nose. He still had an intravenous bag pumping into his arm, however. He wasn't sure if he felt better. He moved, his body screamed. Nope. A groan left his throat.

Chrys looked up. Her legs unfolded from the chair. "You're up."

"How long?" Spencer's voice was hoarse.

His sister put her phone down and in one step was at the rolling table pouring him a glass of water. She poured a little through his lips then stood there waiting. "It's tomorrow. For me it's today, but for you it's probably tomorrow. You were in and out. They tried waking you when they moved you up here, but you were zonked out. Doctor said it probably had to do with your blood loss and your body recouping. They even took x-rays of you. The doctor says even though you had fourteen knife cuts and some other lacerations, it looks like you were electrocuted a couple of times, tied up and have a lot of bruising from being hit and cracked ribs. But you are doing pretty damn well. He also thinks you were drugged, but they won't know with what for a few days. I guess that's a couple days now. Anyway, Wright has been dropping by pretty regularly. I think you're going to have to tell him what happened. At least a better story than you don't remember."

Spencer pushed himself to sitting as his sister moved the pillows. "Jessie?"

"She was here. She went to the restaurant to make sure things are okay. You're going to have to fix

323

things with her, you know. She loves you, you know. You want some more of this?"

He took another sip then shook his head. "I thought about her a lot when … she had me."

"She? Brandi?"

He tried shaking his head, but could barely move it. "She didn't have a name. Not a real one. At least that's what she told me. She had a lot of anger in her."

"At you?" Chrys put the plastic cup on the table. She didn't want to leave his side until he told his story in case her moving would stop him.

"At the world. The men … me, I was just an outlet. I was there and she needed to let go."

"Are you defending her, Spence? I don't know what she did to you, bro, but you shouldn't …"

"She stripped me down and tied me up. She worked her anger out by hitting me and cutting me." He didn't know where they came from, but tears slipped from his eyes and ran down the sides of his face disappearing behind his jaw line. He stared at the episode of Murdoch Mysteries quietly playing on the television. Everything in there was so simple. "She was going to kill me, Chrys. She started with little cuts and rubbed blood on herself. She was going to kill me."

Chrys squeezed his hand. "How did you get away? Who saved you?"

Spencer turned to look at her. His aquamarine eyes were wet with moisture and reminded his sister of snow globes. "You did."

There was a knock at the door. They both stopped and turned to see Constable Wright.

Chapter 29

"You're seriously not going to tell me?" Chrys leaned against the frame of the cooler door. Goosebumps had already formed on her legs under her running shorts. She stared at her brother checking off items on a clipboard. His bruising had gone down somewhat. His eye still had a dark mark under it and a red stain in the iris, but it at least looked like a normal eye, sort of. He had taken the bandage off his cheek. The mark on his neck was starting to look more like a vampire bite.

Spencer said nothing but raised an eyebrow in her direction.

"It's been almost two weeks, Spence."

"I'm not going to talk about it, Chrys."

"Ugh, you're so frustrating." Her brother smiled and squeezed past her. Chrys closed the cooler door and followed him. She touched the dishwasher's shoulder as she walked past toward the dining room. "You have to talk to someone, Spence. It's going to weigh on you and bug you like a cancer. Plus I want to know."

Spencer put the clipboard on the ledge beside the deep fryers. On his left wrist he wore a thick leather wristband with silver buckles on one side and a zigzag line across the rest of it and on his right wrist, he had tied one of the side towels as a sweatband to hide the ligature marks. He wore a long sleeve shirt with the cuffs turned up. As long as he continued to wince from cracked ribs Jessie and Chrys wouldn't let him back into the kitchen. He had over-ruled them a couple of times and paid the price for it afterward.

He crossed in front of the pass heading across the dining room. Mr. O was at his seat by the window. Spencer smiled to Jessie as she looked up from the table she was serving. He wished things were normal with her, but it was slow going. They spoke to each other at least, even outside of work, which was something. The restaurant was slow today, it was becoming a common thing.

In the frame room Wylie and a couple of friends sat around the game table with a board game already set up and ready to use.

"Spence, this isn't fair. I'm worried about you." Chrys stood at the end of the table waiting for a response.

"Chrys, look," he lightly took hold of her shoulders, "I'm fine."

"You don't sleep. I know you don't sleep. I've heard you taking the dogs out in the middle of the night."

Spencer moved his hands to his sister's upper arms. He smiled at the memory of how she had always worried about him. It was a good memory. "Chrys, I'm fine. Now I'm going to play a game with my friends because I don't get to do this often during the day and as long as you and Jess won't let me in the kitchen I might as well enjoy it and forget everything for a little while. Right now I'm telling you that I'm fine. You're more than welcome to pull up a chair and play if you want to keep an eye on me."

She stared at him with a blank expression. Her lips were pulled together making them look thin. "I'm going running. I'll be back later though. Stay out of the kitchen."

Spencer sat on the couch beside Wylie. He had a glass of iced tea sitting in front of him and all of his pieces to play Settlers of Catan. He wanted to soak in the moment. He wanted to roll the dice and place his settlements and laugh at stupid jokes. Twenty minutes into playing he looked up and saw Jessie watching him and smiling. He wasn't too sure where all of that was going now, but seeing her smile was a good thing. It made him smile back.

~ * ~

Chrys crouched down to her knees and let Bullet roll from her arms. Spencer put Breeze down and the little dog took off like a real bullet across the room. He closed, then locked the door. As he stood up, a

327

groan slipped from his throat. He saw his sister looking at him with concern and said, "Don't." The restaurant was closed for the night, the dogs were walked. All was good.

"I'm going to make a snack," Spencer said as he crossed to the kitchen. "Do you want anything?"

Chrys was still by the front door rubbing the bulldog's white belly. She flipped her hair from her face. "What are you making?"

"Chocolate Pop Tarts and ice cream."

She sneered. "No. How do you stay in shape eating that shit?"

"I work out…sometimes."

There was a knock on the door. Spencer's body tensed. He forgot about the bowl of ice cream and his hand instantly went to the handle of the chef knife in the wood knife block. He held his breath and his throat seemed to clench shut.

Chrys stood up without noticing her brother's reaction. Her fingers went to the lock.

"Check who it is," Spencer blurted out. In his mind he saw knives and needles and blond hair flipping over a bare shoulder.

Chrys shook her head and stood on her toes to see through the peep hole. "It's okay." The lock clicked open and she pulled back the door.

The chef knife dropped back into the block with a mild thunk.

The man there almost looked like he came from a magazine. His black suit was perfectly pressed. He didn't smile at all, but looked at Chrys with a pleasant expression on his face.

"What do you want?" Chrys was over being mad at him. She knew how the world worked and being mad at this man was not the right way to go. She was still a little disgusted with him though.

"May I come in?" Lavallee nodded his thanks as the woman opened the door a little wider and he stepped inside to let her closed the door. The only thing not perfect about him was a few scuffs on his shoes. "I saw the restaurant was closed and then saw you two walking the dogs. I'm sorry for arriving so late."

"What do you want?" Chrys asked again, this time with some attitude in her voice and expression.

Lavallee didn't seem to notice or care. "I wanted to let you know that it appears Brandi Reynolds has gone completely off the grid. There are no whispers of her re-opening her club anywhere or being seen in any of her usual circles." He stared across the room at Spencer. "Thanks to your information about her weapons of choice police in at least four other countries have come forward with possible homicides she may have committed. They've dubbed her the Stiletto Madame."

"Catchy," Chrys said.

"Her security force has been taken into custody, all the guards that is except for two that were las seen leaving Club 22 after your brother and Brandi. They must have gone on the run with her."

"Must have," Spencer said with his back to the man as he got the ice cream out of the freezer.

"The city police have been questioning the others for two weeks trying to piece together the whole story.

329

I think there are going to be a few families that will never know what happened to their daughters. "

"What about your terrorist?" Chrys asked.

For a moment it seemed as though he didn't hear her, then he moved his eyes from the man to the young woman. "They've gone back underground. The police raid may have been too close for his comfort, so I'm sure he won't pop his head up for a while. He's out of our country, that I know for sure and we will count it as a win. Anyway, I wanted to let you know what was going on. By the way, you said Mr. O'Donnell was going to a charity banquet the night everything happened, correct? Funny that nobody we have interviewed remembers seeing him there. Have a good night."

Chrys closed the door, locked it and ran across to the kitchen. She even took a shortcut over the arm of the couch. "O'Donnell did it? O'Donnell saved you from Psycho Bitch?"

Spencer put two big scoops of chocolate ice cream into his bowl. "No, I told you, you saved me."

"I saved you? Not O'Donnell who didn't show at his dinner."

He took the chocolate frosted Pop Tarts from the toaster and jammed them around the ice cream.

Chrys' eyes shot wide. "Because I asked him for help. Oh man, what did he do? He tortured that guy in the hospital, didn't he? That guy told him where Brandi had you."

Spencer spooned ice cream onto the corner of the Pop Tart and filled his mouth with the bite so he wouldn't have to say anything. His shoulders

330

scrunched up in an attempt to answer without answering.

Chrys slipped onto one of the stools in front of the kitchen island. "He killed her didn't he? The Irish Enforcer killed the Stiletto Madame." She thought about this for a few minutes. Her mind went over all the possibilities that could have happened, how close her brother came to not being there with her, that the most suspected evil man in the city was, for some reason, on their side. "Holy fucking psycho."

Spencer added another spoon to the bowl and slid it halfway across to his sister. He knew he would tell her someday what really happened. Brandi had been into her cutting - cackling the whole time, smearing handfuls of blood on her body, and licking it from his body, smiling at him with red teeth. When there was a sound outside the room. Spencer couldn't tell what the noises were because he was out of it. The door opened and Brandi flew across the room ending motionless on the floor and it was over. He told the parents of Luke Weston that Brandi and her cohorts had killed their son when he went looking for his phone and walked into a place of evil. He told them that justice had been served and left it at that. He then made them promise never to say a word about it. Someday it could all come out, but for now it was his burden. He owed O'Donnell and his men his life. Someday that was going to come back to haunt him. "Well," Spencer started, "these people weren't the first psychos we've had to deal with and, the way things are going, they won't be our last."

Chrys dropped a spoonful of chocolate ice cream into her mouth and pulled it out slowly, letting her top

lip roll over the cool treat. She smacked her lips and
said, "Do you think that's a commentary on us?"

Author's End Note

What did you think? I hope you loved it. I hope you want to know what other messes Chrys and Spencer are going to get into.

Please get in touch and tell me your thoughts.

Ways to find me

lorneoliverauthor@gmail.com
Facebook.com/oliverauthor
Facebook.com/TheAlcrestMysteries
And @LorneOliver on Twitter

You can get some Lorne Oliver news and merchandise
Lorneoliverauthor.weebly.com

The Alcrest House-Made Iced Tea

2 black tea bags

Sugar or honey

Slices of orange peel

Mint

Blackberries

Strawberries

Raspberries

Bring 2 cups of water to a full boil and pour over tea bags in a pitcher. Let this sit so the tea may brew. Do not stir.

After it has cooled to room temperature, remove the tea bags without squeezing them. Add 2 cups of cold water. Sweeten and garnish. Serve over plenty of ice.